Also by John Burley

The Forgetting Place
The Absence of Mercy

WILLIAM MORROW

An Imprint of HarperCollins*Publishers*

THE
QUIET
CHILD

JOHN BURLEY

HarperCollins books may be purchased for educational, business, or sales promotional use. For information, please email the Special Markets Department at SPsales@harpercollins.com.

FIRST EDITION

Designed by Diahann Sturge

Library of Congress Cataloging-in-Publication Data

Names: Burley, John, 1971- author.
Title: The quiet child : a novel / John Burley.
Description: First William Morrow paperback edition. | New York, NY : William Morrow, an imprint of HarperCollins Publishers, 2017.
Identifiers: LCCN 2016056562 (print) | LCCN 2017003147 (ebook) | ISBN 9780062431851 (trade paperback) | ISBN 9780062431868 (e-book) | ISBN 9780062431868 (E-Book)
Subjects: LCSH: Psychological fiction. | BISAC: FICTION / Suspense. | FICTION / Thrillers. | GSAFD: Suspense fiction.
Classification: LCC PS3602.U758 Q54 2017 (print) | LCC PS3602.U758 (ebook) |
 DDC 813/.6--dc23
LC record available at https://lccn.loc.gov/2016056562

17 18 19 20 21 LSC 10 9 8 7 6 5 4 3 2 1

For my brother, Mark

For God shall bring every work into judgment, with every secret thing, whether it be good or whether it be evil.

—ECCLESIASTES 12:14

I
GONE

1

MICHAEL MCCRAY SQUINTED INTO THE LOW-HANGING SUN as he swung the liberty blue Mercury four-door into the Century Grocery parking lot off Gas Point Road. At 7:45 P.M., the last of the August daylight still lingered, not yet willing to surrender the town of Cottonwood, California, to the custody of the night. Throughout the surrounding neighborhood, shadows spilled out from the bases of homes and businesses, dim expanding pools that merged to cover the quiet streets, the suburban yards strewn with forgotten play-things. On the radio, Kitty Kallen's honey-flecked voice finished singing "Little Things Mean a Lot," and Michael leaned forward and turned the knob to the left, clicking it off. He could feel warm air drifting through the open windows, the oppressive heat of the day finally slipping away with the reluctance of a child heading in for an evening bath.

The churn of the Mercury's whitewall tires across the gravel lot—now all but empty except for the hunkered yellow presence of the proprietor's 1952 Chevy Bel Air—ground to a halt as Michael nosed his car into a spot in the second row. He placed the vehicle in Park and turned off the engine. In the backseat, his two boys sat silently, gazing through the open windows at the parking lot beyond. It was Monday—a school night for ten-year-old Sean and six-year-old Danny—but Kate had been feeling unusually well this evening, her dark brown eyes engaged with her family instead of trapped beneath the hazy effect of her medication. "We should celebrate," Michael had suggested. "How do you and the boys feel about ice cream from the market?"

Kate had nodded, smiling up at him from the living room La-Z-Boy, her expression both foreign and familiar, reminding him of how she'd looked at him twelve years before as he'd leaned in for their first kiss—awkward and wonderful—at the top of that Ferris wheel in Redding. It was the summer after he finished his master's degree in chemistry at UC Davis, the road trip north made on a whim, Michael thinking he'd spend some time in the mountains, maybe cross into Oregon and hit Portland before turning back. He'd made it as far as the small community of Cottonwood before encountering Kate at the late-night check-in desk at the Travelers Motel on the north end of town. It was her summer job between college semesters. By the end of that first conversation, Michael had asked her to the carnival the following night. By the end of August, they were married.

"I'll take Danny with me," he'd told her this evening before heading out.

"I wanna come too," Sean had protested, jumping up from the couch.

"Stay with your mother."

"*Please*, Dad. *Please*," Sean persisted, wrapping his hands around his father's forearm.

"It's okay. Let him go," Kate had said, the latest issue of *Cosmopolitan* magazine resting in her lap. "I'll be fine here by myself for a few minutes."

Michael paused, uncertain, his palm on the doorknob.

"I'll be fine," Kate assured him once again. Then, glancing at Sean, "He wants to go."

Michael had hesitated a moment longer, the memory of the carnival still fresh in his mind. He could almost taste the hint of cotton candy on her lips, the shudder of her body against his, the dip of his stomach as the Ferris wheel lifted them high into the night air, the noise of the world falling away below. He'd wanted the feeling to last forever, not yet realizing how things would change for them—how they always do for young people in love.

Sitting now in the still of the parking lot, the car noiseless except for the soft knock of the engine block as it cooled, he draped his right arm over the seat back and turned to study his two boys, one a constant source of chatter and energy and the other an enigma, silent and indecipherable.

Michael glanced at his wristwatch: still ten minutes before the market closed for the evening.

"Sean, you come with me," he said. "Danny"—he waited for the boy to make eye contact, the only confirmation that he was listening—"I want you to stay here. We shouldn't be more than a few minutes."

There was no dissent from Danny—*Would there ever be?*—and so Michael turned in his seat, grasped the door handle, and swung it wide, stepping out into the parking lot, the gravel loose and shifting beneath the soles of his wingtips. Standing beside the open door of the Mercury, he hesitated, considered not going into the market after all, folding himself back into the car and driving away. He could return home, stop long enough to collect his wife but leave everything else behind. There were other places for them to live besides Cottonwood. The town pulled at them, greedy and unrelenting, demanding more from his family than it had any right to take. Somewhere else, things could be better. Somewhere else, there might be another way.

Instead, Michael closed the door, waited for Sean to walk around the rear of the vehicle and join him on the driver's side. Behind them, along Gas Point Road, the traffic was light. A battered Ford pickup backfired once as it drove past, heading toward the highway, its brake lights winking as it approached the access ramp. On the opposite side of the street, a man in a tan jacket hustled across the empty pavement in its wake.

"Pick out a flavor," Michael said as they headed inside.

"How about two?" Sean asked, hopeful.

"Two then," he replied, "but make one of them strawberry for your mother. And get some coffee and sugar while you're back there." His right hand went to the breast pocket of his shirt, fingers retrieving his pack of Camels, tapping one out, placing it in the corner of his mouth. "Evening, Stan."

"Michael," Stan Eddleworth greeted him from behind the counter and stubbed out his own cigarette in the ashtray on the shelf to his left. The man turned, placed his thick hands on the glass in front of him. At sixty-two, Stan had hair that was more silver than gray, the metallic sheen enhanced by his styling pomade and the pale, granite blue eyes that seemed to observe the world through a light haze of smoke. The market's proprietor leaned forward, his posture canted to the right, his good leg supporting most of his weight. He'd lost the other one during the First World War, a casualty of infection from his time in the trenches. What was left of it merged with a wood and leather prosthesis just south of the knee. If the leg bothered him, as Michael imagined it must, Stan never mentioned it. And despite the black wooden stool behind the counter, he always seemed to stand, keeping vigil, a remnant perhaps of the duties he'd been relieved of long ago.

"How's Kate?" Stan asked, glancing toward the back of the store where Sean had gone to fetch the ice cream.

"Doing well, thanks," Michael said, snapping his lighter closed and returning it to his pocket. He inhaled deeply, tilted his head upward slightly as he blew out a thin train of smoke. He turned to study the rack of newspapers, picked up a copy of the *Chronicle*—EISENHOWER SIGNS COMMUNIST CONTROL ACT the headline read—and placed it on the counter. "Shame we need a law," he commented, tapping the paper.

Stan nodded. "Hoover says it'll just force subversives deeper into hiding—make the FBI's job more difficult."

"Right. But now Senator Watkins and his committee are taking a hard look at McCarthy. Ike must be happy about that."

Sean emerged from the aisle with two cartons of ice cream in hand, the coffee and sugar balanced on top. He set them down on the counter and walked over to the rack of comics in the shop's entryway. A dying glimmer of sunlight spilled through the door's window, illuminating the back of the boy's head, a hint of scalp visible beneath the dusky blond crew cut, the tan neck bent slightly to study the illustrated covers.

"Is he back in school yet?" Stan asked, and Michael returned his attention to the man in front of him.

"Supposed to start up again tomorrow. Me too," he added, thinking of the roster of students he'd been assigned at Anderson Union High this year, how the first few weeks were always a struggle against the inertia that had set in over two months of summer vacation. "It'll be fifth grade for Sean. Seems hard to believe."

And Danny? Stan could've asked, but didn't. And that was

how it was with Michael's younger son, as if the boy's silence gave people the right to ignore him, to pretend he didn't exist. He was a ghost, a quiet child the townspeople referred to only in whispers.

"That'll be a dollar eighty-two," Stan said from behind the register. Michael blinked, and looked up at the store owner. Stan smiled back at him blandly. The two cartons of ice cream, coffee, sugar, and a newspaper sat waiting in a brown paper bag. In the parking lot outside, a car ignition turned over irritably a few times before springing to life.

The cogs of the Ferris wheel turned, lifted them into the night. *Kiss her before it's too late,* Michael thought to himself. *Hold on to this girl in the pale blue dress and the thrum of her heartbeat against your ribs. Let her know that she's yours.*

He dug into his back pocket for his wallet, retrieved it, and pulled out two singles. "Sean, do you want a comic?" he asked, turning toward the shop's entrance.

The last syllable of his sentence ended as a click in the back of his throat. From the parking lot outside, he could hear tires on gravel—not slowing to a stop, but speeding up, spinning slightly as the driver gunned the engine.

"Sean?" Michael called, taking a step toward the door and the abandoned rack of comics, his tongue suddenly dry and gritty.

"Think he went outside," Stan commented, his voice sounding alien and distorted in the small confines of the store.

Tiny beads of sweat erupted from Michael's upper back and forearms as the pieces came together in his mind. The man in the tan jacket crossing the street, heading in the direction of the parking lot. Danny in the backseat of the car, gazing out the open window as he waited for them to return. The engine starting. The spin of tires on gravel. And Sean, standing here less than a minute ago. But now . . .

"Sean!" Michael said again, this time more urgent as he strode toward the exit and shoved the door open.

It swung outward and Michael stepped into the nearly empty lot, looked left and then right. His car was nowhere in sight. The world had taken on the soft golden shimmer of dusk. He could hear light traffic on Interstate 5, folks heading north to Redding or into the mountains upstate, south to Red Bluff or even Sacramento. *One of those cars is mine*, he thought, the shock worming its way through his system like something rancid he'd inadvertently swallowed. *One of those cars is a liberty blue Mercury with a cigarette burn in the front passenger seat and at least one of my boys in the back.*

He hadn't heard Stan's lurching footsteps behind him, the shoe on the prosthetic limb always sounding different—more hollow—from the other. A hand touched his shoulder and Michael jumped, turning quickly.

"Where's your boy?" Stan asked, more as a statement than a question. The owner and sole custodian of Century Grocery had put things together almost as quickly as Michael.

"Give me the keys to your car," Michael said, "and then call Jim Kent. Tell him to close the highway if he can—a roadblock, *something*. Tell him my car's been stolen and that Sean and Danny have been taken along with it. It's a blue 1950 Mercury Eight. Got that?"

"Yeah," Stan responded, reaching into his right front pocket for his keys. He slapped them into Michael's hand, turned, and hobbled back inside as fast as his awkward gait would carry him.

Michael sprinted for the Bel Air and yanked open the driver's door. He threw himself behind the wheel, cranked the ignition, backed away from the building, and then dropped the car into gear and stomped on the accelerator. The rear tires spun on the gravel as he turned the wheel hard to the right, crossed the parking lot, and shot out onto Gas Point Road. He was going too fast for the southbound entrance to the interstate, but he took it anyway, the car sliding dangerously across the lane.

The Bel Air merged with the interstate and hurtled toward the town of Red Bluff fifteen miles to the south. Michael gripped the wheel and pushed the six-cylinder engine as hard as it would go. His blanched knuckles were miniature apparitions in the gathering darkness of the car, hovering along the edge of his line of sight as he stared through the windshield at the road ahead. The steering wheel shuddered in his hands as he topped ninety miles per hour, and his lips—pinched tightly together—began to loosen and then move in a silent prayer, the desperate murmurings of a terrified parent, insanity itself closing in around him.

It was 8:06 P.M. And both of his boys . . . were gone.

2

JIM KENT STOOD NEAR THE SINK IN THE MCCRAYS' SMALL kitchen, his police utility belt pressing into the small of his lower back as he leaned against the counter. The cup of coffee Michael had handed him an hour ago remained untouched, even though his body would have benefited from the caffeine. He'd been up all night, coordinating efforts with the California Highway Patrol and the Shasta County Sheriff's Department. He had taken statements from both Michael and Stan Eddleworth, and scoured the streets in a mix of hope and desperation for several hours before meeting up with the two Shasta County detectives at daybreak and returning to the McCrays' residence to update the parents.

On any other Tuesday morning, Jim might be soldering a pipe joint or snaking a toilet trap. A plumber by trade, he'd inherited his father's business and had kept it running and in the black for the past forty years. Now that he was sixty-five, his police work was a side interest, a diversion. The town of Cottonwood was too small for an actual force of its own, and too poor to pay for something they didn't need on a regular basis. Still, there were times like this when the necessity for law enforcement arose. It was good to have someone who wasn't an outsider, someone who'd lived here long enough to know what they were dealing with. And so Jim had taken on the position of sheriff the same way his brother, Abe, had served with the Cottonwood Fire Department for the past twenty years. His work was as needed and free of charge.

It was different for the men in front of him. At the table, Detective John Pierce ran an open palm across his broad forehead. He leaned forward in his chair, thick forearms coming to rest on the lacquered wooden surface. His partner, Detective Tony DeLuca, was seated to his left, jotting down notes on a flip pad he kept at the ready. The parents sat on the other side of the table: Michael, perched on the edge of his chair, body rigid, the muscles of his clenched jaw working rhythmically beneath the skin; and Kate in a wool sweater despite the early heat of the day, her arms wrapped so tightly around her body that, from his vantage point, Jim could see that her fingertips were almost touching at the spine. It was hard for him to look at that. *How much weight had she lost over the past few years?* he wondered. *How much more could she possibly afford to lose before her body stopped functioning altogether?* He didn't know, and didn't like to think about it. She'd been beautiful once, though; he remembered that. Was it the boy or the town or the disease itself that took that away from her? Maybe it was just dumb luck, or the hand of God telling another one of his faithful in Cottonwood that their time had come. When he really thought about it, it didn't make much of a difference. Twelve hours ago, the children had been here, sitting at this very table. Now they were gone. For the time being, whatever disease was eating away at Kate McCray from the inside didn't matter. Getting those boys back did. *That* was what he should focus on.

"Here's what we have so far," Detective Pierce said, looking back and forth between the parents, Kate never lifting her eyes to meet his, Michael's expression so intense that Jim wondered whether he was truly hearing any of this.

"We managed to establish roadblocks fairly quickly to the south," Pierce told them. "Interstate 5 and Route 99 are the major thoroughfares heading toward Sacramento, and we already had cars along those stretches at the time of the . . . at the time your children were taken. The store owner, Mr. Eddleworth, contacted Sheriff Kent here within two minutes of the incident. The sheriff wasted no time in notifying the state police, and roadblocks were set up sixty miles south of here within twenty minutes. It's extremely unlikely this guy got past them."

Pierce touched his wedding band with the thumb and index finger of his right hand, turning it slowly back and forth as he spoke. "Side streets were closed down or patrolled, and we were also able to establish road blocks on Route 36 east and west of Red Bluff. It took a little longer—fifty minutes to be exact—to position a car along Interstate 5 to the north at Mount Shasta. But it's seventy-four miles between Cottonwood and Mount Shasta. In order to make it past that point before the roadblock was in place, your Mercury Eight would've had to be traveling at a hundred and twelve miles an hour through twisty mountainous terrain."

"Impossible," Detective DeLuca commented without looking up from his notebook.

"Yes, I agree," Pierce said, nodding. "Which means the man who stole your car and abducted your children didn't head north or south, but rather east or west from Redding, likely along Route 299. As you know, the mountains and national forest lie to the west of here, and ultimately the California coast, although I don't think he'll go that far. Too risky, too much chance of being spotted. To the east is the northeast section of the state, which is flatter but very sparsely populated. Not much out there."

"Plenty of places to hide a car," Michael said, and from where Jim stood at the kitchen sink his mind silently filled in the remainder of that sentence: *and a pair of bodies.*

The room fell silent for a few seconds before Kate McCray emerged from her shell-shocked state and sat forward in her chair. "I don't give a shit about the car," she said. "What are you doing to find my sons?"

Michael reached over to take her hand, but she pulled it away, held it firmly in her lap.

"Finding your sons is our top priority, Mrs. McCray," Detective Pierce replied, "which is why we have both state and county agencies scouring the areas to the east and west of here at this very moment. We'll also be canvassing the town of Cottonwood, speaking with every resident we can. We'll be asking about this man in the tan jacket that your husband noticed crossing the street in the direction of the market shortly before your car was stolen. Since this is a small town and your husband didn't recognize him, chances are he was a drifter—a small-time criminal and an opportunist who saw a chance and took it—not a hardened kidnapper. My guess is that he was mostly interested in the car, not your boys, and that he'll come to his senses and drop them off somewhere before continuing on."

"And if he doesn't?" Kate asked, her voice cracking around the edges.

"If he doesn't, we'll find them," Pierce assured her. "We have a lot of good men working on this right now, Mrs. McCray. The man who took your children is most likely an amateur. He's outnumbered, outskilled, already boxed in, and running scared. He's in way over his head, and probably realizes it's only a matter of time before he's apprehended. There's no reason for him to harm your boys. That would only make things worse for him. Sooner or later, these people almost always turn themselves in."

Her eyes focused on the detective's face. "Do I have your word on that?"

"My word?"

"That this man will turn himself in? That my boys will be found alive and unharmed?"

"Mrs. McCray—"

She was looking expectantly back at him, waiting for his answer.

"We're at the beginning of this process," Pierce said. "Every case is different. There can be unanticipated variables."

"That's not what you just said. You said that he'll come to his senses and drop them off somewhere—unharmed—before continuing on."

"Statistically, yes," he replied, watching her, the fingers of his right hand letting go of his ring and settling themselves on the table.

"Well, I'm not interested in statistics," she said, crying now, yet her voice seemed stronger—not weaker—than before. "This is about two sweet children named Danny and Sean McCray. They are six and ten years old." She paused a moment, unfolded her arms in order to wipe at her face with the side of her hand. "Danny doesn't talk much, but his brother watches out for him. You will find them, Detectives," she said, looking at both of them in turn, "and you will bring them home to me, safe and unharmed. Is that understood?"

"Yes, ma'am," Pierce replied as he and his partner rose from their chairs. "We'll need recent pictures of the boys."

"I'll get those for you," Michael said, rising as well.

Kate remained at the table while Jim led the detectives to the door. They stood there in silence, the clock on the wall ticking off lost seconds. Outside, the sun rose farther in the sky, but despite the windows and open doorway, little of its light seemed to penetrate the dim interior. To Jim's eye, there was no architectural reason for why this should be so, only that this was what he'd come to recognize as a waiting house: a homestead turned inward, sheltering its occupants from crisis or illness, attempting to protect them until the worst of it passed. In the case of the McCrays, the house had been waiting for Kate to recover, or to die. And now, with the children gone, the place had drawn inward even further, the walls tightening, the windows rebuffing the unwelcome light from the outside world. In a place like Cottonwood, where death and illness visited more often than they should, Jim had seen more than his fair share of waiting houses.

"What can I do?" Michael asked, returning with the photos and handing them over to the detectives. He stepped outside with them, closed the door behind him. "How can I help?"

"You should be at home as much as possible," Pierce told him. "Your wife needs you. And someone should always be here to answer the phone in case he calls."

Michael's gaze moved across the suburban street, silent and unoccupied even at this hour of the morning. In the house across the way, Betty Savage's face appeared in the large bay window that looked out on the yellowing, weed-infested acreage of her modest front yard. Her hair was in curlers. A forgotten cigarette drooped from the corner of her mouth as she studied the loose circle of men. Michael watched as she plucked it from between her lips, pressed them together and shook her head slightly before drawing back into the darkness of her living room.

"And if he does call?" Michael asked, returning his attention to the detectives.

"Talk to him," Pierce replied. "Don't be confrontational. Find out where he is and what he wants. Then call us immediately." He handed Michael a card. "And if you think of anything that might be of assistance—no matter how small or seemingly insignificant—please contact me or Detective De-Luca right away, day or night. Is that understood?"

Michael agreed, took the card and stared down at it as the two detectives turned and walked to their car.

Jim Kent lingered, placed a hand on Michael's shoulder.

"You okay?"

The father swallowed, closed his eyes for a moment. When he opened them and spoke, his voice was barely above a whisper. "I left him in the car, Jim. Sean went out to join him."

"This is not your fault," the sheriff replied. "Don't go thinking it is."

"If I'd brought them *both* into the store with me, though. Then neither one of them would've been—"

"Or maybe they both would've gone back outside," Jim told him, "and this would've happened just the same."

Michael shook his head, brought a hand to his temple.

"Listen," Jim said, his right hand tightening a bit on Michael's shoulder. "I understand why Danny was in that car instead of the store. The detectives are out of towners, though. They don't get it yet. I'll explain it to them. It's important they know."

"He's just a boy," Michael said. His right hand was shaking now, the tremors—subtle at first—becoming stronger and more pronounced. Standing beside him, Jim was reminded of an earthquake, the slow-building frenzy. It continued for a good ten seconds before dissipating. Neither man spoke as they waited for it to pass.

This is a waiting house, Jim thought again, and shuddered. In his experience, things didn't get better in waiting houses. They just . . . proceeded to completion. Both Michael and Kate were getting worse—had been getting worse for some time now. But what was the point in mentioning it? What could be done?

"We'll find them," Jim said. "I promise you that." And it occurred to him now that he believed it. Because Sean would be with Danny, and a boy like Danny doesn't disappear into the world without a trace. *A boy like that*, he thought as he turned to leave, *will find his way home.*

3

KATE LAY ON THE BED IN WHAT MICHAEL STILL THOUGHT OF
as their living room, her back to the doorway leading to
the kitchen. The heavy shades were drawn, casting the
room in a bronze and ghostly twilight. She'd turned on the
Zenith Trans-Oceanic shortwave radio, its gold faceplate peering out from the dark plastic chassis, the metallic sheen of the
telescoping antennae rising above it like a strand of spiderweb
in the darkness. Doris Day was singing "Secret Love," a song
they'd first heard less than a year ago at the drive-in theater in
Red Bluff. Kate's head had rested on his shoulder for most of
the movie, her breathing slow and even—the way it was now
in the stillness of the room. If he remembered hard enough, he
could feel the cool touch of her hand against the inside of his
elbow, the soft fold of her fingers interlaced with his own. Her
hair had smelled faintly of lilac—or so he recalled—and he told
himself that for the space of that evening he had simply enjoyed
being close to her, that her illness had been the furthest thing
from his mind. When *Calamity Jane* was over, they'd stopped
off at a malt shop on the north end of town, and rode home
afterward in comfortable silence. Only later, lying in bed that
evening, had Kate asked him if he'd enjoyed the movie. He'd

immediately said yes, although the details faded quickly in the months that followed. Only the presence of his wife remained and the feel of her body against him. He wanted more memories like this one, wondered whether there was enough time left for such things, or if this would become the moment he'd remember with bittersweet regret after she was gone.

HOW HAD THEY come to this? The truth was, they hadn't noticed at first. Danny was born prematurely, and spent his first two months in the NICU at the UC Davis Children's Hospital in Sacramento. During that time, they were too preoccupied with worry and the parade of doctors' visits. Four-year-old Sean went to stay with Kate's sister, Lauren. It had been a mistake to ask that of her. Still, they couldn't have known, couldn't have anticipated the things that would follow.

So often the worst trials in life do not appear at once. Instead they're heralded by minor incidents whose true significance is recognized only in retrospect. By the time Danny was five months old and catching up on the growth chart, they'd all begun to breathe a little easier. Sean had moved back home, Kate had recovered from childbirth, and Michael had the distinct sense they'd been granted a reprieve—escaped catastrophe by the narrowest of margins—and were well on their way to resuming some semblance of a normal life.

He'd taken the year off from teaching, yet during spring break they were invited to his colleague's house (this was a time when they were still invited to such places) for a backyard barbecue. It was early April and the weather was spectacular, the sky blue, nearly cloudless, and a light breeze danced and swayed through the recently budded leaves on the maple and dogwood branches.

Kate tripped at the party and bloodied her knee. Michael

remembered that specifically because she'd been holding the baby when she fell, and his first impulse was to reach for Danny, not his wife's outstretched hand as she struggled to her feet. He wanted to see if the baby had been hurt. They'd laughed about that later. Six months before, there was no Danny, but now Kate and her bloody knee would have to wait until the child was thoroughly inspected. Michael had corrected himself, took his wife by the arm and helped her to a chair, the child—held close to Kate's chest—wailing, but otherwise fine.

"That was stupid," Kate muttered, embarrassed, handing Danny off to another woman while she examined her knee. "I tripped over my own feet."

She was wearing shorts. As they watched, a rivulet of blood tracked down her lower leg, turning the cuff of her white sock a burgundy hue.

They went inside to clean the wound; it wasn't deep. She had limped on it for a few days afterward, and it healed fine. And that was the end of it.

Except, of course, it wasn't.

Over the next three months, tripping over her own feet became something of a specialty for Kate, who'd never before been particularly clumsy. At first they joked about it, her new-found awkwardness, the result of hormonal fluctuations or the profound and chronic loss of sleep that all parents encounter to some degree after the birth of a child. Then in late July, Kate fell and broke her wrist. Michael took her to the ER. Although the break wasn't a bad one, things stopped being funny after that.

"I don't know why this keeps happening to me," she'd said as the doctor pressed gingerly on the bones of her hand and lower forearm.

"What do you mean?" he asked, scribbling his findings on the chart.

Kate sighed. "I'm just a lot more accident prone than I used to be. Getting older, I guess."

"You're twenty-six," the man said, looking up at her now. "How many falls have you had?"

"I don't know, maybe ten or twelve," she said. That had scared Michael. He hadn't realized it had gotten so bad. From past experience, he also knew Kate had a tendency to minimize her symptoms. *Maybe ten or twelve was actually more like twenty, or even thirty.*

"Well, let's take a closer look at you," the doctor replied, and asked her to squeeze his hands and to follow his finger with her eyes, to push and pull in various directions. He watched closely as she walked to the waiting room door and back. When he was finished with his examination, he sat in silence for a moment before speaking.

"You've got a foot drop," he said, scowling slightly, his eyes moving back and forth between the two of them.

"A foot drop, what does that mean?" Kate asked, and Michael could hear the alarm in her voice, but also something else. Was it resignation? Was the doctor telling her something she already knew, or at least suspected?

"The muscles that control your right foot and ankle aren't as strong as the ones on your left. Ordinarily, your foot should flex upward at the ankle when you take a step forward. Yours does, but not as well as it does on the left. It's weak. It droops a little and affects the way you walk. I'll bet that's why you've been tripping." He paused, considering. "You should see a neurologist—a specialist in this sort of thing."

"*A specialist?*" she replied. "For a small difference in the strength of my feet? Do you really think that's necessary, Doctor?"

"Yes, I do," he said, closing the chart and resting it on his lap. "This worries me. It's subtle now, but it may be the beginning of something."

"The beginning of what?" Michael asked.

He'd shaken his head. "I don't know. I don't mean to alarm you and your husband, Mrs. McCray, but this could get worse. A lot worse." He pulled a prescription pad from the pocket of his white coat. "I'm going to write down the name of a colleague of mine in Redding. He's a bad golfer, but a hell of a nice guy and a good doctor. Call his office and schedule an appointment. He'll know what to do."

Michael blinked away the memory, taking in the familiar features of his surroundings once again. On the radio, "Secret Love" had given way to Frank Sinatra's rendition of "Young at Heart," and he watched his wife from the doorway. It wasn't a living room anymore. It was a bedroom. He'd converted it for that purpose two years ago when it became clear that Kate was no longer strong enough to safely negotiate the four stairs leading to their old bedroom in the rear of the house. The bed, dresser, and vanity table provided easy access to the things she needed—and the kitchen and bathroom were only a short distance away. And for the times when Michael wasn't home or the short trip to the bathroom was too far, a bedside commode stood against the far wall. When he'd purchased it eighteen months ago, Kate broke down in tears, begged him to take it away. He complied with her wishes, but before long even that basic dignity gave way to necessity, and now she used it more often than not.

A sliver of sunbeam shone through the slightly parted drapes, and Michael studied his wife from behind as Sinatra moved into his second verse.

You can go to extremes with impossible schemes
You can laugh when your dreams fall apart at the seams

The onset of Danny's symptoms was less subtle. The premature birth was one thing, and for a while they believed his slow progress through the usual developmental milestones a mere lingering effect—the fact that he never babbled as a baby, never spoke as he grew older. His pediatrician, Dr. Besson, had tried to reassure them. "He's a bright boy of normal intelligence. I wouldn't let it worry you. Children talk when they're ready. You'll see." But as the years passed, Danny's speech did not flourish—it never emerged at all. *Elective mutism* was the term Dr. Besson now used. "It is what we once called *aphasia voluntaria*," he'd explained. "The child can speak, but chooses not to. There is nothing wrong with Danny's brain or vocal chords, you understand. Anatomically, he has all the tools he needs to speak."

"Then why *doesn't* he?" Kate had asked, wiping away tears of frustration and bewilderment.

"The underlying cause is a type of social anxiety," the doctor replied. "Tell me, does Danny seem interested in interacting with other children? How do they respond to him?"

Our children are gone, Michael thought, surfacing from the memories of those early struggles. He wondered if she blamed him—not just for what happened to the children, but for all of it. Was there something he should've done, some action he could've taken before their lives came to this? He was the husband, the father. What kind of man assumes those roles and then does nothing to protect his family?

He noticed Kate had left her walker near the kitchen table, behind him. Somehow she had managed to make it to the bed without it. That worried him—not because she'd found the strength, but because she could've fallen, could've broken her hip or struck her head on the floorboards. She no longer had the strength or reflexes to catch herself if she stumbled.

"This worries me. It's subtle now, but it may be the beginning of something."

"The beginning of what?"

"I don't know . . . but this could get worse. A lot worse."

Michael went to the dresser and turned off the radio, thinking maybe she would sleep. He started to leave, intending to fetch the walker and bring it to her bedside so she'd have it when she woke.

"Leave it on," she said, her voice quiet but fully awake. Of course it would be, he realized. What mother could sleep while her children were missing?

He went to her, sat on the edge of the bed and rested a hand on her hip. There was no soft contour to her body, only the unyielding jut of bone beneath skin.

"I can't stand the silence," she said, and Michael nodded to himself in the darkness. It was the first thing he had noticed, as well—how the rooms had taken on a deathly stillness in the boys' absence.

"They'll find them," he said, because there was nothing else to say—and no other acceptable outcome.

He wanted her to tell him that she knew they would, that their boys would be returned to them, a little shaken but unharmed. He wanted her to place her hand over his, to squeeze just enough to reassure him they were in this together, that they would somehow make it through.

She did neither. And when the song changed again to something slow and lonesome by an artist he didn't recognize, Michael stood and left the room, careful not to disturb her.

4

OFFER YOU SOMETHING TO DRINK?" JIM ASKED THE TWO detectives as he switched on the overhead light and ushered them inside his small office. The room wasn't much to speak of: a desk and a few chairs, a single window facing the street, a standing fan in the corner for when the summer heat rolled in. The office was a hand-me-down of sorts, used for two decades by Ira Sokolov, a local accountant, before he'd succumbed to cancer five years ago. After Ira passed, the town bought the place from his widow, Shawna, for considerably more than it was worth. Accountant or not, Ira had left her with very little. *But the town took care of its own*, Jim thought. A widow left with nothing was not destitute for long. And outsiders bringing trouble were strongly encouraged to move on. It was the town's business to protect its inhabitants. And in Cottonwood, all business was personal.

There were jails in Redding to the north and in Red Bluff to the south, but nothing like that here—which was ironic because the municipality had started out as a stagecoach town in the 1840s. But times had changed. What had once been a saloon was now Century Grocery. A former house of ill repute over on Chestnut Street had been converted to a post office.

And the original sheriff's office and town holding cell had been demolished twelve years back to make room for a gas station and a drive-in burger joint, where the carhops would bring a vanilla shake and a burger with fries to your window for just over a buck. It was expensive, yes, but there was something about a pretty girl wearing a skirt and a smile that made it seem like a great deal every time, and Jim imagined *that* kind of marketing was one thing that would never change.

Detectives Pierce and DeLuca waved off his offer of a beverage—good because he would've had to run next door to the apothecary to buy them—and they settled into the uncomfortable wooden seats as best they could. Jim moved around his desk and sat down, pushing a small mound of papers to one side. He reached into his breast pocket, pulled out a pack of Lucky Strikes, tapped one out and extended it toward the detectives. DeLuca nodded and took one. He leaned across the desk to light Jim's and then his own. Pierce waved away the offer.

"So," Jim said, settling into his chair. "You have questions."

"Yes," Pierce replied, glancing at his partner.

"You want to know about the boys—particularly Danny."

"Why did the father leave him in the car?" DeLuca asked. "Two boys and their old man stopping for ice cream. What kind of six-year-old stays behind in the car?"

Jim leaned back in his chair, studied the ribbon of smoke that rose from his cigarette. "Doesn't make sense, does it," he said. "Not for a normal six-year-old." He looked from one expectant face to the other. "Of course, Danny's not what you'd call a *normal* boy." He reached out and pushed the ashtray toward the far side of the desk where it would be within easy reach for DeLuca. He thought about getting up and turning on the fan—already hot as blazes at this hour of the morning—and then decided to hell with it. Instead, he reached behind him and opened the window.

"Danny was born too early," Jim commented. "Lungs and heart hadn't been given a chance to mature enough in the womb, I guess. A pound and a half at birth is what they said. Spent the first two months of his life in the hospital attached to all kinds of tubes and gadgets. They didn't think he was going to make it."

The detectives were silent, watching him.

"But he did, of course—wouldn't be here otherwise. It was a damn miracle if you ask me," he said. "The things they can do these days, huh? They can take a picture that can see right through to the bones on the inside of your body, can hook you up to a machine that does the breathing for you." He leaned over and tapped the ash of his cigarette into the ashtray. "Did you know they have a contraption now that can bring the dead back to life? Sends an electric jolt right into the heart and gets it started back up again. I read about it in *Popular Mechanics*. A few years ago they saved a boy's life with one of those things in a hospital back east. In fifty years, I wouldn't be surprised if they had one on every street corner. People won't even be allowed to die without someone lighting 'em up like a Christmas tree." He shook his head. "I imagine that ought to be considered a good thing, bringing a person back to life—but I don't know. Seems a little too close to playing God for my liking."

"So Danny lived," Pierce said, getting him back on track.

"Oh, yeah. He made it, all right. I've lived here all my life, Detectives, and I've known Kate McCray—'course she was Kate Bennet back then—since she was nothing but a child herself. Got to see her grow up, get married, have two children of her own. That's a hell of a thing, you know: to watch a life unfold like that, to see people come into their own. Folks ask what's so great about livin' in a small town, and you know what I say? I say it gives you a chance to watch people grow. It gives you a chance to get to know 'em." He paused, considering this. "Michael and Kate were well-liked back then, and when Danny McCray beat the odds and made it home from the hospital, we all breathed a sigh of relief. Because losing him would've been like losing one of our own. You understand?"

Detective DeLuca nodded. He came from a family of five boys. There were five siblings in total but there used to be six. His little sister hadn't lived past her first month. At twenty-six years of age, there was seldom a day that went by when he didn't think of her—when he didn't feel the loss of that short life and the person she might have become.

"My father was a staunch Lutheran," Jim went on, "so I grew up in a God-fearing family. I don't go to church these days as much as I should, and I certainly don't pretend to know the will of God. But the way of the world is that everything has its price, and when God reaches down and spares you from dyin', I figure there's a price to be paid for that as well."

He sat back, studying them.

"Now, God don't explain himself to us, Detectives. And when he spares us for some higher purpose, you never know what that price is gonna be." He shrugged. "Could be you're like Moses, destined for great works—to deliver your people out of slavery and into the Promised Land." On the other side of the rising smoke, his eyes narrowed. "Could be you're like Job, destined to suffer."

A school bus—empty except for the driver—trundled past the building on its return trip to the dirt lot over on First Street. It was now 9:30 A.M. A good part of the morning was already behind them. And Sean and Danny McCray had been missing for more than thirteen hours.

Jim drew a long breath, and released it through pursed lips. "So, the boy lived," he said, "but he's never spoken—not a word. He can hear just the same as you and me, could maybe moan or scream if he had to, although in six years I've never heard it. But talk? No. He's as silent as a leopard in the high grass, and just as watchful."

"Mrs. McCray said his brother watches out for him," Detective DeLuca commented.

"Yes, he does," Jim agreed. "He's always been a good boy in that way. Fact is, they're almost inseparable. Still, it must be hard for him—having a brother like that."

The room was silent for a moment. Jim stubbed his cigarette out in the ashtray, thought about having another one.

"What's the deal with the mother?" Pierce asked. "She's got some sort of condition?"

"Yeah," Jim replied. "A condition. I guess you could call it that." He looked up at the ceiling, back down at them. "Started a number of years ago, not long after Danny was born."

DeLuca's notepad was in his lap, his pen poised to write.

"At first it was small things," Jim continued. "I've known her all her life, like I said, and she's always been what I'd consider to be a graceful woman." He smiled. "Does that sound odd, coming from an old-timer like me? Well, maybe it is. The thing about a small town, though, is that exceptional people are easier to spot. They don't blend in the way they might in a big city. You notice people's abilities right off. And Kate Mc-Cray had a certain elegance about her that was hard to miss. Or maybe that's just how I remember it. The mind does funny things in retrospect."

"So she became ill shortly after the birth of her second child," Pierce said, but Jim frowned, scrunched up his face as if deciding whether this was true.

"I don't know that *ill* is the right word," he said. "There's no denying it now, of course, but back then it wasn't clear what was going on. The early symptoms were subtle, the changes so gradual you could fool yourself into imagining it was nothing. That's how the worst diseases—the ones you never recover from—start out, I guess." He thought for a moment of Ira Sokolov, the accountant who had once occupied this very desk, working over his orderly columns of numbers as the tickle in his throat became a cough—nothing too bothersome really, just . . . persistent. By the time Ira was coughing up blood and too winded to climb the short flight of stairs to the office, it was too late for the doctors to do anything about it. Then again, maybe there was never anything to be done. Maybe Ira was doomed from the start.

"There comes a tipping point when you realize things are not going to get better on their own. Kate McCray is well past that. She's been to more doctors, has had more tests, than any person I know. There's a neurologist she sees up in Redding. Sounds like a nice enough guy. Michael told me this doctor thinks she has Lou Gehrig's disease. You know, the Hall of Famer for the Yankees who died back in '41? Well, apparently she's got the same symptoms, or many of them anyway. It's a bad disease to have. No cure for it. The body just stops working. Everything just . . ."

"Shuts down," DeLuca finished for him, and Jim nodded.

"Do they know how much longer she has?" Pierce asked.

"Don't know," Jim said. "I haven't heard one way or the other." His metal lighter was in his front shirt pocket next to the pack of Lucky Strikes. He brought it out, flipped the top open and then closed again, a restless habit. "Why do they feel the need to tell a person how much time they've got anyway? Who wants to know a thing like that?"

Neither of the detectives answered. Instead they rose and offered their handshakes and gratitude to the town's only plumber and part-time sheriff.

"There's something else," Jim said, knowing he should tell them everything, yet not wanting to repeat the rumor. It was nonsense, he realized, fearmongering and pointless speculation. In Cottonwood, there was certainly plenty of that to go around. Still, there were people in this town who believed it, who might even act upon it if given the chance. That was motive enough to take a child—at least *this one* anyway. Nonsense or not, the detectives needed to know.

Pierce and DeLuca sat down again, a little reluctant, eager to get back out on the street before the trail got any colder. Jim understood that, and he didn't keep them for long. He folded his arms in front of him, elbows resting on the desk, and told them the rest.

5

D ON'T GIVE IT A SECOND THOUGHT, MICHAEL," DENNIS
Volkmann, the principal of Anderson Union High,
responded on the other end of the line. "Jim Kent
contacted me earlier this morning—he figured you would be
occupied with other concerns."

"I'm sorry," Michael said. "I just didn't . . . it didn't occur to
me until later."

"I can't say how upsetting this is for all of us. I mean—
Jesus—what a thing to . . ." Dennis paused, and Michael
pictured his chubby face reddening the way it always did
when he was distraught, the sweat beading on his forehead
and trickling from his temples, the pudgy hand moving to
the handkerchief in his pocket, swiping it across the back of his
neck. "This is . . . it's unthinkable. I can't imagine what you
and Kate must be going through. Have you . . . has there been
any word?"

"No, nothing."

"Do they have any idea where he might have taken them? I
mean, surely there must be—"

"There were two detectives from the Shasta County Sheriff's
Department here this morning. They think he might've headed

east or west from Redding along Route 299. They're combing the area now."

"Well, they'll find them," Dennis said. "That's all there is to it. Those guys at the sheriff's department don't mess around. I've got a nephew on the force. I'll call him today and tell him to—"

"I appreciate that," Michael said, cutting him off, unable to listen to any more false reassurances.

"Oh, you betcha. Anything I can do. And listen," Volkmann told him, "don't worry about your classroom. We've got you covered. I spoke to Sally Henderson this morning. She's available for the next several weeks—longer if we need her."

"Well, that's very kind. Tell Sally I said thank you."

"Of course, of course. You just concentrate on your family right now. We'll take care of everything else. This is a"—there was a sigh on the other end—"well, it's a hell of a thing. I never thought I'd see the day when something like this happened here. I mean, L.A. or San Francisco sure, but . . ."

Michael placed a hand on the windowsill, looked out at the side yard, at the gray-painted exterior of the Cassidys' place next door. Already, the sun had reached its pinnacle in the sky, and the neighbor's house cast only a sliver of shadow on the lawn. *Almost noon*, he thought, *the day half over.* He struggled with the horror of this, tried to swallow it. They'd received numerous calls from neighbors expressing their concern. He'd cut the conversations short, desperate to keep the line free in case the kidnapper tried to contact them. *I should hang up now*, he told himself, *find some distraction to occupy my time.* Kate had fallen asleep a half hour ago. He would sit by the phone and read—try to, anyway.

"Listen, I've got to go," he told Volkmann. "Thanks for handling things."

"No problem, Michael. If there's anything I can do—anything at all . . ."

"I'll let you know," Michael said, and hung up the phone.

He walked slowly around the kitchen, opening a cupboard and then closing it, drumming his fingers on the teal Formica countertop, running a hand across the raised chrome lettering of the top-loading dishwasher they'd splurged on two years ago. His footsteps echoed on the linoleum. In the middle of his third lap, he stopped, asked himself what he was doing. Making noise, he realized, not wanting to listen to the silence. It was impossible to stand here and do nothing, to wait for the phone to ring with what he feared would be horrible news: *We've found them, in a ditch off Route 299 about forty miles west of here. I'm so sorry.*

He went to the family room, sat down on the davenport, picked up a magazine. The cover was a picture of Eddie Mathews midswing in front of a sold-out crowd at the newly opened Milwaukee County Stadium, for the first issue of what they'd creatively titled *Sports Illustrated*. *I should go outside*, Michael thought, *put my energy to use on some project I've been putting off.* He tossed the magazine aside, stood, made another sweep of the room, and then stopped. No, he wanted to be here when Kate woke. He should be waiting by the phone in case it—

The phone rang. The sudden sound caused him to jump.

He stood there, openmouthed, staring at the thing.

It rang again, a hollow, mournful sound—like the rattling throes of a dying animal.

The third time he was across the room and snatching up the receiver before he even realized he'd moved.

"Hello? Yes, hello?"

No one spoke on the other end. There was only breathing, deep and slightly labored.

"Hello?" he said again, suddenly sure it was him. His hand clenched around the receiver, squeezing so tightly his fingers tingled with the effort.

Nothing. Just breathing. And in the background—muffled and barely audible—*was that the sound of a child talking?*

"Listen," Michael said, and his voice shook. As if following suit, the familiar tremor in his right hand and forearm began.

He wrested the receiver from his right hand and put it in his left, pressed the flesh of his right palm hard against his thigh, willed the tremor to pass. *Not now, not now,* he thought, but his arm continued to spasm, the shaking more violent with each passing second. His knuckles smashed against the lip of the kitchen counter, the blood seeping from the small pores of the newly formed wound. With his left hand, he held the phone to his ear while his right side convulsed in a wild, chaotic dance. He leaned against the counter for support, and almost fell. His shoulder bumped the toaster and it tipped over, its metal casing striking the countertop with a loud crash, the electric cord snapping taut.

Wait, wait! he wanted to scream into the phone, *I'm having a . . . I just need a few seconds!* But he couldn't do or say anything. Suddenly he thought of his son, and how it must feel to have so much to say and no voice to say it, or to have every person in your life—the entire world, as you know it—simply stop listening.

It was coming to an end. Michael could feel it now, the tremors abating, the muscles in his right arm beginning to ache, the fatigue settling in. He was breathing hard, heard only silence on the other end. He stood straighter, tried to pull himself together.

"Hello? Are you still there?" he asked, but there was only a trace of static now.

"*Shit!*" he exploded, slamming down the receiver. He turned, walked to the far wall, spun around, and came back. In the other room, he could hear Kate stirring, moving the walker into position as she readied herself to get out of bed.

Michael went to the phone, lifted the handset to his ear once again. He placed his index finger over the zero in the rotary dial, and spun it around until it stopped.

"Operator," a voice answered.

"Hello, yes. I'd like to . . . I just received an important call, but was disconnected. Are you able to reconnect me with the caller?" he asked.

"Do you know the number of the party you were speaking with?"

"No, I . . . I don't."

There was a slight pause. "I'm sorry, sir. The cords have been disconnected from the switchboard. If you have a name or address, I might be able to—"

"No, I don't have either of those," he replied. He could hear the slide of the walker, the shuffle of Kate's feet in the doorway behind him.

"I'm sorry, sir," the operator repeated. "Would you like to make another call?"

Michael closed his eyes, took a deep breath. "No. Thank you."

"Have a good day, sir," she said, and the line was dead once again.

"Who was that?" Kate asked.

Michael turned and went to her, placed his hands on her shoulders. He leaned forward and kissed her on the forehead. "No one," he said, and tried to smile. But it felt all wrong on his face, plastic and artificial.

Kate's body tensed beneath his hands, her eyes widening, the deep hollows of her cheeks caving in on themselves even farther. "Was that him? Was that about Sean and Danny? Did he—"

"No," Michael lied, not wanting to upset her when there was nothing to be done. "It was no one, a bad connection."

"What if it was him?" she asked, the pitch of her voice rising. "What if it was the man who took—"

"It wasn't," he said. "It was a woman's voice. I couldn't make it out."

She turned away from him. Or at least tried to. Her feet faltered a bit and she lurched forward, her hands catching herself on the walker.

Michael reached out and steadied her. "Careful," he said. "Let me help you to the—"

"I can do it myself!" she snapped. "Let go of me."

He did as she asked, watched as she made her way to the couch.

"Can I get you anything?" he asked after a while. "You haven't eaten all day."

She didn't answer, only picked up a magazine and began flipping through the pages.

"Kate. Honey."

"I'm fine."

Michael sat beside her, placed his hand where her upper back merged with the knuckle of bone at the base of her neck. "Listen," he said. "The detectives, they're going to find them. It's only a matter of time until—"

"If you don't take your hand off me, I'm going to scream."

He withdrew, interlaced his fingers and placed them in his lap.

"Where are they?" she asked, her voice quiet but steady in the still of the room.

"I don't know," he answered. "They have scores of police officers out looking for them right now."

"Will they find them?"

"Yes."

"Don't lie to me." She turned, looked at him through eyes sunk deep in the emaciated contours of her face. The tendons in her neck were cables, the outline of her windpipe clearly visible beneath the mottled gray of her skin.

Michael took a deep breath. Closed his eyes and opened them again. "I don't know if they will find them," he told her. "I have faith that they will. I trust that God will protect them."

"Don't talk to me about God," she said, and actually grimaced at the word. "God shouldn't have allowed them to be taken from us in the first place. He should've given Danny a voice, should've kept me healthy enough to raise my own children into adulthood instead of forcing them to watch their mother waste away into . . ."

She turned her head, staring forward once again, the cartilage in her throat rising and falling as she struggled to control the grief that had grown over the years with her illness, that was forming still, massive and inescapable.

"You know what I've been thinking about?" she continued. "The time we sent Sean to stay with my sister. During those first two months while Danny was in the hospital." She brought a hand to her cheek, but there were no tears, only a thin film of regret that couldn't be brushed away. "You remember that?"

He nodded. "Of course."

"Back then it seemed like the right thing to do. It didn't seem healthy for Sean to spend all that time in the hospital, visiting a brother who might not live. He was too young, I thought, to deal with that kind of thing." She leaned closer to him. "Back then I was thinking, *What if Danny dies? How can I subject a four-year-old to that kind of emotional trauma?*" She shook her head, turned to her husband. "But do you know what I ask myself now? What if Danny *had* died? What if a few months was all he had, and I denied his brother the opportunity to spend that time with him?"

Michael held her gaze. Said nothing.

"Do you understand what I'm telling you?" she asked. "This"—she looked down at the wasted landscape of her body, then back up at him—"is not what I wanted. But it's what I have. I can't change that. And even if I could, it would come at too great a sacrifice." She took a breath, lifted her hand and traced her fingertips across the familiar lines of his face. "*I want to live*," she said, "but even more than that, I want to be with my children for whatever time I have left. And I refuse to let you, or the man who took our boys, or even God himself take that away from me."

Her hand fell to his chest, palm pressing against his rib cage, against the steady tread of his heart. "I don't want to know how, and I won't ask you about it later. But I need you to do whatever it takes to get Sean and Danny back."

He placed his hand over hers, felt her warmth, her will to live. "I'll cooperate with the detectives in every way that I can. We'll—"

"That's not what I'm talking about," she said, and her voice turned hard. "Promise me: whatever it takes."

Michael swallowed, and considered all that promise might entail.

"Swear to me."

"Whatever it takes," Michael said.

She nodded, and leaned her head against his shoulder. He wrapped his arms around her, her body slight and fragile, as if it were made of folded paper.

"Do you remember how it used to be?" she asked. "Between the two of us? Do you remember how you used to love me?"

The question startled him. "I never stopped loving you."

"I know," she said. "But now you love me in a different way. I'm okay with that. It happens to everyone."

He said nothing, didn't know how to respond.

"Can we go back?" she asked. "Do you think that's still possible for us?"

He looked at her upturned face, at the tears welling in her eyes now. Was this the same girl he'd kissed at the top of the Ferris wheel twelve years before? Or was she somehow different, wiser, stronger, embattled by the pain and indignities she'd endured over the years? She had lost her innocence. They both had.

"No," he answered. "But we can go forward." And when he leaned in to kiss her, he found that her lips were still sweet, the way he remembered them from that first time. He pulled her closer. "I love you," he said. "I would do anything to protect you."

"I don't need you to protect me," she whispered. "I just need you to bring them back."

6

DAVE SCHRADER WAS STANDING IN THE FRONT YARD WAIT-
ing for them, leaning up against his black-and-white
police cruiser as Pierce swung the unmarked gray
Ford sedan into the driveway. Dave tipped the brim of his hat,
greeted the detectives as they stepped from the car.

"Afternoon, sirs."

"Dave," Pierce said, nodding to the deputy. DeLuca walked
around the front of the car to join them.

The deputy removed his sunglasses, squinted a bit in the
bright afternoon sun. "She's in the living room waiting for
you," he said. "Tends house and takes care of the children
while their father's at work. The kids' mother died of spinal
meningitis year before last." Schrader shook his head. "Got to
be hard on a man." He looked down at his shoes, then back
up at the front door. "Not sure how much help she'll be," he
continued. "Woman says she saw a man in a tan jacket cross
the street, climb into the car, and drive away. Didn't get a look
at his face."

"Well, that's something at least," Pierce said, letting his eyes
wander over the single-story brick ranch house, the poorly

tended flower bed in the front yard. The house faced away from the market. Gas Point Road was on the other side.

The three men went to the door and knocked, though it was partially opened.

"Come in, please," a female voice called, and they entered, wiping their feet on the mat outside.

A young colored woman sat on the couch, hands folded in her lap. She looked to be in her early twenties, straightened hair in a pixie cut that framed her smooth, broad forehead and the high cheekbones that tapered toward the jawline. Her dress was a light blue with short white sleeves. She rose to greet them, and walked across the room.

"Miss Tucker, these are the men I told you about," Schrader said. "This is Detective Pierce"—the senior investigator stepped forward, shook her hand—"and this is Detective De-Luca."

"Ma'am," DeLuca said.

"Hello," she replied, her voice quavering as she spoke. She looked anxious.

"I was hoping you could tell them what you told me," Schrader said.

The woman looked from one face to the next.

"Why don't we sit," Pierce suggested, motioning to the couch and the two chairs that faced it. He turned to the deputy. "I think we can take it from here."

Schrader nodded. "I'll continue my rounds through the neighborhood. See if there's anyone else you should talk to while you're in the area."

"Thank you," Pierce told him.

The man glanced at the woman, then turned and left, closing the front door behind him.

The three of them—Pierce, DeLuca, and their only eyewitness so far—stood facing one another in the center of the room.

"We appreciate you coming forward like this," DeLuca said. He stepped around one of the chairs and sat down.

She returned to the couch, sat, and pressed her palms against her thighs through the fabric of her dress.

"First day back at school for the children," Pierce said.

"Yes, sir," she replied, her eyes not quite rising to the level of their faces.

"Well, you've done a good thing in agreeing to speak with us," he reiterated. "Witnesses are crucial in these types of situations."

She said nothing, simply sat there, awaiting their questions.

"Why don't you walk us through what you saw. This was . . . what time exactly?"

"A little before eight, I reckon." Her voice lifted at the end of the sentence, turning it into a question. She looked up at them, as if hoping for confirmation.

"Your employer—the father of the children you care for—was he home at the time?"

She hesitated. "I was—"

Pierce held up a hand, stopping her. "Miss Tucker," he said. "My partner and I realize that speaking with police officers can make many people nervous. But let me assure you of something. We're not here to investigate you, but rather a crime that you may have witnessed. So please, try not to be anxious. You have an opportunity to help the boys who were kidnapped. The truth is always the right answer."

She sat there, considering. "Mr. Gladstone got home around six thirty," she said. "I had dinner ready for him and the children. That's one of my jobs." She looked up briefly, made eye contact with both of them, and then dropped her eyes to the carpet. "Afterward," she continued, "Mr. Gladstone went to the study. He said he had some work to do and asked me to stay late to put the children to bed."

"Okay."

"That's why I was still here at eight o'clock."

"We understand," Pierce told her. "And it was around that time that you saw the man heading toward the car parked in front of the market."

"Yes, sir." She nodded. "The children took their baths and I was putting them to bed. Lilly—that's the youngest—left a stuffed bear under the table in the dining room." The woman lifted a hand from her lap and pointed toward the room in the back of the house. "I went to fetch it," she said, "and that's when I looked out through the sliding glass door and saw him heading across the parking lot. He had his back to me. I didn't see his face."

"But he caught your eye," Pierce said, "enough to stop what you were doing and watch him." He leaned forward. "Why was that?"

Restless fingers fidgeted in her lap.

"The truth, please," Pierce prodded. "What was it about this man that made you stop and watch?"

She shook her head. "Wasn't the man at all that caught my eye. It was the car."

"The Mercury," DeLuca said, and she nodded.

"Liberty blue Mercury Eight. Belongs to the McCrays. Everyone knows that."

The younger detective frowned. "Why does everyone know that?"

"Small town. People take notice."

"Of the make and model owned by every resident in this town?" Pierce asked. He sat back, placing his right hand on the

armrest. "Sheriff Kent tells us there are about a hundred and
sixty families living in Cottonwood. Are you familiar with the
cars driven by all of them?"

"No, sir. Not all."

"But you know the McCrays' car. Would you say that most
people do?"

She looked toward the corner of the room, hesitated before
nodding.

"Why is that?"

She was silent, lost in her thoughts.

"Miss Tuc—"

"Because of them boys, I reckon."

"What about them?" Pierce asked. "What's so special about
Sean and Danny McCray?"

She winced at the question, tucked her lower lip inward.

"Miss Tucker."

"Nothing," she told them. "Nothing's special about them
at all."

"If you know something . . ." DeLuca pressed

She shook her head. "People talk. That's all."

"What do they say?"

"Foolishness, mostly. People get sick and die. It's a part of
life. Can't put that on no one but God himself."

They sat in silence for a while, the woman resolute now, the
detectives thinking back to the things Sheriff Kent had told
them earlier that day.

"He was a big man," she said at last. "White fellow with
black hair. Broad in the shoulders. Had on a tan jacket that
was too heavy for the weather. I don't like to say this about
people, but I could tell he was trouble from the moment I laid
eyes on him."

"Why was that?" DeLuca asked.

She shrugged. "The way he walked, for one thing: long quick steps, heading straight for Mr. McCray's car across the lot. I said to myself, 'Bernice, that man is going to steal that car right this very minute. You just wait and see.'"

"The store was about to close," Pierce told her. "What made you think he was going for the car instead of trying to make it to the store before the owner locked the doors for the night?"

"Stan Eddleworth?" she remarked with a thin smile. "He's not going to lock no door against anyone around here. But that man wasn't from Cottonwood, and he wasn't going for the store, neither. He was going for the car." She seemed less timid now, more angry, as if caught up in her story. "I shoulda picked up the phone and called Jim Kent myself, told him there was something about to happen at the Century Grocery. I shoulda done that. Or called Derik—Mr. Gladstone, I mean—and asked him to come look for himself. I wasn't sure, though—or didn't think I had the right to *be* sure." Her hands gathered the soft material of her dress, clenched it in her fists. "And I didn't know. I didn't know the quiet one was in the car."

"The quiet one?"

"Yes, sir. The quiet child, that's what people call him. On account of he doesn't talk."

Pierce and DeLuca exchanged a glance, turned their attention back to the woman.

"Miss Tucker," Pierce said. "Does the town have a special relationship with Danny McCray?"

"'A special relationship'?" she asked, repeating the words. "I don't know what you mean."

"Do people treat him differently from the other children? Because he doesn't talk."

She considered this for a moment, glancing up at the door as if she expected a new arrival, someone to be standing in the threshold. When she spoke again her voice was softer, a little guarded. "People leave him alone, I reckon."

"Why? Because he's different?"

"That's part of it."

"Is there another reason?" DeLuca pressed. He was leaning forward in his chair, his left forearm resting on his knee.

"No," the woman replied. "Nothing else. He's just . . ." She shook her head, glanced at the door once again before returning her eyes to the two faces in front of her. "I don't want to talk about that."

"It may be helpful to our investigat—"

"It can't be helped. There's nothing anyone can do. I don't want to talk about it."

The room went quiet. For the space of ten seconds, none of them spoke.

Pierce shifted in his seat. "You were telling us about the man you saw crossing the parking lot," he reminded her. "What happened next?"

She sat there with her head down, trying to refocus.

"The other boy came out of the store. Sean McCray. I couldn't see his features, not all the way across the lot, but I recognized the car and so I knew it was him." She paused a moment, recollecting. "The man had reached the Mercury by then. He was standing with his right hand on the driver's door, about to open it. Sean walked out, and then stopped when he saw him. The two just . . . looked at each other for a moment. I expected Sean to run back into the store and get his father. But he didn't do that. The man opened the car door and got inside, and with the door still open Sean ran right up and grabbed him, tried to pull him out like the guy didn't outweigh him by two hundred pounds." She shook her head. "The man shoved him, sent that boy sprawling in the lot. He cranked the ignition once, twice, and when it started he began to swing the door closed. But Sean was back on his feet by then and charging right for him. This time, when he got to the car, the man grabbed him by the shirt and yanked him right in, across his body and into the front passenger seat. Then he gunned the engine and tore out of that lot like he was running from the devil himself. Got out onto Gas Point Road and shot toward the freeway." She took in a deep breath. "By then I had the phone in my hand and was dialing the operator. But Stan Eddleworth, he beat me to it."

"Could you tell whether the car was heading north or south?" DeLuca asked.

"Couldn't say for sure," she responded. "My view was blocked by the house next door. If I had to guess, I'd say it was north."

"Why north?"

She shrugged. "It's what I would do if I was trying to get away from the law. I'd go north to Redding, then west into the mountains."

"Why not east?" DeLuca asked. "Try to make it to the Nevada line."

"It's what I would do later," she said, "but not right away. Too much distance to travel. Too much chance of getting caught." She gave it some further consideration, and then nodded. "Right now he's in the mountains, someplace remote and off the main roads. And I wouldn't waste time looking for that car if I were you. Probably in a shed somewhere, or abandoned altogether. You're not gonna spot it—unless he's a fool, which he might be, but still . . . I'll bet he's got that car hidden real good."

She stopped then. "Listen to me go on like that, as if I know about such things. 'People talk,' like I said. And I'm no better."

"You've given it some thought," Pierce commented, rising from his chair. "More than our kidnapper, I hope." He nodded. "Thanks for your time, ma'am."

"It was no trouble," she said, leading them to the door. "I hope I was able to help."

"You were," DeLuca replied. "Men like this"—he gave her a reassuring look—"it's only a matter of time until the law catches up with them. The guilty, they run out of road pretty quick."

"I'm sure that's true," she said. "The Lord stands in judgment of each of us. But sometimes judgment comes sooner. People have a way of taking matters into their own hands."

"Is Cottonwood that kind of town?" Pierce asked her. "A place where people take matters into their own hands?"

"If pushed hard enough, every place is that kind of a town," she said. "And that scares me, Detectives." She stood there, her hand on the door. "Because sooner or later, we're all guilty of something."

7

MICHAEL SAT ON THE FRONT PORCH AND LISTENED FOR the phone to ring. He'd been hovering around it all day, fielded a few more calls from neighbors and one from Jim Kent, but nothing with any real news. In his mind, he kept returning to the missed call, the one he'd let slip through his fingers. At first, he'd been convinced the caller would try again, that the phone would ring and this time there would be more than silence and the sound of breathing: a voice on the other end, telling him where to go and what to do, how things were going to play out from here. But the hours had passed. The sun had descended from its angry perch in the sky, leaving behind a fading glow on the horizon, and still there was no word of his boys.

Sitting here in the gathering darkness, Michael had time to consider other possibilities. *What if the caller had been Danny? What if his younger son had somehow gotten to a phone, tried to contact him?* That would explain the silence on the other end. Maybe he'd been trying to communicate in some other way.

Sound of tires on the asphalt.

Michael looked up, half-expecting to see Sean coasting toward the house on his red Schwinn, the frame speckled with dirt and a few scattered blades of sun-burnt grass.

But no, it was not his son—*how could it be?*—but rather Bill Travis's boy Kenneth riding past on his bike, the machine-gun sputter of a baseball card clacking away at the spokes. Michael raised a hand, waved to him as he rode, but the kid didn't look up; instead he leaned into the turn. A moment later, he was gone.

It had not been Danny on the phone earlier, Michael decided. He would've known—would've sensed it with a parent's unfailing ability to hone in on the signal of his own child. These days, it was so hard to be certain of anything. *But it hadn't been Danny*, he reassured himself. He could be certain of that.

There was a small pinch at the side of his neck and Michael brought his hand up quickly, the surface of his fingers smacking against the skin. He looked down at the smear of blood, the broken body of the mosquito whose attempt to feed had cost it its life. Crushed wings and demolished appendages. The things one must do to survive always came with a price.

At the living room window, a light blinked on, its shaft spilling across the lawn to his right. It illuminated part of the neighbor's driveway—the right-rear quarter panel of the Napolitanos' Chrysler.

Not even eight o'clock yet, and Kate was getting ready for bed. She slept so much these days, could barely manage more than a few wakeful hours in between. There was a time not so long ago (or so it seemed) when they'd taken evening walks together, engaged in quiet conversation as the tapering daylight gave way to night. Back then it was only the two of them, and he'd had the notion that every good thing still lay ahead, that their lives had only just begun. *There will be children*, he'd thought, the idea sending waves of giddiness through his body as they lay together in the afterglow of intimacy, her head resting on his chest, his fingertips brushing against the warm embrace of her skin. If he awakened in the night, disoriented from sleep, he had only to turn his body or to reach out in the darkness to find her, always present, a promise that would never be broken.

Michael stood, stretched his limbs. It was time to go inside. He could barely make out the hulking shapes of the cars parked in their neighbors' driveways on either side. They were everything that was wrong with this town that no one ever mentioned: the way you could live simply, mind your own business, and find yourself surrounded just the same.

The screen door creaked and slapped shut behind him, and he swung the heavier door closed and turned the dead bolt, locking out the night. He was halfway down the hall to check on the boys when he suddenly stopped, realizing their room would be empty. He leaned against the wall, eyes closed, placed the palm of his right hand against his chest, the place where it hurt the most.

"*We'll find them*," Jim Kent had promised, but a full day had come and gone and the bedroom at the end of the hallway remained empty. *What if tomorrow is no different*, he thought, *and the day after that? What if the days and eventually the years stack on top of each other like perpetual shovels of dirt being tossed into the mouth of an open grave? What then?*

The walls of the hallway swelled and receded, moved in and out with a steady rhythmic oscillation. He could hear it breathing, the house—could stand here and listen to the sound of its suffering. A wave of dizziness passed over him. He fought it, clenched his teeth until the worst of it was over. Then he turned in the hallway and made his way back to the makeshift bedroom he shared with his wife.

Standing in the dark, Michael shucked off his clothes and slid in beside Kate, wrapping an arm around her the way she'd once done to him. The hair on her scalp was limp and thinning, the jut of her ribs and hip bones prominent against his naked torso. He could smell the sickness leaching through the pores of her skin. Still, it gave him comfort to be with her, to feel the beat of her heart against his hand. He breathed her in, all the many things that were a part of her now. Then he closed his eyes and slept.

8

JUNCTION CITY, CALIFORNIA, WAS A BLIP ON THE MAP, THE last town before Route 299 sidled up against the Trinity River and wound its way into the Shasta-Trinity National Forest. Getting here had taken Jim Kent well over an hour, the drive pretty enough but hindered by the serpentine road and the other drivers paying more attention to the scenery than their own forward progress. It was Saturday—five days after the disappearance of Sean and Danny McCray. The Shasta County Sheriff's Department, employing the assistance of the California State Police, had scoured a vast swath of territory within a 150-mile radius. An APB had been broadcast to jurisdictions as far north as Seattle and as far south as San Diego, photos and descriptions of the boys disseminated to post offices within the search area. The story had been picked up by several state and local news agencies. Legions of people were on the lookout for the two missing boys. There was no reason for Jim to expect that his own efforts would tip the scales.

Still: it had been five days.

The sheriff squinted as a flash of sunlight winked through the tall canopy of trees. The foliage here was pine with a few scattered oaks, the branches shielding his eyes from most of the direct rays. He kept his sunglasses within easy reach, though, allowing them to slide back and forth on the front passenger seat as he guided the Ford Crestliner around the unending succession of curves.

Up ahead, a deer stood near the edge of the roadway, head erect, black nose twitching, broad ears standing at attention. Jim slowed to a stop, considered tapping the horn, but the animal was already turning and making for the shelter of the woods.

Jim eased the car forward, and rounded the next turn.

It didn't make sense to him that there had been no word from the kidnapper. If he'd meant to take the boys, he reasoned, then the man had done so for a specific purpose. Ransom was a common motive, but the McCrays didn't have much money. Michael taught science at Anderson Union High and Kate raised the children—or at least used to before her illness had really taken hold. And the medical bills had no doubt decimated any savings they once had.

From the Tucker lady's account, it seemed the man was mostly interested in the car, even pushing Sean away when he'd attempted to intervene. Chances were, he hadn't even noticed Danny in the backseat. Then when things started to go wrong, he'd panicked, pulled Sean into the car and taken off. So he now had two boys he didn't know what to do with instead of one, witnesses who could identify him if he ever let them go. Was that reason enough to hold on to them, or to do something far worse? Jim didn't think so. But people make bad decisions all the time, and allow situations to escalate beyond their control.

Or, Jim thought, the kidnapper was intending to take the boys all along—if not for ransom then for another purpose altogether. That line of thinking led him down a different path, a darker one that might culminate—statistically speaking— with the eventual discovery of two bodies in the woods. *That* would explain why the kidnapper hadn't tried to contact them, and probably never would. It was something he didn't like to contemplate. But there were times—times like this—when he could hear it shuffling around behind a closed door in his mind, scratching to be let out.

The trees closed in on the roadway as he entered the national forest, the route itself becoming narrower and more tortuous than before. With drivers distracted by the view of the river, it wouldn't take much for a head-on collision, a slight drift across the center line, an oncoming vehicle taking the curve too fast. He'd been Cottonwood's sheriff for enough years to see it happen in his own community: that sudden shift of fortune, the random, deadly nature of it barreling down on you from the other side of a blind curve. No time to react.

He slowed a little, gripped the steering wheel tighter, his eyes moving back and forth as he scanned the forest on either side of the road, the river below. There was something out here, some trace of them. There had to be. People do not just disappear. There was a concerted law enforcement effort under way. They would find them—*soon*, he thought.

He only hoped it would be soon enough.

9

MICHAEL THANKED THE DRIVER AND SWUNG THE PASSENger door open, stepping out of the car and into the bright afternoon sunlight. He donned his Stetson, tilted it forward to keep the sun off his face as he made his way up the steeply graded driveway. There wasn't much to this area of the county: a few farming houses; hawks circling overhead, hunting for rabbits; a smattering of scrub brush amid the brown rolling terrain. Middle Fork Creek sometimes overflowed during the rainy season, carrying with it waste and debris from the small chemical plant to the north. By August it was a broad, dry trench of cracked earth and sage grass, dead and forgotten until the rains returned five months later.

He climbed the front steps, stood on the wraparound porch, one hand on the railing. Michael had helped Kate's sister, Lauren, paint it the year before, a blazing white that matched the trim on the windows and helped to mask the house's steady physical decline. A rotting board creaked beneath his feet and he stepped away from it toward the door. Since Lauren's husband's passing, there was a lot of work to be done here, more than she could manage on her own. Michael visited often and did what he could. But the paint from the year before had already begun to fade and chip beneath the sun's furious glare. The shingles on the roof were in desperate need of replacing. In the colder months, the furnace emitted a low whine that drove Michael crazy, although Lauren no longer seemed to notice it.

He rapped on the front door with his knuckles, and stepped back. The board creaked again beneath his weight and he took another step backward, just to be safe. Within the house, there was only silence. Michael turned and waited, hands on the rail as he looked out across the land. There was something—a coyote maybe—skulking along the field in the distance some three hundred yards away on the far side of the creek. He watched it, listened to the sound of footsteps as his sister-in-law made her way toward the front of the house.

"Michael," she said, opening the door and stepping out onto the porch.

"Lauren."

She gave him a half hug, planted a kiss on his cheek. "How are you?"

"Not good," he said.

She touched his arm, said nothing.

"It's been a week now."

The words and their implication lingered on the porch between them.

"Two detectives from the Shasta County Sheriff's Department drove out here to speak with me on Thursday," she said.

He nodded, wrapped a hand around the wooden support beam beside him.

"They said there was an eyewitness, a lady who saw it happen. At the time, they were following up on a few leads. I was hoping that by now they'd have . . ."

"Nothing." Michael turned to study the valley below, and

she joined him at the rail. He could no longer see the coyote. It must have slipped away while his attention was elsewhere.

"I worry that she won't make it," he said. "Kate." He glanced at Lauren, at the subtle lines etched along the corners of her eyes and mouth. Her blond hair had been pretty once, her figure attractive before the surgery. The cancer was gone now, carved out of her right breast three years ago. She should be better, recovered. But she moved carefully, like a woman twice her age, her body hollowed out by the disease and something else. He could see it in her face, in the hunch of her shoulders. She wasn't as bad off as Kate—not yet, anyway—but she would be. It was only a matter of time until she crumbled in on herself, completing what had already begun. And she knew it. Michael could see that as well.

"They want me to stay at home, to be there in case the kidnapper calls," he told her. "I don't know if I can do that anymore."

"What else *can* you do?"

He shrugged. "I can go looking for them myself. It's something I should've done already."

Lauren shook her head. "Kate needs you. Don't go driving off and leave her. She can't get through this alone."

"She can't get through this at all unless I find them," he replied.

A hawk cried out in the sky above, a piercing screech that unfurled itself across the open landscape. Michael removed a handkerchief from his pocket, wiped at the sweat on the back of his neck.

"Where will you go? Where will you look?" she asked. "There are so many people out searching for them already."

"I'd be one more."

"And if the kidnapper *does* call while you're away?"

"If he was going to call, it would've happened already." He turned, looked at her. "Can I ask you a favor—two, actually?"

"What?"

"I'll need to borrow your car," he said. "We don't have a replacement."

She glanced toward the driveway at the Buick Special, its dark blue paint reflecting the sunlight, shining it back in her eyes. She'd always thought of it as Gary's car—something her husband had loved to tinker with on the weekends. She'd never felt completely comfortable driving it, even after he was gone. *Especially* after he was gone.

"I hitched a ride out here," Michael told her. "It's hard to find a driver heading in this direction. I wish you lived closer to town."

In the front yard, a rabbit darted from the relative safety of the bushes. Then it quickly disappeared around the corner of the house.

"What's the other one?" she asked.

"The what?"

"The other one. The second favor."

It struck him then that he was asking a lot of her. This house—this whole godforsaken place—was her refuge. She'd settled into it after the surgery, had become comfortable here despite its many shortcomings, venturing into town only once a week for her necessary trip to the market. Michael was asking her to change her routine, to upset the delicate balance of her life.

"Would you stay with her, Lauren," he asked, "while I'm away?"

He could see her draw back at his question, the apprehension rising to the surface.

"I don't . . . I don't like that house, Michael."

"I know," he said. "But it's just your sister."

She took a deep breath, held it for a moment before slowly releasing it.

"Does she know?" she asked. "Have you even told her that you're going?"

He nodded. "She knows." But she didn't know all of it. None of them did. And for now—and maybe forever—that was for the best.

10

WHAT DO YOU MEAN, 'HE LEFT'?" JIM ASKED. HE WAS standing in the McCrays' kitchen, hands on his police utility belt, speaking with Kate's sister, Lauren. This day was not going well. Two hours ago, he'd been at the regional medical center in Redding, where a fourteen-year-old colored boy had been hospitalized after his classmates attacked him on his way home from school. The bus driver, William Bradford, had witnessed the fight and done nothing to stop it. The injuries were severe: a broken cheekbone and a lacerated spleen; several cracked ribs and an eye injury that the surgeon Jim had spoken to felt fairly confident would result in permanent vision loss. The whole thing had put him in a foul mood, and on the drive back to Cottonwood Jim had chastised himself for thinking that—in *his* small town, at least—the path to a desegregated school system would be peaceful.

"I'm sorry, Jim. I thought you knew," Lauren replied, bringing him back to the situation at hand.

"That Michael was leaving town to go after them?" he asked. "Where the hell did he go?"

"I don't know. He didn't tell me," she said, and this was true, or maybe half-true. Lauren hadn't asked for details, doubted Michael would've given them to her if she had. *It was better this way*, she thought. *Not knowing*. There was nothing to hide.

"Did he tell Detectives Pierce and DeLuca where he was heading?" Jim asked. "You know, they've been searching the area for over a week. It does no good for him to just . . ." He shook his head. "Well, *damn*. I wish he'd said something. This guy we're looking for, he's . . ." He looked at Lauren. "Your brother-in-law could be in danger, you know."

"I'm sure he's aware of that," she said, holding the sheriff's gaze. "But, Jim. Someone's got to do *something*."

"We're doing plenty," he countered, "more than you know. It's being handled by professionals."

She stared back at him, and Jim sighed. His words rang false, even to his own ears. Lauren was right. *Plenty* had not been enough. *Plenty* had gotten them nowhere.

"Well, he's gone," she said after a few seconds. "What do you want me to do?"

Jim lowered his head, thought for a moment. "Did he take your car?"

"Yes, he did." It was obvious, she guessed. No use lying about it.

"Does he have a weapon?"

"*A weapon?*"

"A gun? Anything? Do you know if he owns any, if he took it with him?"

"I don't know," she said. "I don't think so."

"So he went after this man unarmed," Jim mused, talking more to himself now. "And even if he knows where to look— which, I presume, he doesn't—what does he plan to do if he finds him?"

Lauren glanced over her shoulder in the direction of the bedroom. Her sister was sleeping. These days Kate was always sleeping. It scared her, the accelerated rate of Kate's decline, the striking difference in her condition from the last time she'd visited. *And when had that been?* her conscience inquired. *A month ago? Maybe more? Your sister is dying. She needs you. It doesn't matter if you're scared to be around the child. Kate's scared too.*

She shook her head, tried to clear it. "I'm sorry, Jim. I don't know what else to say. It's been eight days since the boys were taken. How long was Michael supposed to sit here and wait by that phone?"

Jim glanced in the direction of the Western Electric rotary sitting quietly on the table by the window. She was right, of course. The kidnapper hadn't contacted them in a week. There was no reason for Michael to wait any longer. And so? With no specific knowledge of where to look, the boys' father had decided to go after them? He'd left his sick wife at home and struck out on his own without bothering to coordinate his efforts with law enforcement. *Why?* Was it sheer desperation, the need to act, to do *something* as Lauren put it—even if that something stood no better chance of success than all the attempts that had gone before him? *What was it that Michael knew, or thought he knew,* Jim wondered, *that the rest of them didn't?*

Suddenly, it struck him. His stomach did a slow turn and the hairs on the back of his neck stood at attention. He heard a distinct clunk as the pieces of the puzzle slid together. "Oh," he said, and he leaned against the counter for support. "Of course."

"What?" Lauren asked. "What is it?"

He looked at her, wondered if she'd known.

"I'll need a description of your car," he said. "Make, model, color, license plate number. Do you have any pictures?"

"Of the car?" She looked surprised—also a little scared.

"Yes," he said. "Any pictures of the car."

"A few, I think . . . photographs Gary took before he . . . before he passed away."

"The photos, they're black and whites?" Jim asked.

"Yes, of course. They're at the house, in an album some-where. I'd have to check. It might take me a while to—"

"Let's go."

"What? Now?" She glanced around the kitchen.

"Yes, now," Jim told her. "Get the keys to your house and come with me."

"I don't understand," she protested, but he refused to say anything else until they were in his car, hooking a right onto Musket Way and then a left onto Main Street.

"Your brother-in-law is in danger," he told her, his jaw set, hands gripping the wheel. "I think he knows where they are now. He's decided not to involve the police—to go after them on his own. That's a big risk to take—a mistake that could cost him his life, or the lives of his children."

"How?" she asked. "How does he—?"

"I suspect he got the phone call he was waiting for. The kidnapper contacted him within the last forty-eight hours, I'd guess. It's why he took off," he said. "It's how he knows where to go. When you think about it, it's the only logical explanation."

"I . . . I don't—"

"He's got a head start on us, and we don't know where he's heading. It may be . . ." *Too late already*, he was about to say, then decided against it.

The interior of the car was quiet, the only sound the thrum of the whitewalls on the hot asphalt. When he spoke again, his voice was softer, enough to make Lauren wonder if he was talking only to himself.

"But we've got to try," he said, slowing for the stop sign at the next intersection, then stomping on the accelerator and gunning through it. "We've got to try."

11

MICHAEL ZIPPED THE FLY OF HIS PANTS, EMERGED FROM the woods, scanned the road for any approaching vehicles, and made his way back to the car. It was one of the details that hadn't occurred to him when he first started out, avoiding businesses and rest stops as much as possible—any populated area where he might be spotted and possibly remembered. Not that he was breaking any laws, of course. He was a free man, could do as he wanted. Still, he knew it was only a matter of time until the sheriff's department tried to track him down, and that could jeopardize things for everyone. He'd been told to come alone, and he intended to do just that.

He opened the driver's door and plopped himself down behind the steering wheel. His pack of Camels was lying on top of the map on the passenger seat. He grabbed it, tapped one out, and planted it between his lips. With his left foot he depressed the clutch, then turned the key in the ignition and gave it some gas, listening as the engine sprang to life. He'd filled up the tank before leaving Cottonwood, a smart move he realized now. When they discovered that he was gone, they'd put out an APB on the vehicle; he was pretty sure of that. The fewer stops at gas stations, the better. The fewer stops *anywhere*, really.

At highway speed, the V8 got about fourteen miles to the gallon, which wasn't too bad. It would be close, getting there on one tank, but he thought he could make it.

With the index finger of his right hand, he reached out and depressed the cigarette lighter, and waited for its coils to heat. He scooped up the map, studied it. He'd been torn about taking the main highway—faster, more efficient—versus cutting across the mountains and sticking to less traveled routes. It was important to stay off the radar. Still, the time he would lose negotiating the mountain passes could cost him. He wasn't sure how much time he had—how much time *any* of them had—and so he'd stuck with the interstate. It was simpler, more direct. He wanted to keep the variables to a minimum.

The lighter popped out and he snatched it from its housing, pressing it to the tip of his cigarette. The tremor was back in his hand and he moved the lighter away from his face, waited for it to pass. It was the damnedest thing—unpredictable and getting worse. *Was this a variation of the disease that was destroying Kate?* he wondered. Would it continue to worsen until he was bound to the walker himself, resigned to using the bedside urinal because it was easier than attempting the long and arduous trip to the bathroom? What other symptoms—nasty and humiliating—awaited him? How much time did he have, until he had no time at all?

It took three minutes for the tremor to pass—not as violent as it had been in the kitchen a week ago, but this one lasted longer, and he thought to himself: *Maybe this isn't the answer. Maybe I'm wrong and it won't make any difference at all.* But he stopped right there because . . . well, because he couldn't think that way. There was no hope in that line of reasoning, only madness. The best way through was forward. He believed in that. He had to. There was no turning back. Not now. Not ever.

A tuft of ash dropped from the tip of his cigarette and landed on the map in his lap. He brushed it away, ran his eyes along his intended route. He was about halfway there, should make it to town before nightfall, although he'd save the hike for tomorrow. It wouldn't do any of them any good if he got lost in the woods after dark, or took a step off a cliff he hadn't seen. But tomorrow, yes; he would see his boys tomorrow. It was something to tell himself, something to keep him going.

He put the Buick in gear, checked his side mirror, and pulled back onto the roadway. He'd turned off the interstate a few miles back to find a more remote place, but now he pulled a U-turn and headed back toward the main thoroughfare.

Closer. He was closer now. He could feel it—could feel *them.* They called to him, his children. And when he found them, he would . . . put things right. *Yes,* he decided. *That's* what he would do. He owed it to them—Kate, Sean, Danny, even himself—to do everything he could to protect them. *Isn't that what a husband and a father is supposed to do?*

The Buick growled as he accelerated onto the interstate. He wasn't aware of it, but he was smiling, just a little. "Coming for you," he whispered, and emptied his mind of everything except the road ahead.

II
BROTHERS

12

"STOP IT!"

The man yanked the steering wheel hard to the right. Danny slid across the backseat, his shoulder hitting the inside of the door. In the front seat, Sean slid as well, right toward the man who was stealing their daddy's car.

Danny could only see the top of his brother's head above the seat in front of him. But he could hear them fighting, his brother grunting and struggling. The big man's head was like the cinder block he and Sean had found in the dump last summer, the one they'd lifted into the wheelbarrow together. Sean had wanted to take it to the bridge and throw it over, so that's what they did. Watched it fall to the street below and crack into three separate pieces, two big and one small.

"*Get off me*," the man said. His thick neck was covered with black hair that looked like tiny worms. But Sean wouldn't quit. He kept punching and scratching. *I should help him*, Danny thought. He stood, wrapped his arm around the headrest in front of him, grabbed the man's right ear and twisted as hard as he could.

"*Goddamn it!*" the man yelled, and slammed on the brakes. Danny almost went over the seat back in front of him, which was scary because he didn't want to be up there where the man could grab him more easily. He held on to the headrest, pulled it against his chest as hard as he could. When the car finally stopped, he was flung backward, landing hard on the seat, his teeth snapping together. He bit the right side of his tongue and could taste blood in his mouth, frightening and familiar. His eyes filled with tears, his vision blurred and sparkly. But then he remembered Sean in the seat in front of him, how he'd heard a thud and then silence.

A few weeks ago, their daddy had taken them to the movies. It was a cowboy story with guns and horses and a guy named Roy Rogers. Roy Rogers could punch bad guys and make them fall to the ground and not move again. Sean said they were *knocked out* and that when you hit someone real hard and in just the right way, they fall over and go to sleep. Danny thought that was pretty scary. He didn't want someone to do that to him. But now he thought that might have happened to his big brother. He wiped the tears from his eyes, stood, and looked over the seat.

The man turned and tried to grab him. Danny moved, but the man caught him by the wrist and dragged him into the front seat to sit beside his brother. Blood was coming from a cut on Sean's left ear, but he was awake. Sean leaned over Danny and went right back to punching then, but the man stuck out his giant hand, pressed it against Sean's forehead, and shoved him backward.

There was a loud crack as his head struck the window, and this time Danny thought he was knocked out for sure. But his brother didn't go to sleep. He just shook his head and stared at his sneakers like he was trying real hard to remember something.

"You give me any more crap and I will kill you both," the man said. "Starting with him," he added, poking Danny in the chest with a thick finger. He reached out, put a hand under Sean's chin and tilted it upward, fingers digging into his cheeks. "You want to watch me do that? Kill your brother before I kill you? It makes no difference to me."

Sean stared back at him, lips pressed together. He looked mad, not frightened—the way Roy Rogers did when he fought the bad guys. This made Danny feel a little less scared. Heroes never lost. The good guys always won. This meant they were going to be okay.

"You want me to kill him? Is that what you want?" the man asked, and Sean stared him in the eyes and slowly shook his head.

"Well, sit still then," the man said, releasing his brother's face. A moment later, the car rolled forward, the trees and wooden poles moving past the window faster and faster.

Sean sat back in the seat and looked straight ahead. There was a red mark on his cheek where the man's thumb had pressed. Danny reached out and touched his brother's arm. *Heroes, right?* he wanted to say, but of course he couldn't. Still, his brother would understand. He gave Sean's arm a squeeze, but his older brother pulled away, crossed his arms in front of his chest and didn't look at him.

Danny crossed his arms in front of his chest too, and looked straight ahead. He wouldn't cry. He would be brave like his brother. Didn't the man know the good guys always won? All they needed was a plan. Sean would come up with something. He was always coming up with plans. So Danny waited, stared at the radio and the inside of their daddy's car. The way he was sitting, he was too low to see anything but the sky through the front window. But his brother could see. His brother knew where they were going. *That was the important thing*, as their father would say. That was what mattered.

13

JIM KENT, JOHN PIERCE, AND TONY DELUCA STOOD IN THE small office, hats in their hands. There was only one chair, and it was occupied by Marion Guthrie, a pretty, slender woman in her early twenties who sat in front of a medium-size switchboard. One of six girls who staffed the telephone communications office in rotating shifts, she was dressed in a gray skirt and white button-front blouse with a wing collar. She'd grown up in Cottonwood, and Jim knew Marion and her family well. Still, she seemed nervous in front of the three of them, her hands fidgeting in her lap.

"This would've been yesterday or the day before," Jim was telling her. "We're not sure of the exact time of the call."

Marion shook her head, the brushed-under bob of her reddish-brown hair swaying from side to side. "I wasn't working yesterday, Mr. Kent," she said. "Candice Lockhart worked the day shift and Paula Seeger worked the overnight. I'm not sure who covered the early evening."

"We were hoping there would be some sort of log of incoming calls," Jim said. "I'm sure you've heard about the McCrays' unfortunate situation. Something has . . . come up," he added. "This could be very helpful to the investigation."

"I'm sorry, Mr. Kent. I—"

A jack lamp lit up on the panel.

"Excuse me a moment," she told the officers. She swiveled to face the switchboard more directly and placed a cord into the jack, flipping the front key forward. "Operator," she said. "Oh, hello, Mrs. Kimble. Yes . . . yes, she did, thank you. My mother has them sitting in the bump-out window in the kitchen where they can get plenty of sunlight. She says they're very beautiful. It was kind of you to send them . . . She's feeling better, thank you. Dr. Silver expects her to make a full recovery." She glanced toward the men standing against the wall. "Mrs. Kimble, I have some people in the office right now who need to talk to me. I can ring you back in a few minutes if you like . . . Okay . . . Did you need me to put you through to anyone? . . . Mrs. Cravitz, yes, ma'am, I'll connect you. And thank you for the flowers."

Marion reached up and placed the front cord in another jack and pulled the front key backward, ringing the Cravitz residence. She turned in her seat. "I'm sorry about that. Where were we?"

"A call log," Detective Pierce reminded her, running his fingers along the brim of his hat.

"Oh, right," she said. "I'm sorry, but . . . we don't keep a log here. Most of the calls are local connections. Within the community."

"What about long distance?" Jim asked. "Something coming from outside the community?"

"For Cottonwood, long-distance calls—both incoming and outgoing—are routed through Redding."

"Walk us through the process," Jim said.

"Well," she replied, smoothing her palms over the fabric of her skirt, "the office here in Cottonwood is run by a private company, but we're interconnected with PT and T—the Pacific Telephone and Telegraph Company, that is. They have local and long-distance offices throughout California. Large cities like San Francisco and Sacramento have designated long-distance offices. Redding's a bit small for that, but there's a switching center there—a central office."

"Go on," Jim said.

She looked past them, considering.

"Let's say I was in a small town in Northern California," she continued. "If I wanted to make a long-distance call to Cottonwood, I would pick up the phone and speak to the manual toll operator in the town I was calling from. She would pass my call along to the closest central office and they would connect me to the CO in Redding, who would then contact the local operator—that's me—here in Cottonwood. It's a step-by-step process."

"A relay," Detective DeLuca suggested, and she nodded.

A jack lamp lit up on the switchboard and she turned to it, placed a cord into the jack, flipped the key forward.

"Operator. Yes, Mrs. Felton, it's Marion . . . Thank you, ma'am. I'll tell her you said so . . . I will . . . Sam Donovan, yes, ma'am. I'll connect your call."

She placed a cord in a different jack near the bottom of the panel, flipped the key backward, then turned to them once again.

"What if we needed to know where the call originated?" Jim asked. "Does anyone keep a record of that?"

"The central office in Redding would have a log," she said. "They have to, for billing purposes. How much you're billed for a long-distance call depends on how many points along the relay—as well as the amount of time you spend talking, of course."

"So they would have a record," Detective Pierce said, "of all the points along the relay—*and* the exact start and stop time of the call."

On the panel, a supervision lamp lit, signaling the end of a call. Marion reached up and pulled the cord from the two jacks. She looked at Pierce, nodded. "Yes, sir," she said. "They would."

14

THANKS FOR BRINGING US OUT HERE," LAUREN SAID AS
Nathan Reed straightened the steering wheel and eased
the car to a stop, the rubber of the passenger-side tires
whispering against the curb. "It's good to get some sun, to be
out of the house for a while."

The pastor smiled. "It's a pleasure to share part of this beautiful day with the two of you." He climbed out of the driver's
seat, walked around the rear of the car, and opened the front
and back doors for Lauren and her sister.

Kate was slow getting out. He took her by the hand and upper arm to steady her.

"I'm sorry I'm so weak these days," she told him, but his
smile only broadened.

"'I can do all things through Christ who gives me strength,'"
he quoted. "Philippians four, verse thirteen. God's presence is
beside you every step of the way, Kate. Don't you forget that.
He's all the strength you'll ever need."

It was late afternoon, but the summer sun was still high above
them. They walked to the wooden bench that overlooked the
meager lake and the dry track of riverbed beyond.

"I'd better sit," Kate told them, lowering herself onto the weathered boards.

Lauren and Pastor Reed sat beside her. They studied the rippled surface of the water, noted from the marks along the bank how much it had receded during the rainless months since early April. Near the water's edge, a child of about eight or nine plunged a stick into the mud and pulled it back. He dragged it a short distance before repeating the motion, over and over, as he made his way around the perimeter.

"There used to be a lot more of them," Kate commented. "When I was a kid, we came down here by the dozens. Remember, Lauren?"

"I remember," she said. A gust of wind tousled her hair and she reached up, tucked the blond strands behind her ear. "I lost a new pair of shoes in that muck. Mom about killed me."

"She made you go back and search. Only you never did find them, did you."

"They were completely submerged. I thought I knew where they were, but when I went back to try to dig them out they were—"

"Gone."

"Gone," Lauren agreed. She glanced at her sister. "Part of me always wondered whether you'd taken them, pulled them out after I left and hid them somewhere."

Kate looked puzzled. "Why would I do that?"

"Because you knew Mom would send me back for them."

Kate shook her head. "That would've been mean."

"I know. And you're not the type. You helped me look for them, remember? When we couldn't find them, you offered to give me yours."

"You should've taken them."

"If they'd fit, I would've," Lauren said. "They were two sizes too small."

There was silence between them, then they both laughed.

"She offered to give me hers, Pastor Reed," Lauren told him, "as if *that* would've solved anything. Either way, one of us was coming home with no shoes."

"I thought maybe we could trade them back and forth," Kate explained. "Only one of us would go outside at a time."

"Great plan," Lauren said, still laughing.

"What did I know about great plans," Kate said. "I was six, same age as Danny."

Their laughter stopped then, and they sat watching the high grass sway in the soft breath of afternoon breeze.

"God walks with them too," the pastor said. "'The Lord will rescue me from every evil deed—'"

"'—and bring me safely into the kingdom of heaven,'" Kate finished. "That's from Second Timothy, isn't it?"

"It is," Pastor Reed said.

Kate was quiet a moment. Lauren placed a hand on her leg, studied her sister in her peripheral vision. *She will want to go home soon*, she thought. She was getting tired.

"I don't want them to go to the kingdom of heaven yet," Kate said. She turned to the pastor. "When you pray for us, can you tell God that we need them here in Cottonwood? That we want them home?"

"God is with you even now," he said. "You can tell him yourself."

"I don't think he listens to me," she said. "I've been"—she shook her head—"angry."

"He listens, always. Even when you're angry."

"Yes, but . . . maybe if it comes from you, it would carry more weight. You know?"

The pastor offered her a faint smile. "I don't think that's how it—"

"Want to see something?" a voice asked, and they turned their heads to the right, suddenly aware that he was standing there, the boy with the long muddy stick still clenched in his hand.

"What is it?" Lauren asked, annoyed by his interruption.

"A dead bullfrog," he said. "A big one. Down by the lake. Want to see it?"

The adults said nothing, simply gawked at the boy with muddied shoes, dark green shorts, and a thatch of thick red hair that shifted ceaselessly in the wind like a pile of earthworms freshly excavated from their home.

Pastor Reed leaned forward. "Thank you for the offer, son, but—"

"Why would we want to see *that*?" Lauren asked, interrupting him. Her eyes narrowed as she stared at the boy. "Why would you?"

The small figure to their right shrugged. "I don't know," he said. "It's kinda cool."

"Is it?" Lauren turned her body and looked at him more directly. "What makes it cool?"

"Nothing," Kate interjected. "He's only curious—"

"Did you kill it? With that stick of yours?"

The boy stared at Lauren, said nothing.

"Charlie? Stop bothering those people," a woman called from her front yard on the other side of the street. They turned in her direction—except for Lauren, who kept her eyes on the child and his stick.

"Mary Sanders," Pastor Reed said, rising from the bench. "How are you? We were just talking to Charlie here. He's been having some fun down at the lake."

"Oh, hello, Pastor Reed," she said. "I appreciate you taking the time to talk to him. But Charlie's not supposed to play down there anymore, after—you know—everything that's happened."

"I'm right here," Kate muttered. "Does she not—"

"Charlie," the woman called. "Charlie, get over here."

"Want to see?" the boy asked again, his voice low and conspiratorial. He spoke only to Lauren now.

"No," she answered. "No one wants to see what you did to that thing."

Charlie shrugged, dropped the muddy stick at their feet, and skulked across the street to join his mother.

Mrs. Sanders snagged him by the upper arm, bent low, and whispered something to the boy. She turned, gave them a brief wave, and then hustled Charlie inside, closing the door behind her.

Lauren stood, and kicked the stick with the toe of her shoe. It rolled toward the water, came to a stop halfway down the hill. "What a little creep," she said.

"One of God's children, same as you and me," Pastor Reed commented. He turned to Kate. "You want to sit awhile longer?"

"No," she said, allowing him to help her to her feet. "I want to go home."

15

THE ONE-STORY BRICK BUILDING AT 1629 MARKET STREET was located in a business and industrial district a few blocks south of the Sacramento River. It was late afternoon, almost 5:00 P.M., and much of this area was closed down for the evening. Workers heading off their shifts climbed into cars and buses bound for home or the local bars, their thoughts turning toward their evening rituals. There was a busier feel to Redding than Jim was used to in Cottonwood, a hurried pace that carried with it a sense of perpetual servitude, as if the tasks ahead were more than anyone could ever hope to manage. It made Jim eager to return to the recognizable streets and faces of his own town, a place that was unwell, but familiar nonetheless. He found some degree of comfort in that, wondered if it was the same for many of them—the reason they stayed. *How loyal we are*, he thought, *to the things that hurt us the most.*

Kate's sister, Lauren, for example, had lost her husband the year before. Gary had served in the marines during the war, took part in the amphibious landings at Normandy. The invasion cost him his left arm, and that was bad enough. He then returned home to a wife who loved him and a town that embraced him as a hero. Nine years later, Lauren found him sitting in the garage in their Buick, his skin cherry red, eyelids closed as if he was sleeping, the engine running. It was easy to understand how the horrors he'd witnessed could have continued to haunt him, how his suicide might have been just another casualty of the war itself. Jim had said as much to Betty Savage at the time. Betty lived across the street from the McCrays, and had spent the entirety of her seventy-two years in Cottonwood. Jim had stopped by to fix a leaking sink, something her husband could've done if he hadn't passed away the previous spring.

"Gary spent a lot of time in that house," she said, peering through the window at the McCrays' residence across the street. "He and Lauren visited every other weekend."

"So?" Jim's head was inside the cabinet as he worked on the fitting. He couldn't see her, didn't turn around to look, but he could picture her standing there, smoking her cigarette, studying the family's dwelling.

"Too much time spent with that child," she said. "He's brought nothing but sickness since the day he was born."

"I've heard people say that," Jim replied. "Doesn't make any sense to me. How can a child bring—"

"Doesn't matter how," she said. "There's a poison to that boy. Everyone can see it . . . including *you*, Jim Kent. Look what's happening to the mother, the father, even Lauren herself. I told my Bill to stay away from that place. 'Ain't no sense goin' over to that house if you don't have to,' I said. 'Kate McCray is sick and there's nothing you or anyone else can do about it. You want to be neighborly?' I said. 'Leave them alone. The sick want to be left in peace.'"

Jim withdrew his upper body from the cabinet beneath the counter, turned to look at her. "We're talking about a five-year-old child, Betty. Do you really believe—"

"I believe what I see," she said. "I've watched that place through this window year after year. I stood in the cemetery off First Street last April and watched as they lowered Bill's casket into the ground. Place is gettin' full, Jim. Pretty soon, there won't be no room left."

"You okay, Sheriff?" Detective DeLuca asked.

Jim looked up to find the man waiting for him, holding open the door to the redbrick building on Market Street. He nodded, stepped past him and into the lobby. There was no receptionist, only a push-button ringer. Pierce stepped forward and pressed it with his thumb.

They stood there for a moment, staring at the bare, window-less walls, the white linoleum beneath their feet.

"Help you?" a man asked, opening the interior door. He was short in stature, neatly dressed in a dark three-piece suit. He stepped into the room, looked at each of them in turn, his quick, darting movements reminding Jim of a small bird rummaging for seeds at a feeder.

"Shasta County Sheriff's Department," DeLuca said. "We called earlier."

"Oh yes." The man nodded. "I'm Frank Henshaw," he said, shaking hands—one brisk pump and then on to the next— with each of them in turn. "How can I help you?"

"We were hoping we could review your call log from the past few days," Pierce said.

"Call *logs*. There would be several," Henshaw replied, the cadence of his speech rapid, crisp, businesslike. There was a touch of condescension in his manner that Jim didn't take much of a liking to.

"Several logs for only two days?" Pierce asked.

"Indeed. Redding is an important point on the long-distance line that runs from San Diego to Salt Lake City by way of Portland. Most people aren't aware of this, but it's actually the longest telephone line in the world. Not all of the calls go through Redding, of course, but we average over two thousand a day and have four to six operators working at any given time. Each of them keeps their own log."

Pierce nodded. "Well, we'd like to see them."

"Right this way, gentlemen," Henshaw said, and led them through the door into a room with a large switchboard staffed by several operators. It was a hectic, somewhat frenzied environment, much busier than the small telecommunications office they'd visited in Cottonwood. From what Jim could overhear of the operators' side of the conversations with callers, there were none of the pleasantries that Marion Guthrie had nurtured.

Henshaw ushered them through the door on the other side of the room, which led to a small back office.

"Ordinarily, I'd have my secretary review the logs with you," he said. "But I had two operators call in sick today—stomach flu and something else, I don't remember—and she had to fill in at the switchboard." He turned to them. "I don't really understand how a touch of upset stomach is grounds for taking an entire day off, but"—he shrugged his shoulders—"you know these girls, calling in sick at the slightest provocation. No doubt one of them is pregnant, and the other isn't far off."

"The logs," Jim said, his patience thin.

Henshaw looked back at him, opened his mouth as if to respond, then seemed to think better of it. There was almost an entire wall of shelving behind the desk. He went to it, plucked out a total of fifteen books and placed them in three stacks on the desk in front of them. "These are the days in question," he said, offering them a perfunctory smile, hands on his hips.

Neither Jim nor the two detectives moved to open them.

"All we know is that the destination town was Cotton-wood," DeLuca said.

Henshaw opened the first, turned it around so they could read it, and pointed to a column. "This is where the girls enter the destination city. Or town," he said with a slight smirk. "Cottonwood isn't really what you'd call a city."

Jim stepped forward, into the man's space, and Henshaw took a reflexive step backward.

"*I'm* from Cottonwood. Lots of good folks there."

"I wasn't—"

"Shut up and listen," Jim said. He stopped, waited for another remark, but Henshaw only stared at him, slack-faced and openmouthed.

Jim took another step forward. "Two children have been kidnapped," he said, his speech slow and deliberate, as if he was explaining a simple concept to someone either very young or very stupid. "And these books may have the information we need to figure out where they've been taken. Now, you will sit yourself down in that chair, go over these logs one by one, and help us find what we're looking for."

Both the color and smugness had drained from Henshaw's face. He looked more like a little boy now, caught dressing up in his father's suit.

"Is anything unclear?" Jim asked.

The man shook his head. "No, sir."

"Then sit," Jim said, and Henshaw did, collapsing into the chair without glancing back to confirm that it was behind him.

He slid the chair closer to the table, turned the open log book back around so he could read it, and traced down the column with a slightly shaking index finger.

The rest of them waited in silence.

In the room next door, they could hear the steady buzz of the operators' voices, the click of cords being plugged into jacks. Jim closed his eyes, told himself to take it easy. Henshaw was not a likable man, but Jim's anger and impatience had mostly come from somewhere else. He checked his watch: five thirty already, the time slipping away.

"Here," Henshaw said, his finger motionless on the page now. "A long-distance call to Cottonwood came through this office yesterday around one in the afternoon. It lasted"—his finger slid to the right, following the row—"six minutes and twenty-two seconds." He looked up, hesitant. "I'd better check to see if there were any more. We don't get long-distance calls to Cottonwood often, but . . ."

He marked his place, and then continued with quick, practiced dexterity. He got to the end of the book, slid it to one side, and grabbed another. "Sorry," he said. "This may take a while."

Detective Pierce nodded. "Take your time. Don't miss anything. Let's get this right the first time."

Henshaw's eyes were back on the pages in front of him, his finger racing down the column. "Here's another one," he said. "It was from earlier in the day, but was to the same destination number in Cottonwood." He frowned. "Only lasted eighteen seconds, though. Not much of a conversation."

"Set it aside and keep going," Pierce told him.

The small man was back at it, moving through the books one after the other until only one remained in the stack. "Ahh," he said, tapping his finger on the page. "A third one. This is interesting—more calls than I expected."

"Keep going," Pierce prodded, and Henshaw did. When he was finished, he looked up.

"Three incoming long-distance calls in twenty-four hours. That's a lot." He opened the three separate books to the pages he'd marked. "What was the specific phone number you were interested in?"

Jim removed a piece of paper from his pocket, read it to him.

"Well, there you go," he said. "That fits these two." They all leaned forward for a better look. "Both calls occurred yesterday, one at ten thirty-six in the morning lasting only eighteen seconds, and another at one fifteen in the afternoon lasting six minutes and twenty-two seconds. This other call—here—that's to a different number."

"Where was the third call from?" Jim asked.

"Looks like . . . St. Louis, Missouri," Henshaw replied.

"And the other two?"

"See this notation here?" Henshaw asked. "That means these calls were made from a pay phone."

"A pay phone," DeLuca said. "Where?"

"Grants Pass, Oregon. The call was routed from a pay phone to a toll operator at the switching center in Grants Pass, then on to the central office in Medford, then to us, and finally to the local switchboard operator in Cottonwood. It took the same route both times. Same pay phone."

"We'll need to know exactly where that phone is located," Pierce said.

"Well, the only information I have," Henshaw responded, "is that it's somewhere in Grants Pass." He glanced up at Jim. "'Course, I could contact the switchboard operator there. She could probably tell me the location."

"Thank you," Jim said, placing a hand on his shoulder and giving it a squeeze. "We appreciate your assistance."

"Anything I can do to help those kids," Henshaw said, looking from one face to the next, and then excusing himself to gather the last bit of information.

16

I T WAS DANNY'S FAULT THE MAN HAD FALLEN. "KEEP YOUR EYES on the ground," he'd told them. "Don't trip over the roots."

Adults were always saying stuff like that. *Watch where you're going. Don't forget your coat. How did your shoes get so wet?* There were so many rules to remember. If he closed his eyes, he could hear his father. *"What are you doing? I just told you not to touch that."*

He missed his father. His mother too. It made him happy to hear their voices, even if they weren't really there. He was looking up at the trees—not down at the ground like the man had told him—when one of his feet tripped over the other. It was Danny's fault, what happened next. There hadn't even been a root in front of him.

The path was steep and full of rocks. He banged his knee on one of them, and slid backward down the trail.

"Goddamn it!" the man said as Danny collided with him. The sound of sliding rocks, and then a *whomp* as the man hit the ground himself.

Sean's hands were on Danny's right arm then, pulling him to his feet. *"Run,"* he whispered, and Danny did as he was told. He ran down the hill away from the man—feeling not happy or scared, only worried because he didn't know where he was supposed to run. Sean would catch up with him, would tell him where. But as Danny rounded the curve in the trail he heard his brother scream, and that stopped him. He turned back to see what was happening.

"Your brother's hurt," the man said. "Better come quick."

"*Run away!*" Sean yelled from around the bend, and then he screamed again like there really *was* something hurting him.

Danny moved back up the trail, far enough for him to see Sean lying on the ground, his feet facing down the hill, blue shoes kicking. The man was kneeling on his brother's shoulder, one hand on Sean's wrist and the other on the back of his head, pushing him into the dirt.

"You get back up here, Danny," the man said. It was weird to hear the stranger say his name. "You get back up here right now or I will rip your brother's arm right off of his body."

"*Run away!*" Sean said again, his voice muffled by the dirt, and then he screamed as the man twisted his arm.

Danny took a few steps toward them. He wanted to go to the man and make him stop. But Sean had a plan. He had told him to *run away*. When his brother told him to do something, he almost always listened. Sean was smarter and better than him in every way. That's what people said. And even when they didn't say it, that's what people thought. He could tell by the way they never spoke to him, the way they pretended he wasn't there. If he walked into a room, people would leave. If he followed them, they would tell him to go find his parents.

A better brother shouldn't lose his arm because of me, he thought, and his lower lip trembled, the world becoming splintered and blurry. Sean was still screaming as Danny marched up the trail and placed his hand on the man's shoulder to get him to stop.

"Okay then," the man said, releasing Sean's arm but still

holding him down. He turned to look at Danny. There was a big cut on the man's forehead. Blood ran along the side of his nose, over his lips, and dripped from his chin. "That was a smart thing for you to come back like that." He looked past Danny toward the trees. "I don't feel so good," he said, and Danny wasn't sure if he was talking to him or not. "I'm dizzy and sick to my stomach." He lowered his head, closed his eyes. The blood dripped from the tip of his nose now.

"Got to do something," the man said. "Got to do something or they'll run."

Danny stood, watching him. He wondered if he could punch the man once and knock him out, the way Roy Rogers did in the movies.

"A leash," the man said, opening his eyes. "You need a leash." He paused, thought for a moment. "Take your arms out of your T-shirt, but leave it around your neck."

Danny didn't move.

"Like this," he said, pulling Danny's arm from one shirt-sleeve and then the other. He twisted the cloth around itself until it became tighter at the neck. "Got something to hold on to you with now," he said. "A leash for the little mutt." He laughed at this, then his chest rattled and he leaned over to cough three times in a row, draw in a short breath, and cough twice more.

He stayed hunched over for a while, staring at the ground. "Blood," he said at last. "Why am I coughing up blood?" He pulled on the shirt-leash, and Danny stumbled, almost fell. "You better hope that's from the gash on my face and not something worse," the man said. He paused, thinking, held a hand to his head. "They say you . . . They say you got it in you. Is that true?"

"Leave him alone," Sean said, still pinned against the ground.

The man ignored him, lifted his eyes to meet Danny's and gave the shirt a little tug.

"No one wants to be around you. Is that it?" he asked.

"Don't listen to him, Danny."

"Everyone thinks it would be better if you just"—he drew his fingers together, opened his hand and let them fly outward like a dandelion in the breeze—"disappeared."

"No one thinks that," Sean hissed. He squirmed and wriggled beneath the weight of the man's body.

"*Everyone* thinks that," the man said. "And do you know what?" He smiled, the center of his lips red with blood. "I'm beginning to think that too."

"Stop it," Sean said. He tried to get up, but couldn't with the man's knee on the back of his shoulder.

"What do *you* think, Danny? Would it be better if you just disappeared?"

"I'll kill you," his brother threatened, but the man still stared, waiting for an answer that would never come.

"Can't even speak for yourself, can you?" he said after a while. "Let your brother do all the talking. That about sum it up?" He sighed, and then stood, swaying on his feet.

Sean was up as well, punching at him, but the man used Danny as a shield against his brother. He pulled the shirt-leash tight, making it difficult for Danny to breathe.

"You'd better settle down, or I'll strangle him right in front of you," the man said, and sounded like he meant it, like all of a sudden he was really mad.

The shirt was a hand squeezing away the air. Danny grabbed at it, fingernails digging into his neck. He was floating, moving up through the trees toward the white of the sky. He reached down, tried to catch Sean's hand and pull him up too. But he was too far below. There were too many branches in the way. Only the ends of their fingertips touched.

"Okay, okay," he heard his brother say, which meant it was okay for Danny to go without him.

"Will there be any more trouble?"

"No. I promise. Let him go."

Something loosened. There was a shriek, like the noise Daddy's record player made if you bumped it during a song. *Rrrooooop.* Quiet. *Rrrooooop.* Quiet. Over and over.

He was going down again, back through the trees to join his brother. The sky was no longer white but dark green, the leaves and branches above him.

Rrrooooop. Quiet. *Rrrooooop.* Quiet.

"He's dying."

"He's catching his breath. You think about that noise the next time you want to start punching."

Rrrooooop. Quiet. *Rrrooooop.* Quiet.

"Get the shirt off his neck."

Rrrooooooop.

"The shirt stays. This is what happens when you try to run."

Rrrooooop. Quiet. *Rrrooooop.* Quiet. The sound, Danny realized, was him. He tried to make it stop, didn't want Sean to think he was crying.

"Take some deep breaths and work it out," the man said. He coughed four or five times, leaned over and spat a big red blob on the ground.

Danny concentrated on his breathing, tried to do as he was told. The noise was softer now, more a whisper than a shriek.

"Look at that," the man said, pointing at the thing he'd spat onto the ground. "*You* did that to me. That fall of yours is going to make it a lot harder on all of us." He wiped at his face with the palm of his hand. "Feel like I'm gonna throw up," he said. "Am I still bleeding?"

"Yes," Sean told him. "Really bad. You'll probably die."

Shut up!" the man said. He swung his hand, smacked the boy on the left ear. The noise startled Danny—a loud clap in the forest—but Sean took the blow without a flinch, stared back at the man like he was daring him to do it again.

The stranger tilted up Danny's chin with the same hand he'd used to strike his brother. "Well," he said, "am I? Still bleeding?"

The blood had stopped and was drying on his face now. Danny nodded anyway.

"Hmm," the man said. "You think I'm gonna die too?"

Again, Danny nodded. He didn't know if the man would die or not, but Sean said he would. That was enough for him.

"Yeah? Well, the hell with both of you," the man said. "I'll be glad to get rid of you, one way or the other." He looked up the trail, turned Danny at the shoulders. "Let's get moving," he said. "Your brother goes first, then you. I'll be holding on to your leash from behind." He coughed, spat again. Bright red. "If I die, I'm taking you both with me. Remember that. If you have any control over this," he said, yanking the leash, "you'd better stop." He reached out and pushed Danny forward. "Like it or not, we're in this together."

The three of them moved up the trail. With the shirt pulled tight around his neck, it was harder to search the ground for roots, but Danny tried. He did not want to fall again. "*If I die, I'm taking you both with me,*" the man had said, and Danny believed him. He could still hear the crack of the man's hand on Sean's ear, see the way he'd tried to rip off his brother's arm. "*If you have any control over this, you'd better stop.*" But Danny didn't know how. All he knew was that people got sick around him.

Sometimes they died. *"Everyone thinks it would be better if you just . . . disappeared."*

Sean was ahead of him, leading the way. *Did he think that too?* Danny wondered. *Would his life be better if I disappeared?*

He could feel it in his throat, the tightness that came before he cried. It was only the shirt, pulling on his neck. Silent and ashamed, he stumbled, almost fell. The man gave him a jerk. "Watch where you're going," he said, and that got him coughing all over again.

The path was a blur, so Danny focused on the outline of his brother's shoulders: turned when he turned, slowed when he slowed. When branches blocked their way, Sean ducked beneath them, and Danny—shorter and less hindered by the obstacles—ducked as well. The sticker bushes were trolls, grabbing at their legs. Behind them, feet thudding against the ground, was their pet dragon. *"Hold it. Not so fast,"* the dragon said, and Danny paused, waited for him to catch up.

At the top of the mountain was a castle. Danny couldn't see it yet, but could picture it in his mind: pale stone against the sky. If there was a moat, they would use the dragon to cross it. If they were met by guards shooting arrows, they would block them with their shields and fire back.

"Do the good guys ever lose?" his brother had asked their father one night before bed.

"Never," he told them, closing the book and handing it to Danny, who liked to leaf through it and look at the pictures.

"Why not?" Sean asked.

"Because those are not the stories I choose to believe." Their father walked to the door, and turned out the light. "Did you clean your room today?"

"No."

"Then tonight your room is dirty. Tomorrow you have another chance. The world can be anything you want it to be. You just have to make it happen."

"Dad?" The door started to close.

"Yeah."

"I want Mom to get better."

Their father stood in the shadows, one hand on the knob. "Me too."

"How can we make that happen?" Sean asked.

"I don't know," he answered. "But I believe it's possible." He walked back across the room, went to one bed then the other, and kissed them both on the forehead. "We'll figure out a way," he said, then closed the door behind him.

"I'll think about it really hard," Sean said, and lay on his back, staring at the ceiling.

Danny was still holding the book in his arms. He thought and thought, but nothing came to him. Eventually, he fell asleep. In the morning, the book was back on the shelf, and he had only the slightest memory of his father returning to their room, and standing over him in the dark.

17

CAMILLA NAPOLITANO SWITCHED OFF THE STOVETOP BUT left the pot where it was. A slim curtain of steam rose from underneath the section of the lid that canted upward. It would be another ten minutes before dinner was ready, but the artichoke would serve as an appetizer for them to pluck while her husband sipped a glass of wine and told her about his day. Aldo owned the town's only barbershop and heard more news and gossip than any of her friends, which was saying something given the enthusiasm with which the girls chattered over their weekly bridge game. Still, her husband was more of a listener than a talker, and while this made it easier for people to confide in him during their trim or shave, it was difficult for her to extract anything more than a few passing comments during their evening meal. He rarely related personal stories or discussed his own emotions, and was of the opinion that most people shared more of themselves than they should. The only time she ever heard him cry was after the miscarriage. That was three years ago, and it hadn't happened here in the privacy of their own home, but at the McCrays' residence next door—back when she used to babysit their boys for extra cash and to get out of the house.

Aldo hadn't liked her work, didn't like her working in general. "I make enough to put food on the table," he said. "It's not something you need to worry about."

She should've listened. But she was young and didn't have any children of her own to look after. And so many families needed someone to watch their little ones so they could go out and enjoy themselves every now and then.

When Camilla discovered she was pregnant—already three months along—she knew her time away from the house was drawing to a close. With the promise of a new baby, her interest in caring for other people's children seemed to melt away. She was relieved, actually, and felt that all this time had merely been preparation for her own turn. She loved her husband, but in her mind they did not feel like a *true* family. A child would change all that. A child would be the start of a new life, one that would continue beyond their own. Perhaps she and Aldo would even become grandparents someday, although that was so far off it seemed an abstraction, not something real and tangible like the life growing inside her.

Aldo was proud and happy when she told him. If it was a boy, they would name him Christopher after Aldo's father. If it was a girl, they would name her Sophia. They planned to convert the small room he used as an office into a nursery. They would sell his desk, and replace it with a crib. She phoned her parents, and made travel plans for them so they would be here when the baby arrived.

She agreed to continue watching the McCrays' children until they could find other arrangements. There were rumors— even then—that there was something wrong with the younger child. For one thing, he never spoke, and that was odd enough. And his mother was unwell—not as bad as she was now, but on a steady decline since the child's birth three years before.

Camilla had seen her navigating the steps at church, noted how careful she was with her feet, and how tightly she gripped the handrail for balance. She always wore flats, nothing with heels, and held on to her husband's arm when she walked. Some believed it had to do with the child, that whatever was wrong with Danny had infected her as well. Camilla thought this was nonsense. Just because two things started at the same time didn't mean one caused the other. As a second-generation immigrant, she knew what it was like to be labeled different, to have others form opinions about her based on her ethnicity rather than the reality of who she was. Maybe that's why she continued to watch the McCray children. She also saw how Michael and Kate struggled, not only with Kate's illness but with the shifting currents of public perception about their family.

Camilla's miscarriage occurred on a Thursday in mid-October. The season had begun to turn. It was chilly in the evenings, and the sun sank below the horizon a bit earlier each day. The boys had eaten their dinner, taken their baths, and were already in their pajamas. Camilla helped Danny brush his teeth, gave Sean a glass of water, read them a story, and turned out their light. She planned to read for a while until the McCrays returned home, and after closing the bedroom door most of the way—Sean preferred it open a crack and claimed Danny did as well—she walked down the hallway to the living room and settled into the davenport.

She didn't recall the name of the book she'd been reading, and the pregnancy had a way of draining her energy, especially once she crossed over into the second trimester. She fell asleep without realizing it, the paperback slipping from her hand onto the floor, the pages on which the open book rested—facedown—bending and creasing. If she dreamed, she couldn't recall the details later, only the vague sense that they had been easy and blissful, like a downward slide through soft white snow.

She awoke to a hand on her stomach to the right of her belly button, above the swell of her uterus. At first she assumed it was Aldo, and that it was already morning—time for him to go to work—and he was leaning over to kiss her good-bye. But the hand was small, light against her clothing. When she opened her eyes it was three-year-old Danny McCray who stood beside her, not her husband. The sharp smell of ammonia filled her nostrils, and when she looked down she could see that his pajama bottoms were wet, soaked through with urine.

"Wha—" she began, clearing her head from sleep and propping herself up on one elbow. "Honey, you wet your pants," she said, although that was probably why he had come out here to begin with.

He stared back at her, his face expressionless, the small hand still resting on her abdomen.

"We need to get you changed," she said, and started to rise, then realized her own clothing was wet. She looked down and saw a dark stain—no bigger than a child's palm—on the front of her skirt.

She stood and felt the back of her skirt, and realized that most of the fluid had collected there as she slept.

"Oh . . . oh, no," she said, her tone one of surprise and embarrassment more than despair; but by the time she was halfway to the bathroom she knew.

"Oh. Oh God, no. Please, don't let it be . . ." She closed and locked the door behind her, stripped off her clothing until she stood there in her bra, looking down at the trail of blood that ran down the inside of both legs.

If there was any physical pain, she wasn't aware of it, only the emptiness in her chest—an excavation almost—that made her think of a small plastic shovel scooping sand at the beach, creating a hollow place where there had once been something more.

She was still in the bathroom when Michael and Kate came home. She told them to call Aldo, to contact the hospital in Redding and tell them she was on her way. By the time she arrived, there was nothing they could do except to reassure her that this was a common occurrence, and that she was young and there would be other pregnancies in her future. "Sometimes children in the womb do not develop correctly," the doctor had explained as he completed his exam. "Sometimes there's something very wrong. God understands that. God has ways of letting them go."

Aldo handled things with the same measured composure and practicality with which he handled everything else. He never talked about it later, and she never saw him cry—only heard the stifled sound of his sobs once, a week later, through the closed door of their bathroom as the water ran in the shower.

As for other pregnancies, there were none—at least not yet. And although Camilla was only twenty-seven, she was beginning to feel like her time for building that kind of family—a *true* family—had passed. Even now, as she lay awake in bed at night, she could feel the press of that small hand against the side of her abdomen. She would turn her head and imagine him standing beside her in the dark, studying her with that expressionless face, waiting for her to open her eyes.

Now he was gone—*both* of them—taken by a stranger. The police were out there searching, following their leads, desperate to track them down. *Did she hope they would find him?* She supposed that she did. Even if she allowed herself to believe the child was responsible, she did not think it was intentional. She could not go so far as to wish him harm.

And if they looked and looked and he was never found? Well, maybe that would be okay too. Not every life could be saved. Not every life *should be* saved. Sometimes children in the womb do not develop correctly. Sometimes there's something very wrong. God understands that, and God has ways of letting them go.

18

I T WAS EIGHT THIRTY IN THE MORNING WHEN MICHAEL EXITED the highway, turned right onto NF-742 and then left onto Butcherknife Road. He'd spent the night in the car in Grants Pass, and drove the twenty minutes to Wilderville as soon as he woke. He should've eaten and picked up supplies—a canteen and a hunting knife, at least—before setting out. It would've been wiser. He wasn't sure how long the hike would be, and if he got turned around or became lost in the forest, he could be in real trouble.

But he was already in trouble, wasn't he. They all were. Things had gotten out of hand. It was hard to know the exact moment their lives had begun to derail, like a locomotive rounding the track too fast, the passenger carriages tilting to a critical angle, the massive steel wheels beginning to lift. By the time he'd realized what was happening—by the time he'd *truly understood*—it was too late for them to continue on the planned trajectory of their lives. For a while, they had been suspended as if in midair: Kate's rapidly declining condition; his own sporadic tremors; Gary's suicide; Lauren's struggle with cancer. *And how many others?* As the collateral damage broadened and the casualties continued to mount, the town slowly turned against them. Now they were heading toward the final crash. There was no way to stop it—not all of it—and Michael would have to live with the responsibility for the rest of his life, and wonder if there was something he could've done to stop it.

When he reached the end of the road, Michael eased the car into the dirt driveway next to the tarp-covered mass of what he presumed was his Mercury Eight. He opened the door, stepped out of the Buick, and went to inspect it, lifting the plastic cover enough to see the liberty blue exterior, the California license plate, the small dent in the right-rear bumper from when he'd accidentally backed into a light pole a year and a half ago. It was his, all right. There was no doubt about it. And the car's last occupants couldn't be more than a few miles from where he now stood. He wanted to run and find them, to slash his way through the woods, the brambles clutching at his clothes and carving deep red gouges into his skin. He wanted to act without thinking, just this once, to undo the years of indecisiveness in a single endeavor.

A few miles, he thought. *So close now. It could be over. All of it.*

Michael returned to the Buick, opened the rear passenger door, and lifted the brown leather satchel from the backseat. He scanned the driveway and the road beyond. It was empty, nothing but tall weeds on either side, a few crumpled beer cans lying against the curb, no one to observe him entering the woods. That was good. It was important for him to remain unnoticed. Because what happened from here on out would be a private matter, something that concerned only himself, his boys, and the man who'd taken them.

"The Mercury . . . is parked beneath a blue tarp at the end of . . . Butcherknife Road off NF-742. It's about . . . sixteen miles west of Grants Pass. The house . . . will be empty. At the edge of the yard

you'll find . . . a trail head entering the forest. Take it. We're not far from there."

"Put Sean on the phone," Michael had said through clenched teeth, his hand squeezing the receiver so hard that the muscles of his forearm still ached, two days later.

"You can talk . . . to them plenty when you get here," the man responded. His voice sounded odd, his speech halting and strained, the words gurgling up through the phone line.

A bad connection, Michael had thought. But he'd replayed the conversation hundreds of times in his mind since then. And now . . . now he wasn't so sure.

He swung the Buick's rear door closed, moved past the shrouded carcass of the Mercury and into the side yard, walked the perimeter until he found the spot where the trail began.

"*Come alone,*" the man had said. "*Don't . . . tell them where you're going. Don't bring anyone with you.*"

"I won't," Michael had promised, and he'd stayed true to his word. But now that he was here, it was hard to know what waited for him at the other end of this dark and narrow stretch of path.

He paused, looked back over his shoulder one last time to be certain he hadn't been followed. Then he turned, stepped beneath a tangled arch of overhanging branches, and disappeared into the woods.

19

THEY STOOD ON THE NORTH END OF THE COUNTY FAIR-
ground, the three of them eyeing the metallic Pacific
Bell phone booth with the same contemplative expression. The glass-paned accordion door stood partially ajar,
and the pay phone's black-and-silver exterior peeked out at
them through the opening. Except for a few semipermanent
structures—mobile trailers atop concrete blocks, a green-framed
ticket booth to the south—the fairground was empty. A hundred yards ahead, the Rogue River stretched out before them,
running east into Grants Pass, west toward the mountains. A
light breeze wafted in off the water, scattered bits of restless
trash in the otherwise deserted parking lot behind them.

"This is the one. She's sure of it?" Detective Pierce asked,
pushing aside a crumpled red-and-white popcorn box with the
toe of his shoe.

"Yeah," his partner confirmed. "This is it. Figure the kidnapper made his call from here two days ago."

"Why here?" Pierce asked. He seemed irritated, and Jim
reckoned it was the same thing that was eating at all of them:
the feeling that they were so close now, that the man they were

looking for had stood in this very spot, made his call, and then just walked away.

"Traveling carnival came through this past weekend," De-Luca said. "Lots of people. No one stands out at events like that."

"You think this is the closest pay phone to where they're staying?" Pierce asked.

"No," DeLuca answered. "That would lead people right to you. I mean"—he shrugged, palms turned up at his sides—"here we are."

"I don't think he's staying in town," Jim said. "He needs someplace remote, where there's no chance of the kids being spotted." He stepped forward, slid the booth's door all the way open. "But he's not far from here. No more than a forty-minute drive, I'd guess."

"In the stolen Mercury?" DeLuca asked, but both Pierce and Jim shook their heads.

"Too risky," Pierce noted. "That thing won't resurface until we've found him."

"Agreed," Jim said, surveying the inside of the booth. Finger-prints would be useless: time consuming to collect and evaluate, and obscured by the scores of people who'd used the phone during the carnival.

Pierce turned slowly in a 360-degree circle, taking in the river, the fairground, a few nearby houses, Redwood Highway to the south. To his left, a rat scurried out from beneath the raised foundation of one of the trailers, snatched up the stale remnant of a hot dog roll in its teeth, and disappeared again.

"He came in off the highway," Pierce said. "Had another car or hitched a ride. This is the west end of town. I'll bet he came from that direction. It's mostly forest and mountains out there—a good place to hide."

"With all the people here two days ago," DeLuca said, "there's no way he brought the kids with him. He would've locked them up somewhere while he was gone. Bet he worried the whole time about them getting loose."

Pierce nodded, turned back toward the river. "So no more than forty minutes to the west of here is what we're thinking."

"Hmm," Jim muttered, "that's interesting." He stood inside the phone booth now, bent slightly at the waist, staring not at the phone itself but at a pane of glass along the back wall.

"What?" Pierce asked, moving forward and looking over Jim's shoulder. "What do you—?"

"Blood," Jim said, "at least I think it is." He stepped out of the booth to allow the others a closer look.

Pierce placed a hand on each knee and brought his face close to the glass. There were small red droplets—like scattered bits of punctuation—on the interior side of the panel. They were denser in the center, the area between them becoming greater toward the edges. It reminded him of the scattered spray of a shotgun fired at medium range.

"You think it's his?" he asked.

"Could be anyone's," DeLuca said. "Anyone's at all."

"But you don't think so," Pierce replied, looking at Jim. "You think it's his."

The sheriff's eyes shifted toward the horizon before refocusing on the men in front of him. "I do."

"What makes you so sure?" Pierce asked, but he felt it too. This was from the man they were chasing. *Was he wounded?* He wasn't sure, couldn't fit all the pieces together yet. But they were right there in front of them, each one turning, changing positions with the others, trying to merge into something whole.

Jim was the closest to understanding, could feel the full story locking into place. *Was it possible for things to move that quickly?* He didn't know. *Couldn't* know. There were some things he didn't want to believe.

"He's not a bad child," Camilla Napolitano told him on the day after Danny was taken. He was canvassing the neighborhood, talking to folks who knew the McCrays best.

"You used to babysit the boys when they were younger."

"I did," she said, "and I can tell you this: if any harm has come to Danny McCray, he doesn't deserve it."

Jim turned to look at the house next door. "I'm glad to hear you say that. Not everyone in this town thinks the way you—"

"But he is broken," she continued. "Anyone who spends time with him can see that."

"Broken?"

"He didn't come out right." She placed the palm of her right hand on her stomach. "The McCrays aren't the only ones who've had to pay for that."

Jim tucked his thumbs into his belt. "If you've seen anything . . ."

"I've seen plenty, and so have you." She shook her head, leaned against the wooden frame of the door. "Broken things can hurt people." She glanced over at her neighbor's front yard, at the child's bike left lying in the grass. "They need to be fixed," she said, "or they need to be put away."

Jim's gaze shifted away from the phone booth toward the mountain range to their west. They were close now, but not close enough. There was still so much territory to cover. He turned and headed for his car. "We need to find them," he said to the detectives. "There's even less time than I thought."

20

BANES HAD BROUGHT ENOUGH SUPPLIES FOR ONE BUT NOT two, and had only a single pair of handcuffs to use for the boys. So he looped the short chain around the wood-burning stove's metal support post—but that meant they each had a hand free to get up to mischief. He didn't like that, didn't like the way the older one whispered to the mute, and the way they watched him.

"*No talking. Eyes on the wall,*" he would say, but before long they would be watching him again, likely planning their escape.

He had a pistol and a shotgun that he kept between the wall and the mattress. But the presence of the guns made him feel *worse*, not better. What if one of the boys got free while he slept? The younger one seemed complacent enough, but his brother was a real fighter, and wouldn't think twice before snatching a weapon. *Better make sure the chain on the cuffs won't snap. That boy'll put a hole in you real quick.* And so he checked and double-checked the cuffs, and tested the tightness of the bolts that fastened the support post to the floor. *You know he's working on them with his other hand,* he thought. *It's only a matter of time until a boy like that figures out a way to get loose.*

Why had he pulled him into the car in the first place? Why

hadn't he dumped him? The kid had seen his face, sure—might be able to point him out in a book of mug shots—but bringing him along was an even greater risk. And now that Banes was sick, coughing up blood and dizzy as hell from the knock he'd taken on the head, it was difficult for him to concentrate and figure a way out of this mess.

He sat at the table, and dealt himself a hand of solitaire.

"Eyes on the wall," he said, "or I'll take that ax in the yard and cut off your finger." From the top of the deck, he turned over two cards, then the jack of diamonds. His only queen was a queen of hearts. But he plopped the jack on top of it anyway, figured what the hell.

There was a knock on the door.

Banes was up in a half second. The chair clattered to the floor as he dove for the mattress and grabbed the revolver.

"Come in," he said, a little too gruff, once he held the gun in his hand. He leveled the sights at the door.

A full minute passed. He counted it in his head.

"I said, 'Come in,'" he yelled. "Door's open."

Not a sound from the front porch.

Banes stood, went to the window, and looked outside. There was no one that he could see.

He took a deep breath, set his hand on the doorknob, and slowly turned it. On the count of three, he threw it open, and stepped to the left behind the wall so he wouldn't be an easy target. The door banged against the interior wood paneling.

"Hello?" he called, hazarding a peek. The porch and front yard were still empty.

Banes hid the gun behind his right leg, and stepped out onto the porch. "If you're out there, you'd better show yourself," he said. "I'd be happy to put a bullet in one of these boys if you don't."

He descended the steps, circled the house. No one was out here—no one but himself. The knock had been nothing: the cabin settling, a branch tapping the roof in the wind. Except the cabin was surrounded by a small clearing, and the closest tree was more than fifty yards away. Maybe he had imagined it. It was certainly possible. He couldn't think straight around that boy.

He was almost back to the porch when a wave of dizziness passed over him. His knees buckled and he pitched forward, caught himself with his hands as he went down on all fours.

The gun went off in his right hand, the report deafening.

There was no pain, only a small spray of blood on the grass in front of him.

A moment later, he noticed that the tips of both the index and middle finger on his left hand were missing.

He was surprised at how long it took for the pain to surface. He left the gun where it was, stood, and climbed the four uneven steps to the porch. On the second one, it hit him, an overwhelming agony in his hand that bent him double at the waist. He lowered himself to the wooden planks, and squeezed his eyes tight against it.

"*Aaaaaaaaaaagghhh,*" he groaned, folding into a fetal position. The sound of his voice was muffled in his own ears, as if it came from under the mattress within the cabin. For a brief period, he felt like two people: the one lying here on the porch, cupping his injured hand against his belly, and the other witnessing it from a distance. He moved back and forth between these two states until the worst of it passed, then righted himself enough to scoot the rest of the way inside, using his right hand to push while keeping his left tucked tightly against his body. With considerable effort, he pulled himself up to stand at the sink. There was a meager water supply to the cabin—tinged with brown but better than nothing—and he held his wounded fingers under the faucet, watching the reddish-brown runoff pool in the sink, the bits of clotted blood bob and circle in the current like tiny ships before disappearing down the drain.

Banes rinsed the fingers as best he could, then turned off the water and searched for something he could fashion into a bandage. There were no medical supplies, only the mattress, a bookshelf, the table and chair, some canned food, and the clothes they wore. The boys had their eyes on him again, sizing up this new development. They appeared *glad* that this had happened to him. He wanted to punch them over and over until their faces swelled and they could no longer stare at him, or turn up the corners of their mouths in that subtle smirk.

He held up his hand in front of them. Slim rivers of blood slid down the two fingers.

"What d'ya think of that?" he asked. "Does *that* make you happy?"

"Yes," said the older one, and Banes lowered his hand, stared at the boy.

"Oh yeah? Makes you happy, does it?"

The kid didn't reply, merely looked at him with a hint of satisfaction in his eyes.

"Okay," Banes said. Turning and crossing the room, he opened the wooden drawer beneath the sink. There were two knives in there. He pulled out the one with the serrated edge, the larger of the two.

"How'd you like it if I chopped off some of *your* fingers? Or maybe"—he paused, standing in front of them once again—"maybe your brother's." He dropped to one knee in front of the younger boy, and grabbed him by the wrist that was not tethered to the handcuffs. "You think two will do it, or should I cut off more?"

"He'll kill you," the older boy said. "The stuff that he's do-ing now, that's just the beginning."

Banes paused, the knife poised above the fingers. "What are you talking about?"

"You know," the kid said. "Everyone knows."

"What do they know?"

The boy smiled. "Everything bad that's happened to you since you took us, it's because of him. He's making it hap-pen. You shot off your own fingers," he said, nodding at the wounded hand that was wrapped around the younger boy's wrist. "That's not an accident. Neither is your cough or the cut on your head."

"He's making it happen?"

The older boy nodded. "Sooner or later, he's going to kill you. He doesn't want to do it, but he can't help it. It's not his fault. Right now it's happening slowly."

"You call this *slowly*?"

"It's worse with people he doesn't like. Still, it's not as bad as it could be. He's holding back, trying to fight it." The boy studied him, lowered his voice. "But if you hurt him—if you hurt either of us—you'll be dead by morning."

"I don't think so," Banes responded. "I can tell a bluff when I hear one."

"How are those fingers feeling?" the boy asked, and Banes realized he had released the younger one's wrist, and slid away from him.

"You should take us back," the kid said, and rapped the knuckles of his free hand twice on the floor—a sound that bore a close resemblance to the knock Banes had heard earlier. "It's the only way you make it out of this alive."

21

FOR THE FIRST MILE OR SO, THE PATH THROUGH THE WOODS followed what Michael presumed—from the small wooden sign he'd spotted—to be Butcherknife Creek. The terrain was uneven, thick with tree roots, the earth loose in spots and prone to sliding beneath the soles of his shoes. The thorny arms of blackberry vines stretched across the narrow path, snatching at his shirt and pants. He recognized other plants as well: sword ferns and western redbuds; common nettles with long stems that stung when they brushed against his arms and neck. The creek beside him was still and swamplike, its surface covered with a dull film on which dragonflies and water bugs rested. Within thirty seconds of entering the woods, mosquitoes took to him with relentless persistence. A haze of no-see-ums danced in front of his face, penetrating his nostrils until he snorted them away.

He pushed on, and hoped the path would clear up ahead, that his progress would become easier, faster. The creek forked to the right and the trail followed for a short distance before the water ended and he turned northward, ascending a gradual incline. The swarms of insects were less dense now, but the trail was narrower. The grasses and weeds grew together in the middle, obscuring the ground beneath him. He stumbled often, and his breathing became deeper and more rapid as the pitch of the hill intensified. It was difficult to gauge how far he had traveled. He had been walking for nearly an hour. In the distance, he could hear the flow of other waterways, the far-off rumble of thunder. Otherwise, it was silent—except for the sound of his breathing and his body passing through the dense underbrush. The thought occurred to him that he might've taken a wrong turn, and could be heading in the wrong direction. How much farther should he walk before turning around and retracing his steps? What would he do if he couldn't find them?

The wind picked up and threaded its fingers through the trees. The thunder sounded closer now, and he felt a drop of rain—fat and pregnant—strike the back of his neck, slide beneath his collar, and ripple its way along his spine. A storm was coming, would be upon him soon. If he turned back now, he would have to navigate the hill's steep decline and root-strewn topography in the rain. He'd likely fall and break an ankle or strike his head on a rock, rendering him unconscious or physically incapacitated—and of no help to his boys. Then all of this would be for nothing.

No, he decided, *the only way through is onward. There's no turning back now.* He took one step forward, then another, and focused his mind on the faces of his sons. They were waiting—somewhere ahead—and he would not stop until he found them. Dirt crumbled beneath his right foot and he nearly fell. Instead he planted an open palm on the ground, steadied himself, then straightened and continued up the hill.

Ten minutes later it was raining, and building to a deluge.

Forked tongues of lightning sizzled through the sky, blanching his vision. Thunder rolled across the landscape like the sound of massive bodies being tossed from a truck. Half-blinded from the downpour and now moving by feel and instinct alone, Michael pressed on, shoulders hunched, head lowered against the storm.

22

I T WAS RAINING OUTSIDE. DANNY COULD SEE IT THROUGH THE window, and hear the water hitting the roof above, like the sound of his mother's shower each morning. Back when she was strong enough to stand in the tub without falling, she used to sing in the shower. Sometimes Danny would sit outside in the hall and listen. He liked the sound of her voice. It was even prettier than the ladies on the radio. At night, she would sing to them before bed. He thought about it now, and pretended she stood just outside the window singing a song only he could hear.

The man was pacing the room. "Eyes on the wall," he said, but it was hard for Danny to not look at his hand and the two fingers with their missing ends. It was scary, seeing all that blood. The man was angry. He had wanted to cut off Danny's fingers too.

"He'll kill you," Sean had said. "The stuff that he's doing now, that's just the beginning."

"What are you talking about?"

"Everything bad that's happened to you . . . he's making it happen. You shot off your own fingers. That's not an accident."

Danny had listened to his older brother and tried to understand. Sean had never said anything like that before. He told people to shut up whenever they said mean things about him. At Danny's birthday parties, it was always only Sean and his parents, Aunt Lauren, and Uncle Gary. Then Uncle Gary died and could no longer visit, and Aunt Lauren stopped coming too. His mom said it was because she was sad and that sometimes adults died for no good reason. That sure seemed like a sad thing to Danny.

"Sooner or later, he's going to kill you. He doesn't want to do it, but he can't help it. It's not his fault."

Why did his brother say that? Everything about it was scary. Was it true what he said, or a trick to make the man leave them alone? He looked over at Sean, and tried to figure out what he was thinking. His brother stared back at him, and shook his head. Danny didn't know what that meant either.

The man continued to pace in front of them. The wood floor shook with each step. Danny tried to look at the wall, but his eyes kept returning to the bloody fingers with their little missing pieces.

"Eyes on the wall," the man said again, but he didn't seem to be paying attention to them. Danny turned his head to the wall anyway. He didn't want to anger the man. He might try to cut off his fingers again. And even though he wasn't a nice man, Danny wished he had not shot off his fingers with the gun. He didn't mean for him to do it, and didn't like to think that he might have *made* him do it. If he could put the fingers back, he would.

Danny was a good boy, or at least he tried to be. He knew people didn't like him, didn't want him around. If he could talk, maybe they would like him more. He imagined walking up to the kids who played stickball in the street and sharing a joke. Everyone would laugh, slap him on the back, and tell him to catch the ball if it came to him. When it was his turn at bat, he would swing the stick hard and hit the rubber ball past Joey Inzana at shortstop. It wouldn't be a home run—he wasn't strong or fast enough for that—but he would make it to second base. And then he could tell his parents about it over dinner.

"Got to keep moving," the man said. "Can't stay here for long." He stopped at the window and looked out at the rain.

Danny turned to his brother. Sean smiled and winked. It made him feel better. Sean didn't believe the things he had said earlier. It was all part of his plan. Even now, he was figuring out their escape. Pretty soon, it would be time. When they ran from the man, Danny would pretend he was running the bases, only straight ahead this time instead of in a circle. In his head, he practiced. Sean would need him to be fast, and he didn't want to disappoint his brother. When the time came, he would be ready.

23

JIM KENT CAME TO THE END OF SLATE CREEK ROAD AND
negotiated a three-point turn in the black-and-white
cruiser, pointing himself in the direction from which
he'd just come. He was a little less than three miles in, but
the road was narrow and potholed and the going slow. He'd
split from Detectives Pierce and DeLuca to search the area for
signs of Michael's Mercury or Lauren's Buick Special. They'd
contacted the Oregon State Police and the Josephine County
Sheriff's Department, who were now organizing a formal
search. But it would take time to assemble enough men and
decide on an appropriate line of attack. For now, it was only
the three of them—way out of their jurisdiction and unfamiliar
with the territory. Jim had his money on the kidnapper hiding
out in the mountains and national forest west of Grants Pass.
Pierce and DeLuca were searching farther south. They would
use their radios to stay in contact, though reception in this area
was patchy.

So far Jim's thirty-minute drive along Route 199 had yielded
nothing, but he would keep looking. He was convinced they
were close.

The key to finding someone was to think like them. He'd read that somewhere—in a police procedural manual or his wife's copy of *Reader's Digest*, he couldn't remember which. But it made sense, no matter where it had come from. You can't catch a rabbit unless you think like one, except they weren't after a rabbit. They were hunting a man who, from the look of the dried blood in the telephone booth, was either sick or injured—and an injured man will seek cover, lay low. But an injured man could also be dangerous, and strike out unexpectedly with lethal intent, knowing that surprise was his only advantage.

For the moment, assume that the kidnapper doesn't have access to any other car but the Mercury, Jim thought. The day before yesterday, the kidnapper hitched a short ride into town, and asked the driver to drop him at the fairground. He made a phone call to the McCrays' residence at 10:36 in the morning. According to the switchboard operator's logbook, it lasted only eighteen seconds. *Why?* he asked. *Who makes a trip all the way into town to talk for only eighteen seconds?*

He glanced at the second hand on his watch, noted its position, and cleared his throat. "I've got your boys," he said aloud in the otherwise empty car. "If you ever want to see them alive again, bring five thousand dollars to the bridge just north of the county fairground in Grants Pass, Oregon. Be there at midnight tomorrow. Involve the police and I'll kill them both." He looked down at his watch again. The short monologue had taken him twenty-two seconds. Only, the kidnapper wouldn't have started speaking right away. He'd have waited for someone to answer on the other end. And the chances were that he would have paused at the end of his speech, waiting for some kind of response, an assurance that his message had been received. Jim figured a conversation like that would take at least thirty seconds. So how to make sense of an eighteen-

second phone call, too short to convey the necessary instruc-
tions, too long for a simple hang up. And then, two hours
and forty minutes later, a second call lasting six minutes and
twenty-two seconds. That was too long, in his opinion, for the
conversation one might expect. The duration of that call meant
something, he *knew* it did. As he stood before the phone booth
at the county fairground he'd considered the possibilities, until one—the scenario he least wanted to be true—seemed to
emerge as the only option.

Jim's eyes moved back and forth as he surveyed the woods
on either side of the slender roadway. He was halfway back
to Route 199, he guessed. There were other secondary roads
much like this one, and he would search them all until he
found those boys. Rain spattered the windshield now, blurring the details of the world beyond the glass. "This is not
what I need right now," he said, flipping the lever to activate
the car's wipers. The rubber blades arced across the windshield, smearing muddy streaks from the dust that had settled
there. In California, and even here in this southwest corner
of Oregon, a summer rainstorm was a rare event, something
people gawked at from the shelter of their front porches. Statistically speaking, it wasn't supposed to happen, and yet here
he was in his car as the rain furiously pounded the roof a few
inches above his head. It was difficult to see the road ahead,
and he eased the cruiser to a stop, waiting for the worst to
pass. It wouldn't last long, he thought, but it would wash away
any signs that might help in his search: footprints in the dirt,
a sporadic trail of blood left by the kidnapper. It would slow
his progress too—the rain—and it made Jim wonder if even
that was intentional.

"This is what happens when you allow your mind to enter-
tain impossible things," he said to himself. "You become para-

noid like the rest of them—start to believe even the weather is against you."

But it is, his mind responded, which made him feel cold and hollow inside. He looked up, studied his reflection in the rearview, and didn't like what he saw staring back at him.

"What are *you* doing here?" he asked himself.

His only answer: the thrum of rain on the windshield and the *whump, whump* of the wipers.

You're no cop, he thought, *not really. You're a small-town figurehead—someone to call when the neighbors are bickering, when the kids go drag racing on Gas Point Road.*

Thunder rumbled overhead and, for a moment, drowned out the sound of rain against the cruiser's metal exterior.

"You're a plumber," he said, "and an old one at that. You've got no business throwing yourself into a manhunt."

The familiar face in the mirror said nothing, only looked at him with deeply sunken eyes. The lines of his cheeks were driven like stitching into his worn and leathery skin, and he followed them to the downturned corners of his mouth.

"You're too old for this shit," he said, and reached out his right hand to twist the rearview out of his line of sight. It broke off in his hand. He stared at it, wrapped in the fleshy envelope of his palm and fingers.

"Well . . . damn," he said, tossing the severed fixture onto the passenger seat.

Outside, the rain continued. He pulled his metal lighter from his front shirt pocket, flipped open the Zippo's top and flicked the spark wheel with his thumb, and watched as the butane-fueled flame sprang to life. He'd smoked the last cigarette in his pack at the fairgrounds, but there was a new one in the glove compartment. He reached over, opened it, and stuck his hand inside until his fingers felt the paper packaging.

". . . about, Jim. Over."

He paused, stared at the Motorola, then dropped the cigarettes on the seat beside him and picked up the mic.

"This is Jim," he said. "Didn't catch your last. Over."

There was a low hiss and crackle from the speaker, but nothing else.

He keyed the mic again. "Can't tell if you're copying me or not. I'm not reading you well from my end. Forget cats and dogs, it's raining pianos out here. I think the storm's messing with the reception. Over."

More static from the dash-mounted radio, then: ". . . nothing to . . . only . . . might ch . . . with you."

"I'm not catching most of that," Jim said. "If you can hear me, let's meet along Route 199 just north of Slate Creek Road in about an hour. Do you copy?"

The speaker was quiet for a moment, then another short burst of static.

". . . the . . . of . . . ack to . . . ver."

Jim hung up the mic. So much for modern technology.

On the other side of the windshield, the rain was starting to slacken, at least. He could make out the general contours of the road once again, and by the time he reached the main route, the visibility would be better.

Jim dropped the car into gear and nudged the accelerator. It was slow going; the road was pockmarked and would give him a flat tire if he wasn't careful.

Twenty minutes later he was back on Route 199. The precipitation had tapered to nothing, and the sky overhead cleared to a deep and cloudless blue. He passed over the muddy bed of a small creek and turned right onto NF-742, just one of a tapestry of fire roads through the Siskiyou National Forest. They would be unmarked, he presumed—crisscrossing and doubling back until he was hopelessly lost. *No*, he decided. *Going in there would be foolish*. There were rangers and local law enforcement who knew the area, and would be far better equipped to conduct an extensive search in the mountains. *If it came to that*, he reminded himself. Because he didn't think it would. The kidnapper would not have risked coming all the way into Grants Pass if it meant an eight-hour round-trip. It would've meant too much time away from his captives—time for them to be discovered, to figure out a way to escape.

They're closer than that. And so Jim turned the steering wheel to the left, and eased the car down the short stretch of Butcherknife Road.

24

WHAT DOES IT LOOK LIKE? IS IT STILL BLEEDING?" THE man squatted in front of them. The cut on his face was no longer oozing, but the skin around it appeared bright red, like he'd colored it with one of Danny's crayons.

"It looks bad," Sean told him. "It's not healing right. There's something wr—"

"Shut up!" the man said. "I wasn't asking you. I was asking your brother."

"He doesn't talk."

"I know that!" A fleck of spit flew off his lower lip and landed on Danny's pants leg. "You think I don't know that? You think I'm stupid?"

"There's something wrong with you. You're getting sicker. I told you."

"Yeah, yeah. You told me, all right. Said he couldn't help it. Said everyone gets sick around him."

"That's right."

"So tell me something else," the man said, poking Sean in the chest with one of his uninjured fingers. "Why don't *you* get sick, huh? Why not you too?"

"Sometimes my breathing is bad."

"That's it? Sometimes your breathing is bad. You're not dying of anything?"

"I don't know," Sean answered. "Maybe I am and I just don't know it."

"Ha! What kind of smart-ass response is that?" The man scratched at the cut; his nails left white lines across the red of his skin. "You wanna know what I think?" he said. "I think it's all a bunch of crap. I mean, who ever heard of a boy who can make people sick just by being around them?" He shook his finger at Sean. "You're a sly one. You think if you scare me enough, I'll let you go."

"You're getting sicker," Sean said. "You're going to die."

"Stop saying that!" the man hollered. He rose to his feet, walked back and forth across the room, speaking low and quiet to himself.

"You've got to let us go," Sean told him. "Pretty soon it'll be too late."

The man ignored him, continued to pace the room. He touched the cut, and looked at his fingers. After a while, he returned and squatted in front of them. This time, he looked only at Danny.

"Hey," he said, smiling and pointing to his forehead. "This don't look so bad, right? It looks like it's getting better, don't it? You can nod if you want to."

Danny looked over at Sean. He wasn't sure how he was supposed to respond.

The man reached out and turned his head so he couldn't see his brother. "Don't look at him," he said. "He doesn't have the answers. Tell me: the cut looks good, right? Things are getting better."

Danny looked at it again. The man's forehead was even redder than before. Maybe because he was so angry.

"Don't you ever get tired of listening to your brother's jab-bering?" the man asked. "Don't you ever wanna speak for yourself? I mean"—he smiled again—"what's stopping you? Ain't nothing stopping you, right? Just open your mouth and say something."

The man's eyes were brown, Danny noticed, like his mother's. She must be worried about them. He wondered when they would get to see her again.

"Come on, kid. You and me, we can be friends, you know. One word is all I'm asking." The man pointed again to his forehead. "Looks good, doesn't it? Healing up well, I'd say."

Danny turned his head slowly to the right, then back to the left. Or maybe it was left and then right. He was always confus-ing the two. He did it again, faster this time. *No, the cut wasn't getting better.* It was getting worse, like Sean had said. He shook his head back and forth, back and forth. Once he got going, he couldn't stop.

"Okay, okay," the man said, standing and going to the sink. "I'll wash it again if that's what you want." He turned on the faucet, cupped the water in his uninjured hand, and splashed it on his face.

"Dirty water won't help," Sean told him. "You ought to go to a doctor."

"Oh, yeah. A doctor. Good idea." The man turned to him. Brown water ran down his face, dribbling to the floor. "Let's see now, where would I find one?" He went to the window, looked outside. "Maybe there's a doctor standing in the front yard right now. Oh, wait: I think I see one." He went to the door, opened it, and stepped onto the porch. "*Hey! Hey, Doc!*" His shoulders slumped. "Nope, nope. My mistake," he said. "That's a tree."

"You should get your gun while you're out there," Sean

called. "You forgot to bring it in after you shot yourself in the fingers."

The man turned. "Why are you so interested in my gun?"

"I'm just saying you forgot to get it," Sean told him.

"I didn't forget, okay? I decided to leave it out there for a while, that's all."

"Why?"

"Why do *you* care?" the man responded. "Mind your own business."

"Are you afraid you'll shoot yourself again? This time in the head?"

"Boy, *shut up*. Don't you ever shut up?"

"No."

"*Jesus*," the man said. "I don't know which of you is worse. Forget *him*," he said, standing in the doorway, pointing at Danny. "How does anyone stand to be around *you*?"

"Go get it," Sean told him, "but not if you're gonna shoot yourself in the head."

"I'm not gonna . . ." The man went to the front steps, and paused with his head down for a moment. A few seconds later he reentered the cabin and walked directly to where Danny and his brother sat with their backs propped against the wood-burning stove. He bent down on one knee, tested the bolts with his fingers. "These seem a little loose," he said. "You been workin' on them when I wasn't looking?"

"No," Sean told him, although Danny had seen him doing it.

"Still trying to escape, huh? Well, I've got someplace I can take you. I didn't want to have to do this, but . . . you're leaving me no choice." The man dug in his pocket for the key to the handcuffs, unfastened the clasp around Danny's wrist, and then refastened it around the metal support post. "Come with me," he said to Danny, pulling him to his feet. "As for you," he said, turning to Sean, "keep working on that bolt of yours. Escape if you can. But if you do, you'll never see your brother again. And that, my annoying little friend, is a promise."

"Where are you taking him?"

"Where I won't have to worry about the two of you anymore," he said, and then started coughing. He went to the sink, dragging Danny with him, and spat into the metal basin. "Come on," he said, pulling Danny toward the door.

"Wait," Sean called after them, and Danny didn't like the sound of his voice. He could tell his brother was scared. That worried him. Sean was almost never scared.

The man stopped, and turned in the doorway. With his hand wrapped around Danny's wrist, he felt warm—almost hot. *Maybe he is dying*, Danny thought, *like Sean said*. He didn't want that to happen, and concentrated real hard on making it stop.

"Where are you going?" Sean asked, but the man only snorted.

"Don't worry," he said, swinging the door closed behind him. "You'll find out soon enough."

25

THEY SAT IN THE FIRST PEW TO THE RIGHT OF THE AISLE. Lauren had rented a wheelchair from Kimble's Apothecary off Main Street. It was a quarter mile from the house to the church on Gas Point Road, and the wheelchair was heavy—seventy pounds empty, another eighty-five with the addition of Kate—but it rolled easily enough along the sidewalks.

It would've been much simpler to go by car, to catch a ride with one of the neighbors. The Assembly of God was well-attended on Sundays. Aldo and Camilla Napolitano frequented the eight o'clock service. Bill and Samantha Travis went to the nine thirty. Against Kate's protests, Lauren had visited both homes to ask them for a ride. They'd offered legitimate reasons for why they couldn't help. Aldo and Camilla were setting up an event, and planned to head over early, their car full of supplies. Samantha Travis appeared well enough, but said she was recovering from a bout with pneumonia and thought it best not to expose Kate. "It was a dreadful thing," she'd admitted. "If either one of you came down with it on my account, I could never forgive myself."

There were others she could've asked—Pastor Reed would've

been happy to drive them—but after two rejections from their closest neighbors, Lauren decided this was God's way of encouraging her to get outside and enjoy the sunshine.

"You're going to push me? All the way there? In the wheelchair?" Kate frowned. "Lauren, no. If we can't get a ride, we'll just—"

"Sit here in the house. Until . . . what exactly?"

"Until Michael comes home with the boys. It won't be long now."

Lauren lowered herself into a chair at the kitchen table.

Kate touched the mug in front of her, turned it with her fingers. "He's going to bring them back, you know. He's out there looking for them right now."

"Yes, I know."

"I don't *need* to go to that place, and put myself on display like that."

"It's just church," Lauren said. "How long has it been?"

Kate pushed away her cup. "Doesn't matter."

"It's not right for you to lock yourself away like this—"

"I'm *comfortable* here. I don't want to be out there anymore. Can you understand that?"

Lauren reached across the table, and tried to take her sister's hands in her own. Kate pulled back, folding her arms across the prominent rungs of bones in her chest.

"They need to see you," Lauren told her. "They need to be reminded that you're still part of this community."

Kate shook her head. "They don't *want* to be reminded. As far as they're concerned, I'm already dead."

"Kate," Lauren whispered, but her sister held up a hand.

"It's okay. I think about it too." She looked toward the window, and the light from it nearly reached her face.

"You're not—"

"Dead yet? No. But it's waiting for me. I can feel it." She leaned forward. "Sometimes it's like I'm standing on a bridge between this world and the next. I look down and my feet are moving, only I'm not sure in which direction they're taking me."

Lauren studied her: the subtle gray pallor of her skin; the lines around her eyes and mouth were too deep, too harshly drawn for a woman so young. "You're getting better," she said, and Kate smiled.

"Yes. I feel that too. Since I've started the new medicine that Dr. Eichner prescribed. There are days when I have hope, when I think it might all just . . . go away." She drew a hand across the side of her face, placed her palm on the table. "It's not about my son. It's never been about my son."

"No," Lauren agreed. "Of course not. Danny is—"

"Just a boy. A little different from the others, but nothing to be afraid of." She leaned forward. "He's missed you, you know. He's shunned enough as it is. It shouldn't happen here in his home. This should be a safe place for him."

"I'm sorry if I've seemed distant since Gary's passing."

"I'm sorry you still have doubts."

Lauren had said nothing in response. The next morning she rose early, planning to return the wheelchair to the apothecary. But there was Kate, dressed and ready, standing beside it.

"It's an ugly thing," she said, looking down at the metal frame, the sling of leather that served as a seat.

"Well, *you* look beautiful," Lauren replied. And despite the caged look in her eyes that never really disappeared, the way the dress hung on her—now three sizes too big—Kate *was* beautiful: her brown hair curled inward at her shoulders; the creased corners of her mouth that lifted as she spoke. They'd left the house at seven, before the heat of the day was upon them. *All of our suspicions will be for nothing,* she thought. *People will see us along the way, and stop to offer a ride.* Only no one did. And as each passing car slowed for a better look, Lauren and Kate stared straight ahead, pretending to be lost in the splendor of the morning and the familiar pleasure of each other's company.

"I'm so pleased you could be here," Pastor Reed greeted them when they arrived. "What a glorious day to rejoice in the fellowship of the Lord."

But still, for all that fellowship, they were alone. When the last psalm was recited, and the lyrics to the doxology gave way to the rising pitch of the organ, the parishioners shuffled outside and stood in the sunlight. Lauren and Kate were met with smiles and polite murmurings—but nothing genuine, nothing that might sustain them.

"So nice to see you."

"Will you be staying for coffee?"

"You're looking well today."

Kate stood with the rest of them, her hands resting lightly on her sister's forearm for support. "You can see it in their eyes," she said when they were alone again. "I've known these people my whole life. Only now, it's uncomfortable for them to have me here."

"I don't think that's true," Lauren said, but there was no conviction in her voice. She could feel it too.

"Thanks for bringing me," Kate said. She turned, and kissed her sister on the cheek. "We've got a long walk home. The day is growing warm."

"I'm sure we could get a ride home if we asked."

"Maybe." Kate scanned the crowd. "But I don't want to ask. Are you ready?"

"Yes," Lauren said. "Let's go."

They found the wheelchair where they had left it, waiting dutifully in the rear of the chapel. It was nearly nine thirty. The second service was about to begin, the congregation filing in, settling themselves in the wooden pews.

"Thank you for coming," Pastor Reed said as Kate eased herself into the chair. "May the grace and strength of the Lord be with you."

"And with us all," Kate replied. Because *this* was her family too. The things that were happening affected them all.

"Maybe *I* should push *you*," she told her sister as they exited the parking lot.

Lauren laughed. "Maybe you should. You're strong today."

Stronger than I've been in a long time, Kate thought, and pictured the bridge again, the one that spanned the world between the living and the dead. *I look down and my feet are moving*, she'd heard herself say the night before, *only I'm not sure in which direction they're taking me.*

They continued in silence, only the churn of the wheels along the concrete, the soft *thunk* as they encountered each seam in the sidewalk. With the interstate behind them, Lauren chose a different route this time. Turning left on Locust, they approached the neighborhood from the east. The sun was now at their backs, and their shadow—the rolling chair and two women—stretched out, long and skeletal before them.

26

I T WAS MOSTLY UPHILL, SLICK AND TREACHEROUS AS MICHAEL pushed his way through the wild, nettled overgrowth. The storm had passed, leaving him soaked to the bone but otherwise unaffected: still upright, still moving forward. His satchel had kept the money relatively dry. *Even if it hadn't,* he thought, *money dried quickly enough.* It made him nervous to carry so much cash. Fifteen hundred dollars was half a year's salary. He had called ahead. The bank had to check his ledger, and ensure the funds were available. He'd brought his briefcase, expecting the stacks of bills to fill the entire thing. Instead the teller handed him thirty fifty-dollar bills. Folded over once, they fit easily into the palm of his hand. Years of savings, and there it was. It was humbling to see how little he had to show for all the time and effort. It seemed your life never amounted to as much as you thought it would.

The downpour had beaten back the insects, at least. He was thankful to be rid of the swarming army of biting things. As he continued, the slope of the land became more even, the foliage thinned, and the trail curved sharply to the left. A hundred yards or so later, it curved right again, and then ended abruptly at the perimeter of a small clearing.

Michael had pictured himself finding them in such a spot: a small cabin in the middle of a meadow, a front door that would open to the sight of his boys.

Only now, stepping out from beneath the pines and standing in the circular clearing, there was no cabin, only shin-high grass and the empty *shush* of a passing breeze.

He turned slowly, scanned the perimeter for any sign of a trail. There was nothing except for the one that had led him here, so he stood and listened to the angry squawk of a scrub jay in the woods to his left.

A wrong turn, he thought, the horrible certainty seeping into him like sewage, rancid and suffocating. *I made a wrong turn somewhere along the way, followed a path to nowhere. And now*—his shoulders sank with the thought—*now there's nothing to do but go back, and search for a less obvious path that I missed before.*

Then he realized that he hadn't missed them before. No, he had seen them all: snarled and thicketed passages he'd felt certain *couldn't* be the right way. How many were there? Five, ten, maybe fifteen possibilities? Which one should he take? How far would he follow each narrowing trail until he turned back to try the next? How many hours would he spend trying to find the right one?

"Hello?" he called out. "I've come like you asked. I brought what you wanted."

He listened for a response, strained to see deeper into the dense shadow-freckled expanse of woods around him.

"At the edge of the yard you'll find . . . a trail head entering the forest," the man had told him between short pauses, the crispness of his words dulled and slightly garbled over the line's long connection. *"Take it,"* he'd said. *"We're not far from there."*

Michael swiped at the sweat on the back of his neck. The sun was already high in the sky, the hours moving faster than he wanted. He cupped his hands around the corners of his mouth. "Hello?" he called again. No answer, only the wisp of the parting grass as he made his way across the clearing, searching for a trail on the other side.

He reentered the woods and moved in an ever-expanding perimeter around the clearing. It was hard to maintain his bearing and not lose sight of the meadow. There was something menacing about these woods, a riptide that seemed to want to pull him deeper into its waters. The completion of each circle brought him back to the only apparent trail in the area, the one he'd taken here. He used it as an anchor as he searched, knowing that as long as he encountered it with each broadening revolution, he wasn't lost. Still, it wasn't long until he had veered off course. Within twenty minutes, he realized what had happened, and turned back, tried to retrace his steps. But nothing looked familiar.

So much had gone wrong over the past two weeks that it seemed inconceivable that luck would be with him now. And whether it was luck, or destiny, or the hand of God that intervened, ten minutes later Michael crested a hill and saw a small wood-framed cabin nestled against the curved base of a cliff. From this direction, the approach gradually declined, and then leveled out as it reached the four meager steps of the front porch. Michael advised himself to be careful, to approach slowly and watch for the kidnapper, taking care not to twist his ankle along the way. But the admonition slipped through his mind like a silk handkerchief in the high wind, and by the time he was halfway there he was almost running. The wooden boards were rotten and threatened to give way beneath his feet as Michael stepped onto the porch. The doorknob was unlocked and turned easily in his hand. He shoved and the door swung open with a petulant shriek from its arthritic, rust-bitten hinges.

"Sean? Danny?" he called, and stepped inside, his eyes adjusting to the dim interior.

First he heard the voice, wafting toward him from some stale, darkened space.

"*Daaad.*"

The boy's breathing was harsh, panicked, audible from across the room. It took Michael a moment to register what he was seeing: his older son was on the floor, his right arm chained to the base of the woodstove.

Michael went to him, dropped to his knees and wrapped his arms around him. "Thank God," he said, bringing his head against his chest. With one hand on the boy's back, he could feel the vibration of air passing through his lungs, the ribs spreading and compressing with each labored cycle.

Sean hugged his father for a few seconds, then pushed him away. "Heee's gone," he said, the words extending at the end to match the patter of his breath. "The man took him awaaaay. I don't know where."

"Calm down. We'll find him," Michael promised. Then he heard footsteps behind him, the *thunk* of boots on the porch.

"You won't find him," Banes said, stepping inside. The gun was in his hand, the muzzle pointed neither directly at them nor completely away, only ready if needed. He crossed the room, retrieved the chair, and dragged it so that its back was against the wall, then sat with the gun resting on his right thigh. "Hello, Michael," he said. "Thank you for coming."

III

COLLECTION OF SOULS

27

JIM KENT STOOD NEXT TO THE DARK BLUE BUICK, STARING UP at the dilapidated exterior of the one-story cabin. Two small windows looked out onto the driveway, the paint on their faded white frames chipped and flaking. A few minutes ago, he'd stepped up onto the porch to peer through them. Beyond the meager panes of glass there'd been nothing but the dark stillness of an empty bedroom: a single cot without linen, a bare wooden floor, the partially opened door to a hallway beyond. He'd gone around to the back of the house, found a single wooden door and another window looking in on the small kitchen. The sink was empty, devoid of dishes, the countertop clear of anything but dust and a few rat droppings. Beyond the kitchen, there was a partial view of the living room, and that too was dark and without movement. If there were people inside—if they'd been living here for even a single day—there was no trace of them that he could discern. He'd banged on the kitchen window with the side of his hand, watched for any response from within, listened for footsteps or the hushed exchange of voices. There'd been nothing.

Still, here was Lauren's Buick and the tarp-covered hulk of the stolen Mercury Eight. The kidnapper had come here, and

Michael had arrived within the last twenty-four hours, he presumed. They were close, or at least *had been* a short time ago.

Jim returned to his cruiser, opened the door, and lowered himself into the driver's seat. With his right hand he reached out and plucked the CB mic from the small metal latch on which it rested, brought it to his mouth, and thumbed the switch.

"This is Sheriff Jim Kent calling Shasta County detectives Pierce and DeLuca. Over."

He waited, listened to the broken thread of static.

"I need all local law enforcement units to respond to my location at the end of Butcherknife Road," he said. "Officer requires immediate assistance."

He listened to the radio silence—the occasional unintelligible squawks—for a full two minutes before returning the mic to its receptacle.

Jim sat back in his seat, considered his options. He could attempt to force entry into the cabin. It was almost certainly vacant, the chance of encountering any of them very low. Still, there was a remote possibility he might find something useful, a clue to where they'd gone. Since both of the cars were here, he assumed they'd traveled by foot. That reduced the search area considerably.

Alternatively, he could drive the cruiser back to the main road, try to radio Pierce and DeLuca again. If that was unsuccessful, he could leave the car there, return to the house on foot, and begin the search without them. It would be safer, he reminded himself, to rendezvous with them first, to conduct the search together. But time was not on their side. Jim could feel the minutes slipping away, the chance of a catastrophic outcome, or losing them altogether, increasing with each passing hour.

He started the car, turned it around, and headed back out to the main road.

There was an envelope in the glove compartment. On the back of it, he wrote, "Found Buick and stolen Mercury at house at the end of this street. Couldn't reach you on radio. Beginning search myself." Climbing out of the vehicle, he placed the envelope under the rubber blade of the left windshield wiper. Then, remembering the sudden rain earlier that day, changed his mind and left it on top of the dashboard instead.

At the rear of the cruiser, he opened the trunk. Inside was an Ithaca 37 pump-action shotgun that had spent most of its life— along with the sidearm currently nestled in the holster of his utility belt—locked inside the gun cabinet in his office. Police work in Cottonwood did not require firearms, and the weight of the shotgun felt unnatural—menacing—as he lifted it and loaded the cartridges in the port in the bottom of the receiver, sliding them forward into the magazine. He filled his pockets with extra shells, tucked a flashlight into his belt, closed the trunk, and made the short walk back to the house in just over seven minutes. It didn't take long until he found what he was looking for at the rear of the property: a path heading into the woods.

They must've started out here, he thought, ducking beneath the branches. If he was afraid, it was a distant emotion, over-shadowed by the realization that it was only him now, that as ill-prepared as he was to face this, *he* was the one whom God had put in a position to save them.

"'For thine is the kingdom and the power and the glory forever and ever,'" he recited. Then he pumped the shotgun once, delivering a round into the chamber, and headed up the trail.

28

WELL, THAT'S JUST GREAT," PIERCE COMMENTED, LIFTing his foot off the accelerator and putting the car in Park. They'd been working their way through the maze of side streets east of Route 199. A few minutes ago, they'd skirted around the north end of Lake Selmac, turned left onto Reeves Creek Road, and were now following it back toward the highway. Or at least they *had* been until the rain came, pelting the windshield with such fury that Pierce began to wonder if the glass might crack under the onslaught. The visibility had gone to hell, and they'd been forced to stop and wait it out, the inside of the windshield fogging up as the rain pummeled them from above.

Sitting there in the car, DeLuca had tried raising Jim on the radio. All he'd gotten was the senseless drone of static—interference from the storm, most likely. Even before the weather had rolled in, the CB's reception had been scratchy, the surrounding forest and mountains playing havoc with the signal. *It was an odd feeling*, Pierce thought. *Disorienting.* Blurred shades of gray and white against the windshield, nothing but static rolling out across the speaker. It was hard to dismiss the notion that they'd been cut off completely from what was happening out there, the ordinary features of the world morphing into something dreamlike, wild and untamable. He was struck with the irrational thought that there were massive creatures—nightmarish and prehistoric—on the other side of the glass, that if he opened his door and stepped out of the car at this moment he would be snatched up in the grasp of a predatory talon and carried away into the deluge. And whether it meant that he was losing his mind or simply losing control of the situation, he came to the same conclusion. Things were starting to unravel, to slide away from them. He could feel it—had worked enough cases to know when things were about to go bad. There was a slippery, helpless texture to it that made him feel sick to his stomach.

"You'll be back in a few days?" his youngest son had asked him before he left.

He'd ruffled the nine-year-old's dark hair, pulled the blanket up over his shoulder, leaned over, and turned out the light. "Yeah," he said, walking across the room to the bedroom door. "Shouldn't be more than a couple of days—a week at the most."

"Back in time for football, though."

Pierce paused, one hand on the doorknob. He'd coached his son's team the year before. Nathan wasn't big, but he was fast. He'd done well as a running back, had that explosive power that hurtled him past the defensive line, left them clutching at his jersey as he passed. Watching him play, Pierce had been proud of his boy, had entertained thoughts of college scholarships and maybe, someday, a shot at the pros. It was strange how that happened, how your imaginings had legs of their own, a tendency to run and run until something—real life—reached out and stopped them.

"I should be back by then," he'd said, but it was little more than a guess. He could feel his family waiting for him, trusting him to walk through the door in a few short days, to slip back into their lives as if he'd never left.

The rain had begun to taper off, the world outside sliding back into focus. Pierce cleared his mind, put the car in gear, and gave it some gas. The vehicle rocked forward slightly, but otherwise refused to budge. He could hear the rear wheels spinning, felt the back end sinking as he let up on the accelerator.

Cursing, he swung the door open and stepped out to inspect the situation. One glance at the left-rear wheel was enough to tell him that it wasn't good. The dirt road had become soft and muddy during the downpour, the whitewall tire sunk at least two inches deep into the muck. Pierce circled around behind the car to check the other side, his shoes getting sucked up into the slop.

"Aw, hell," he said, trying to pull himself free. "How're things lookin' where you are?" he asked his partner, whose head was bent and studying the ground, his right hand pressed against the roof for balance.

"Just lost a shoe," DeLuca replied. He bent down to retrieve it, disappeared back into the car while he slipped it on, then slid across the front seat and exited from the driver's side.

Pierce joined him in the middle of the roadway, scanned their surroundings. In good visibility, he could see now what he'd done wrong. The stretch of land southwest of Lake Selmac was marshy, the earth here soft to begin with. When he'd brought the car to a stop, he hadn't noticed that this was a low point, that water would pool here. Even worse, he'd made the mistake of pulling onto the right shoulder, and although the road was narrow and the left tires weren't hopelessly stuck in the mud, the right ones were.

He lowered his head and tried to think, but he could feel

things continuing to slide away from him, the slow, maddening pull of momentum.

"If we can get something under that left tire for traction," DeLuca said, "we might be able to move it forward and off the shoulder."

Pierce scanned the terrain. "See anything we can use?" he asked. They were pretty much in the middle of nowhere.

"You still got those rain jackets in the trunk?"

"Took them out for the summer. It's *supposed* to be dry season. Besides," he said, "they wouldn't work anyway. Too slick. No traction."

DeLuca thought for a moment. "There's the canvas gun bag. Put that down in front of the left tire, dig out the right one a bit, and we might be in business."

"Okay," Pierce said. "We'll hand-dig a path in front of both rear tires so they'll have something to follow if we can get the car moving."

"Dirty work," DeLuca commented, "but it beats hiking out of here." He retrieved the key from the ignition, went to the trunk, and opened it. "I've gotta tell you, though," he said as his partner rolled up his sleeves and knelt in front of the left-rear tire, "this is one of those moments when I'm kind of wishing I'd ridden with Sheriff Kent."

29

TOOK YOU LONG ENOUGH TO GET HERE," BANES SAID. HIS thumb stroked the handle of his revolver. "I'd about given up on you."

"Where's Danny?" Michael demanded, but the man ignored him, his eyes shifting to where the older boy sat cross-legged on the floor.

"That kid of yours is a real peach. This one too. I can see why you were eager to—"

"You don't know me *or* my boys. Don't talk to me as if you do."

Banes smirked. "You think you can pretend—" He stopped then, coughed several times into the blood-soaked cloth wrapped around his left hand. There was something familiar about it. The fabric was dirty and stained with whatever was coming from the man's body. But the color beneath, it was—

"Is that . . . is that my son's shirt?" Michael asked, and then he knew. Danny was wearing it the day he was taken, an off-white color, almost yellow, like the separated cream in the bottles of milk that were delivered to their doorstep three times per week. The shirt was one of Danny's favorites. Michael had sat in his own kitchen and described it to the detectives.

Banes rose from his chair. He went to the sink, lowered his head, and spit into the metal basin. "It *was* his shirt," he said, returning to his seat. "Now it's mine. I need it more than he does."

Michael went cold. "What does that mean?" he heard himself say. "Have you done something to him? What have you—"

"More like *he* did something to *me*." Banes coughed again, and didn't bother to cover his mouth this time. "Look at this," he said, unwrapping the shirt and holding the hand up for him to see. "The kid cost me two fingers, that's for starters."

Beyond the final joint, the tips of his index and middle fingers had been torn off. Banes wiggled them, offered up a crazed smile. It was hard for Michael to stop staring at the macerated flesh. More striking, though, was the rest of his hand, which had turned purple and bloated, as if it had already been amputated and left to rot in the baking sun. *Infection*, Michael thought. *He will lose that hand if he doesn't get to a doctor. If he waits long enough, he could lose the entire arm.*

"How did he—"

"Oh, you know how he does it," Banes said. "You told me about it yourself, only I—"

"Told you about it? I've never met—"

"—only I didn't believe it," Banes continued. "Though right about now I'm wishing I had."

Michael glanced at Sean, started to get to his feet.

"*Sit down*," Banes told him. "You found me easy enough. Now you can stay."

"Look," Michael said, lowering himself to a seated position beside his son. "I think you're confused. And sick."

"Yeah? And whose fault is that?" Banes coughed again. The gun slid off his thigh, clattered to the floor. With his good hand, he reached down and snatched it up, pointed it at

Michael. "Don't even think about it," he warned. "I've still got enough juice left to put a bullet in both of ya." He bared his twisted rows of teeth at them, half smile, half grimace. The gash in the center of his forehead glistened.

"I don't know what you've heard about Danny—"

"You don't, huh. You of all people should know."

"He's just a child."

"Yeah? Is that right?" Banes scratched the wound on his head. "Then why are you getting rid of him?"

"*You're* the one who took him. I'm trying to get him back."

"Why? Did you reconsider?"

"No. I never—"

"Doesn't matter. He's dead now. Or he will be soon."

"*No!*" Sean screamed, and both of the men jumped. "You're a liar! I'll kill you myself!"

"Shut up," Banes said. "You'll be dead soon too. Matter of fact, I should've killed you first."

"He's not dead," Michael told his son. "He's just trying to get to you. You can tell that he's lying."

"I'm telling the truth," Banes said. "Why would I lie about that? Why would I lie about anything? I'm the one holding the gun."

"*Liar,*" Sean hissed. His breathing had worsened, the small chest rising and falling, the cords in his neck working to lift it, then letting the ribs drop with each wheezing exhalation.

Michael had witnessed this before. When Sean was four years old—six months after the birth of his brother—he took to his bed and barely moved for three long days. Dr. Besson, the family physician, had stopped by the house on the second day to examine him. There was nothing wrong, in the doctor's opinion, only a common childhood reaction to the introduction of a new sibling.

"His breathing is shallow," he'd said. "When I listen with my stethoscope, I can hear a high-pitched wheezing that we sometimes encounter in patients with asthma. When I was in training, we were taught that the condition is psychological in nature—a form of depression, a subconscious cry for the attention of the mother. With a new brother in the house, I imagine Sean isn't getting as much attention as he's used to." He smiled reassuringly, returned his stethoscope to the black bag resting on the bed.

"Could there be anything else the matter with him, Doctor?" Kate had asked. "He's a pretty happy child, not prone to fits of depression."

"The practice of medicine is like all things academic," the doctor replied. "Opinions often change over time." He leaned over, placed a hand on the boy's forehead, felt the chain of lymph nodes along the side of his neck. "If he was an adult, we could try the use of medicated cigarettes with belladonna or stramonium, but"—he smiled—"he's a little young for that. For now, I'd simply make sure he gets enough attention at home from you and your husband. Beyond that, there's no need to worry. He'll turn around in no time."

As it turned out, the doctor was right. By the next day the wheezing began to abate, and by the following day Sean was up and out of bed. It wasn't until the end of the week that he seemed completely back to normal, and although there were additional episodes over the years, none were as bad as the one he'd suffered at the age of four. Until now, that is. Now it seemed that Sean was in real trouble. And with Kate some two hundred miles away, the best Michael could do was pray it wouldn't get worse.

"You know what your boy there told me recently?" Banes asked. "He said that sooner or later his brother was going to

kill me, that he couldn't help it, that it happens with everyone."

"That's not—"

"He said that it happens faster with people he doesn't like.
That's why I was getting sick so quickly." Banes stood and
paced the room. "But as bad off as I am"—he paused, looked at
Sean—"he also said that things could get a lot worse, that if I
hurt either of them, I'd be dead by morning."

"It isn't true." Michael pulled his knees to his chest, watched
the man walk back and forth in front of him. "Danny doesn't
speak. That makes him different. A lot of people in my town
have gotten sick. Some of them have died. I don't know why.
There's a chemical plant to the west of us. It sits adjacent to a
stream that carries waste past Cottonwood during the rainy
season. My sister-in-law lives out that way. I've seen the resi-
due. If it seeps into the ground, it can get into the water supply.
Maybe that's what's making people sick. Maybe it's something
else. Nobody knows for sure. But people are afraid, ready to
blame anyone, especially anyone who's different. It isn't just
Cottonwood," he said. "It's happening across the country.
We've been rooting out communism, hundreds, maybe thou-
sands of lives ruined in the process. You think all those people
are guilty?"

Banes looked at him through eyes that were glazed over
with fever. He swayed a little on his feet. "Maybe not," he said.
"They used to drown the witches. The guilty ones rose to the
surface."

"And the innocent?"

"Sometimes they drowned, as well." Banes shrugged, sat
down again, leaned back in the chair. "We'll have to see," he
said.

"See what?" Michael asked.

"See if he rises to the surface," the man answered. "See if I drown." He looked toward the window. "Be getting dark soon," he said. "This one thinks I'll be dead by morning." He gestured toward Sean, whose eyes had slipped closed. Right now, it seemed, the boy was concentrating on breathing. "If I die," Banes continued, "you'll never find him. I'm the only one who knows where he is."

"He's alive then," Michael replied. His voice was little more than a whisper.

"I didn't say that," Banes told him. "I said you'd never find him. Then again," he said, "maybe you don't want to."

The two men sat there, staring at each other.

Banes lifted the gun. "You brought the money? Is that what's in that satchel there?"

"Yes."

"Well, slide it over. If I live past morning, it'll come in handy."

Michael lifted the leather strap over his head, and slid the satchel across the floor.

"Let's get one of your wrists in those cuffs," Banes said. "I'm getting tired. Think I might try to get some rest."

"If you die, we'll be chained to this thing," Michael told him. "It's unlikely anyone will find us. Sooner or later, we'll die as well."

"Well then," the man said, "I guess we're in this together."

"You should get to a doctor. That's the way you survive this. Not by keeping us here."

Banes chuckled. It turned into a cough, rough and wet. He brought the T-shirt to his mouth, hacked into it. The coughing spell went on for a long time, his face turning as purple as the hand that clutched the fabric. When he finally lowered his arm, the shirt was speckled with fresh blood.

"That's what your son said, that letting them go was the only way I was going to survive this. And you know"—he grinned, looking at Sean—"maybe he's right. Or maybe he's wrong. We'll just have to see." He sighed. "Sundown's coming. Things will be clearer in the morning."

30

SURE WISH PIERCE OR DELUCA WAS HERE, JIM THOUGHT, PUSH-ing through the undergrowth. He estimated he was about two miles in. The ground sloped upward now, and the earth was slippery and unpredictable beneath his feet. Plumbing was a physical job, but it didn't compare with the strenuousness of this. He was breathing hard, and sweating through his shirt. "Don't have a heart attack, old man," he told himself, unconvinced his heart was listening. He could feel it hammering away on the inside of his rib cage, an angry prisoner clamoring to be set free.

He held the Ithaca in a two-handed carry across his body, his right hand on the grip and the other on the fore end. But now, with the changing terrain, he switched the shotgun to a shoulder-carry position so his left hand was free to grab on to tree trunks as he climbed, to reach out and steady himself if he fell forward. There were shoe prints in the mud—relatively fresh and easy to follow—and he guessed they belonged to Michael. It was hard to know for sure how long ago the boys' father had passed this way, but he figured it was within the last few hours. This made him want to hurry.

It was impossible to shake the feeling that he was already too late. In his mind, he pictured it: a man lying on his back in an open field, legs splayed, blood pumping from a ragged wound in the center of his chest, his breathing shallow and labored. But the face—the face was harder to identify. Depending on how things played out, it could belong to Michael or the kidnapper, or even to himself. He could feel it pull at his chest, the pending heart attack or the bullet, he wasn't sure. So he focused on the climb, pushing the muscles of his thighs until they burned, and the stitch in his side dug its sharp fingers into his ribs.

It seemed the only sound for miles was the brisk tread of his forward progress—the soles of his shoes scraping and slapping against the muddied earth. It was hard not to think of the lives that hung in the balance. "You be careful now," his wife had warned as he prepared to leave, but she didn't protest. Instead she trusted that he would know better than to serve as anything more than a consultant, that he wouldn't place himself in any real danger. It was what he had intended all along. He hadn't lived to the age of sixty-five by being reckless. What plagued him now, though, was what she'd said next, the last conversation they had before he left.

"I just hope that family is worth it," Margery said, and Jim had paused, his right hand on the doorknob.

"What?" he asked, before turning to face her.

She said nothing else, and when Jim *did* turn around, her expression was guarded, difficult to read.

"You don't think they're worth it?" he asked, and then immediately wanted to retract the question. He did not want to hear her response. It had not been easy to defend the McCrays against the town's mounting hostility these last few years. Through it all, Margery had been quietly supportive. Or so he'd thought.

"They've put this town through a lot," she said. "And now you're going after them."

"That's right."

"For what?" she asked. "To bring them back?"

"Yes," he said. "To find those boys and their father. To bring them back safely." He swallowed, and felt a catch in his throat. "That's what I'm trying to do here."

"But why, Jim? Why bring them back if they don't want to stay?"

Jim shook his head, and tried to wrap his mind around what she was asking him. There was no logic to it, only a foul and horrible current that ran like sewage beneath the homes and streets of Cottonwood. All this time, he'd imagined that it didn't touch them. And now, here she was asking him this inexplicable question: *Why bring them back if they don't want to stay?*

"Those boys were kidnapped," he said. "They didn't leave of their own free will. It's the town that wants them gone. The McCrays want to stay."

"I know that," she replied. But for a moment, he had a vision of her dropping to her knees and pulling up the floorboards one after the other. *It's down here too*, she said, revealing the same river of sludge had lain beneath them all this time. Jim took a step backward, and blinked it away. Only his kind and gentle wife stood before him now, an inquisitive half smile on her lips. But the realization remained: they were no different from the others.

"Margery, they were taken," he heard himself repeat, but his words sounded distant and unimportant.

"Of course they were," she said, and her smile broadened, as if she had explained something very basic and was simply waiting for him to understand.

You don't know anything about this, do you? he wanted to ask, but he couldn't bring himself to level suspicion at his own wife. "I have to help find them," he told her instead, and she nodded, agreed that it was his duty to do so.

"You believe that this is the right thing to do," he said. He didn't phrase it as a question.

She took a moment to think it over. "It doesn't matter what I believe."

"It matters to me."

"Well then, I believe that you'll do what you think is right," she said, and it wasn't lost on him that she still hadn't answered his question.

"If I can find them and bring them home, then that's what I should do," he said. "It's not for us to decide whether they're worth it or not." He paused, looked at her. "You understand that, don't you?"

She nodded, still smiling. "But how long will you look?" she asked. "If they haven't been found yet, then—"

"I have to go," Jim interrupted, then turned and left the house, closing the front door behind him. The engine cranked once and then came to life. He let it drown out the sound of his wife's voice in his head.

The path opened before him and Jim emerged into a clearing. He stood in the circle of trees, and surveyed his surroundings. The field was quiet, tranquil. There was no sign of an encounter here, no slain body lying in the grass as he had feared.

It took him a while to notice the swaths of grass that had been pushed aside, their bases crimped beneath the soles of Michael's boots. Jim squatted—knees creaking as he did so—for a closer look at the ground. The imprints he'd seen along the muddier portions of the path were here as well, although they were more subtle, a mere trace of the ones he'd been following. The footprints were too vague to point him in any particular direction, yet he studied them anyway, in several locations across the clearing. It seemed Michael had continued into the woods. By now, he was either hopelessly lost or had discovered their location. If he had found the kidnapper, there was a good chance that Jim was close as well. If, on the other hand, he'd become lost in the woods, then following his footprints could place Jim in the same predicament.

"I can follow them back out again," he told himself. But the light was already slipping from the sky. Tracking anything—even an obvious trail—would become increasingly difficult over the next hour. Within two hours, he would be walking around in the dark. He'd had sense enough to bring a flashlight, but the chance of losing his bearings would be much greater. He wondered briefly whether he should go back to the house and wait for Pierce and DeLuca. But that wasn't really an option anymore. He had to make good use of whatever light was left in the day.

Jim returned to the trail and started from there. Most likely, that's what Michael had done. After walking a short section, he found the spot where Michael had pushed into the woods on either side. *He started out here, moved around the exterior of the clearing in a circle*, Jim reasoned. If he kept the field in view, there was less risk of getting lost. When he met up with the trail again, he would know that he'd completed a full circle. And with the completion of each full circle, he would have widened the next one, ventured farther from the clearing.

By that reasoning, it seemed logical to backtrack along the trail to the last point where it appeared Michael had entered the woods. *I need to find his widest circle*, Jim thought. The problem was, it wasn't obvious where Michael had entered the woods. *Look for the footprints*, but the earth was drier here and deciphering the prints was not as easy as he'd hoped.

In the end, it came down to a best guess. He entered the woods and circled the clearing, stepping over tree limbs and catching his clothing on brambles that seemed hell-bent on blocking his path. Occasionally, he spotted footprints, but there were long stretches when he did not. Eventually, one of those stretches went on so long that he realized he'd wandered off course. *Get back to the clearing*, he told himself. *You've got to start over again.* He made a right turn and headed directly for it, but the clearing was no longer in view and he was now relying entirely on his sense of direction. A hundred yards later, he still didn't find it. *Adjust your trajectory and head right again*, he thought, but after another hundred yards he had to admit that nothing looked familiar.

"Lost," Jim said. His voice crackled around the edges. "Well"—he scanned the trees, hoping to recognize something— "goddamn it."

He stood, thinking, considering his options. The worst thing he could do now, he realized, was to continue wandering. He was no more than a quarter mile from the clearing, but he had no idea in which direction it lay. If he pushed on from here, there was a good chance he would end up several miles from his intended destination, and finding his way out at that point was an entirely different matter. "You could die out here," he warned himself. "Don't be a fool."

Jim straddled the trunk of a fallen tree and sat down. He laid his shotgun across his thighs, and tried to think his way out of this. But nothing came to him, only the knowledge that he had been close to finding them, and had screwed it up. "There is a way," he told himself. But, for the life of him, he didn't know what it was. And so he sat there, counting his mistakes, and waited.

31

ALMOST GOT IT THAT TIME," DELUCA TOLD HIS PARTNER through the open driver's-side window. "We need a little more traction is all."

"Are you pushing?"

"*Hell yeah*, I'm pushing. Look at me, I'm covered in mud."

"That doesn't mean you're pushing," Pierce replied. "You've gotta time it for when I step down on the accelerator."

"You think I don't know that? Why are you telling me—"

"Okay, fine. You're pushing," Pierce told him, climbing out of the car. He walked to the rear, and studied the wheels sunk in the mud.

"Why don't we let some air out of those back tires," DeLuca suggested. "It'll give us more traction."

"That's a good idea," Pierce said. He knelt next to the left-rear wheel, removed the pen from his front shirt pocket, and used the tip to depress the valve stem. There was a soft hiss as air bled from the tire. "Do the same on the other side," he said. "But only release it halfway, or we won't be able to drive."

"Right," DeLuca said. He walked around the car and worked on the other tire. When they were both sufficiently deflated, Pierce climbed back into the driver's seat.

"Are you ready?"

"Ready," DeLuca said. He'd switched his position so that he was beside the vehicle with his hands on the B-post. The ground was drier here, less soupy.

"Okay, giving it some gas on three," Pierce said. "One . . . two . . . *three*."

Pierce pressed lightly on the accelerator as DeLuca leaned forward, shoes digging into the dirt roadway. Since he'd grown up with four brothers, it wasn't the first time he'd been called on to get something unstuck, to fix a problem that required cooperation and a little ingenuity. His older brother Carl ran a small construction company north of Redding, and had called on the four of them on more than one occasion when he was understaffed or up against a deadline. It was sporadic and unpredictable—and always inconvenient—but DeLuca liked the way they came together without a fuss. They could count on each other to get things done. He couldn't imagine what his life would be like without them, and found it hard to think about one of his siblings without considering the rest.

"You watch out for each other out there," his wife had said before he left, but DeLuca had been doing that his whole life. Working with a partner came naturally to him. If his brothers were here, the car would be clear by now.

He shoved, using the strength of his legs to drive his body forward. The car shifted slightly, and when it started to rock backward they let it. Pierce eased up on the gas and DeLuca readied himself for another push.

"*Again*," Pierce said, and as the car rocked forward DeLuca put everything he had into it. The wheels turned—slowly and then more steadily—as the vehicle moved into the center of the roadway. Pierce didn't touch the brakes until he'd reached the top of the hill, and then stopped only long enough for DeLuca to retrieve the gun bag, toss it into the trunk, and plop down beside him in the passenger seat.

"Try to raise him on the radio," Pierce said, and gunned the engine. He would have to be careful about his speed. He didn't want either of the back tires to blow.

"This is Shasta County detective Tony DeLuca calling Sheriff Kent," he said into the mic. "Jim, do you read us?"

With the weather clearing, there was less static on the radio, but still no response from their colleague.

"Jim, this is DeLuca. Are you reading us?"

Still nothing from the dash-mounted CB.

"Might as well holler out the window for all the good that thing's doing us," Pierce muttered. He swerved to avoid a pothole, but hit it anyway.

"Careful," DeLuca reminded him. "The tires."

"I know about the tires. You don't need to tell me how to drive."

They rode in silence, listening to the soft rumble of the tires on the roadway. When they hit Route 199, Pierce turned right and headed north. He felt his stomach churning, anxious about the slick and treacherous way their search was unraveling. *The tires want to blow*, he thought, and although it was an irrational notion he also suspected it was true. "Anything left to chance will go against us," he said. DeLuca turned his head, looked at him, and said nothing.

Pierce noticed there were no other cars on the road, and this too seemed a bad omen. The southeast section of Oregon was not a highly traveled part of the state, but still, there should've been someone out here besides the two of them. For no particular reason, he found himself recalling something their only eyewitness had said as she walked them to the door.

"The Lord stands in judgment of each of us. But sometimes

judgment comes sooner. People have a way of taking matters into their own hands."

"Is Cottonwood that kind of town?" Pierce had asked. "Where people take matters into their own hands?"

"If pushed hard enough, every place is that kind of a town," she'd said. And now, looking around at the few scattered houses that speckled the countryside, Pierce wondered if there was a limit to what a community of people were capable of. *We give each other courage*, he thought. *And permission. We are much deadlier together than we are apart.*

"There," DeLuca said, pointing through the windshield.

Pierce slowed, turned left onto the side road, and came to a stop beside Jim's cruiser. He studied it from where he sat, exchanged a brief look with his partner, then switched off the engine, opened the door, and climbed out.

The Ford Mainline was parked on the north side of the street, which made it easier for them to spot, as they'd approached from the south. Pierce placed a hand on the hood. It was cool, devoid of any ticking from the engine underneath. He walked once around the car, saw nothing out of the ordinary.

DeLuca opened the driver's-side door, leaned in, and inspected the interior. "Broken rearview mirror on the passenger seat," he announced. "Along with a map and an empty pack of cigarettes." He reached in, and pulled an envelope off the dash. "And this," he said, straightening.

"What is it?" Pierce asked.

"A note," DeLuca told him. "From Jim." He paused, scanned the writing. "It says, 'Found Buick and stolen Mercury at house at the end of this street. Couldn't reach you on radio. Began search myself.'" He looked up. "That's it."

"He found them," Pierce said, heading back to their car and starting the engine. "Get in."

DeLuca hopped in and his partner floored it, unconcerned with the rear wheels now. Less than a minute later, they pulled up beside the Buick, climbed out, and went around to the trunk. There were two shotguns inside, and a flashlight for each of them.

"Try calling it in," Pierce told his partner.

DeLuca returned to the cab, and keyed the mic. "Officers in need of immediate assistance. End of Butcherknife Road off Route 199. Tracking suspect considered armed and dangerous." He released the thumb switch, and heard only static in response.

"Any luck?" Pierce asked from outside the car.

"Nothing," DeLuca said. "It's like there's nobody out there."

Pierce shifted to his left foot, and heard the grind of loose dirt. The situation continued to slide away from them. It seemed that what he'd said earlier was true: anything left to chance would go against them.

"Forget it," he said. "That thing's not going to work until this is over." He stepped back to allow his partner to exit the vehicle, handed him a shotgun. "Not much light left in the day. We've got to go now."

"Go where?" DeLuca asked. "I don't see any—"

"If Jim found them, so can we."

32

THE HANDCUFF WAS TIGHTLY CLAMPED AROUND MICHAEL'S right wrist. He made his hand as narrow as possible and worked the metal bracelet back and forth with his free hand, the steel ridges biting into his skin. Banes was asleep on the mattress—or delirious with fever, it was hard to tell. His body tossed from one side to the other as he groaned and muttered to himself. Every once in a while, he sat bolt upright, looked around the room as if he had no idea where he was, then lay back on the mattress and resumed his previous restlessness. Michael thought of his missing fingers, the left hand and severed stumps purple and swollen with infection. *How did it get so bad so quickly?* he wondered. But then he thought of Danny—silent and watchful—sitting here in the cabin as the hours passed.

Banes shifted on the mattress, mumbled something indecipherable. He was ill, his life likely in jeopardy, a different man from the one Michael had met the month before at a bar on the outskirts of Sacramento. Michael and Kate had been down that way to see another specialist, a man Dr. Greenwald had recommended at UC Davis. For two hours, they'd sat in the waiting room, wondering if this visit would be different, if there was something the specialist might offer that their own neurologist had overlooked. During Kate's evaluation, the physician—Dr. Eichner—posed the usual questions, and quickly reviewed the thick file Dr. Greenwald had sent over. Then he performed a thorough physical examination. Michael was hopeful, watching him go about his routine, nodding to himself at certain findings, frowning and scratching down notes at others. Greenwald had said he was an authority on degenerative neurologic diseases, and lectured widely across the country. *Surely, something will come from this*, Michael thought afterward, as he sat on the plush leather chair in the doctor's office, scanning the array of certificates and diplomas on the wall, waiting for the doctor to look up from his notes.

"I wonder, Mrs. McCray," Eichner said at last, "if you would give me a few minutes to confer with your husband. There are some things I'd like to discuss with him."

Kate looked from the doctor to Michael, then back to the doctor.

"Just a few minutes," Eichner reiterated. "My secretary Candice will escort you to the waiting room." He pushed a button on his desk. A moment later the secretary rapped lightly on the partially opened door.

"Mrs. McCray has been kind enough to give us a moment to speak in private," Dr. Eichner said. "Would you mind seeing her to the waiting room?"

"Certainly, Doctor," the secretary answered.

Michael stood, and helped Kate up from her chair. Candice took her by the elbow, wrapped an arm around her shoulder. "That's a lovely dress you're wearing," she said, admiring the pattern. "Did you make it yourself?"

"No, I got it . . ." Kate glanced back at Michael, uncertain.

"It's okay," he said. "It will only be a few minutes. I'll come out and get you when we're done."

"Okay," Kate said. As they walked to the door, she turned her head, attempting to look back at her husband once more, but the secretary's arm blocked her view.

"Would you like some tea or coffee?" Candice asked, and then they were gone, the sound of their voices trailing behind them like a tattered banner in the hallway.

Dr. Eichner went to close the door. He circled around to his desk, his shoes silent on the thick orange carpet. Instead of sitting, he turned to a cabinet, opened it, and retrieved a tumbler.

"Care for a drink, Mr. McCray?"

Michael looked at the glass, at the bottle of Dewar's White Label in the man's hand. "No. Thank you."

Eichner poured himself a small amount, screwed the cap back onto the bottle, and returned it to the cabinet. He took a seat behind his desk, his hand still on the tumbler. Michael watched as he took a sip, swallowed. The neurologist slid open his desk drawer, found a pack of cigarettes, tapped one out, and extended it across the desk. Michael shook his head. His mouth was dry enough.

"This is"—Eichner struck a match, held it to the end of the fag until it caught—"always difficult."

"It's bad?" Michael asked. "Over these past few months she's been getting—"

"Amyotrophic lateral sclerosis. Lou Gehrig's disease. It's in the advanced stage of progression."

Michael's eyes were back on the tumbler. Color was reflected in the glass, the room or maybe a small and twisted version of Michael himself. *It's in the advanced stage of progression.* Michael knew Kate was sick, spiraling downward. Was this man offering him anything he didn't already know?

"She uses a walker sometimes," he offered, "when her legs are weak. I've moved our bed into the—"

"She will suffocate," Eichner pronounced. "Sooner rather than later."

"What?"

"The muscles that control her breathing, they will fail her like everything else. Most of the patients I've seen with this condition die of respiratory failure or pneumonia."

"Pneumonia," Michael said, repeating the word.

"The breathing gets shallow and irregular," Eichner explained. "The lungs don't inflate properly. People develop infections."

"But the breathing problem—can't that be fixed? There must be some medication that can—"

"No," Eichner said. "Nothing she isn't already taking. Dr. Greenwald was thorough and prescribed all the appropriate medications."

Michael shook his head slowly. "Some other form of treatment then?"

"I'm sorry, Mr. McCray. I have nothing left to offer you."

Eichner watched him from across the desk. He took a drag from his cigarette, leaned forward, and stubbed it out in the ashtray.

"Dr. Greenwald never said anything about suffocation," Michael told him. He could feel himself growing angry. "That was *never* on the table."

"To be honest, sir," Eichner said, "suffocation was always on the table. Dr. Greenwald knows that as well as I do. But in the early stages of the disease, patients don't need to hear it. As things progress, however," he said, and took another sip of the drink in front of him, "well . . . eventually they do."

Michael closed his eyes, struggled with the reality of the doctor's words. The phone was ringing in the other room. He could hear the secretary—*Candice*, he reminded himself—clacking away at the typewriter.

"I'm sorry," Eichner said. "This is a fatal disease. I just thought you should know."

"How much time does she have left?" Michael heard himself ask. "A year, maybe two?"

The neurologist closed the manila folder that Dr. Greenwald had sent him. "Four to six months, maybe. She won't make it past a year."

Four to six months, Michael thought. *Was it possible? Was it possible that Kate would be gone by then?* He sat in silence, listening to the flow of ordinary life as it moved around him, the hum of traffic from the street below, Candice's voice answering the phone.

("Dr. Eichner's office, may I help you?")

Michael looked up and met the man's eyes. "Can you tell what's causing it?"

Eichner laced his fingers together, placed his hands on the desk. "There are different theories," he said. "Some researchers think the problem rests in a defect in the DNA—the genetic blueprint. Other people think it starts as an infection that invades the nervous system. This is all conjecture, you understand. We don't know enough about it."

"What kind of infection?"

Eichner frowned. "A virus, or some type of bacteria, I'd imagine. Nothing specific has been identified."

"Could it be a person? One person infecting another?"

The neurologist shook his head. "We don't think it's communicable. It doesn't pass from person to person like the common cold."

"But if a person has a tendency to make other people sick . . ."

"How do you mean?"

Michael sat back in his chair. He brought a hand across his face, stared down at his lap. "If you removed the infection," he said, "could the person get better?"

Eichner sighed, glanced at his watch. "I don't know," he said. "We don't know much about the infection—if it even *is* an infection—for one thing."

"And the other?"

"It's probably too late. The nervous system would have a hard time recovering. In theory, removing the infection might stop the *progression* of the disease. But as far as returning the patient to normal, I . . . I don't think that's possible."

"But they could live. They wouldn't die. It might halt the progression of the disease."

"I don't know what would happen. This is all very hypothetical." He removed a pen from his front shirt pocket, and scribbled on his notepad. "I'm going to prescribe her a medication. I don't think it will change the course of her disease. In my opinion, it's not much better than a placebo," he said. "But it will give her hope, something new to try."

Michael stared at the rectangular slip of paper. "That's it? That's all you've got to offer us?"

"I'm afraid so," the man said. "We should bring your wife back in now. I'm going to present her with a more optimistic picture. The things we've just talked about, I'll let you decide how much you want to share with her. If I were in your shoes, I'd share very little. It's important for the patient to not lose hope."

Michael refocused his thoughts on the interior of the cabin. Sean was beside him, his left wrist enclosed in the other metal cuff and connected to Michael's own by a short chain. His breathing had worsened over the last few hours, the exhalations thin and reedy, each one dragging out over the course of eight to ten seconds. They weren't screams, but something softer, more menacing.

Heeeeeeeeeeeeeeeeee. Heeeeeeeeeeeeeeeeeeee.

"When it happens," Sean had once told him, "it's like the air is in another room and I can't get to it. It only comes to me through the small space between the floor and the bottom of the door."

Michael thought of this as he listened to the sound of his son's breathing and recalled the doctor's words.

"She will suffocate. Sooner rather than later."

Of everything they spoke about that day, this stuck in his mind most of all. His wife of twelve years—the mother of his children—would suffocate. The time was coming.

I can't let this happen, he had told himself. *I won't let it happen.*

After the doctor visit, he and Kate had decided to stay overnight in a motel, and drive home in the morning. Kate had climbed into bed, and immediately fell asleep. He was reminded of the physical toll such visits took on her. "*It's probably too late*," Eichner had said. "*The nervous system would have a hard time recovering.*"

Was it too late? Michael had asked himself. *Was it only a matter of time until the muscles that controlled her breathing failed her like everything else?*

He hadn't been able to sleep, and sat on the edge of the bed thinking, searching for a way around this. Eventually, he went for a drive to clear his head. He didn't remember the name of the bar where he'd stopped, couldn't picture the face of the bartender. All he remembered was Banes, and how he'd seemed like a reasonable enough man that night.

There was something liberating about talking to a stranger

in a place to which you would never return. You can say anything—even become someone else for a while. By the end of his first drink, Michael had told Banes about his wife's illness, and that she might not have much longer to live. By the end of his third drink, he had told him everything.

"Sometimes I wish that I could send him away," he'd said, staring at his reflection in the mirror behind the bar, in between the rows of bottles that stood shoulder to shoulder like a line of soldiers awaiting orders.

Banes had gone quiet, considering. "Maybe you can," he'd said after a while. "I know a couple who would take him, no questions asked. They're good people, just never had children of their own."

Michael looked at him. "Send my boy to live with someone else?" He shook his head, pushed away his empty glass, and waved off the bartender when he came to refill it. "I couldn't do that. No matter what happens, it's . . . it's not something I'm capable of."

"No," Banes agreed, "of course not." He jotted a phone number on the back of his napkin. "I'm just saying I could make it happen. If you decided it might be best for everyone, that is."

Michael looked down at the napkin, but left it where it lay.

"No," he said. "I think I've given you the wrong idea. Danny stays with us."

"Sure," Banes replied. "Your wife would want to spend as much time as possible with him. In the limited time she has left."

Michael had gotten up and walked away then, and drove back to the motel in the center of town. He should not have gone out. He should have remained with his wife. As he turned the key in the lock and entered their room, that much became

clear to him. Kate had vomited in her sleep. He smelled it
as he was feeling for the switch on the wall, before he turned
on the light. The puke was drying on her pillowcase. It was
orange, almost the exact color of the carpet in Dr. Eichner's
office. She didn't even wake up, just went right on sleeping, her
breathing raspy and ragged.

"*She will suffocate. Sooner rather than later.*"

He helped her up, and took her to the bathroom. She sat on
the lid of the toilet as he ran hot water in the tub.

"I can wash up tomorrow," she said.

"No," he said. "We should wash your hair now. Tonight."

A week later, Michael called him. *It'll be better for Danny,*
he reasoned. *Better for all of us.* But he was a long way from
believing it, even then. *What if I'm wrong?* he asked himself.
*What if I send him away and it doesn't make a difference? What
if she dies anyway?* He did not think he would be able to live
with it, to bear the grief and loss of them both. But here
was the thing: *What if Kate recovered? What if this was the only
way—the only chance for her—and he didn't take it? Could he live
with himself then?*

Michael hadn't taken the napkin when he left, yet he still remembered the number. He had somehow fixed it in his mind,
even as he rose from the barstool and walked away, which perhaps meant that he had decided in that moment—and he had
thought about little else in the time since. *Did Banes know he
would call?* he wondered. *Had he recognized his desperation?*

The man lying on the mattress before him no longer seemed
like the reasonable, intensely thoughtful man he had met at the
bar in Sacramento. He seemed like a psychopath. But maybe it
was the situation and not the man. Banes was in the midst of
it now—and in over his head—a trapped and desperate man.

"What was that?!" Banes blurted out. He sat up and looked

around, the silhouette of his body nothing more than a shadow in the darkening room.

Michael said nothing, only watched, his back pressed against the bulk of the wood-burning stove.

"Where you at? How come I can't see you?" Banes rose from the mattress, and made his way across the room to the cupboard below the sink. Halfway there the side of his leg struck the chair and nearly toppled it. He cursed and finished the job by planting his foot on the seat and shoving. The chair clattered to the floor. It was not entirely unlike the sound of an office typewriter.

Sean stirred, mumbled in his sleep. To settle him, Michael reached over with his free hand, placing it on his son's shoulder.

"Keep that boy quiet," Banes said. "If you ask me, he's worse than the one I already put in the ground."

Danny is alive. There's still time to save him. Michael closed his eyes, and refused to believe the man's threats.

Banes opened the cupboard below the sink, and fiddled with something, whispering to the thing as if it were an animal that would do his bidding.

Danny is ali—

"What are you *doing* down there?" Banes asked. He struck a match, let the flame build, and then held it as steady as he could. It faltered and sputtered. Banes cursed and repeated the process twice before achieving the desired result: a blue flame flickered in the small glass contraption. For several moments, he didn't speak—only watched it, the small nidus of light that did nothing to brighten the room. It simply hovered near the floor along the base of shadows. Then Banes reached out, turned the knob, and the kerosene lantern filled the room with an eerie glow. He stood, holding it by the handle in front of him, and took a few steps in Michael's direction.

"What are you doing?" he again asked. "Trying to get free?"

"What good would that do me?" Michael said. "I've got nowhere to go."

Banes placed the lantern on the floor between them, then righted the chair and took a seat. The stubble on his face had blossomed into something resembling a beard, full and thick along his neck and the corners of his jawline, but patchy and almost nonexistent where his cheeks caved inward. It made him look thinner than he was already, and the large gash along his forehead seemed to pulse and glisten in the light. He sat there silent for a long space of time, arms slack, chin resting on his chest, like a wooden marionette forgotten on a shelf. Michael watched him and felt something between disgust and pity. Banes had proved incompetent in the one task Michael had asked him to perform, but the man's rapid physical decline was difficult to witness. It reminded him of Kate, and made him feel sick with worry and longing. He wondered how she was doing, and if Lauren was still watching over her. He wondered if she was already dead.

"Why'd you come all the way out here to get him?" the wasted figure asked, and for a moment it was Kate in the chair and not Banes. Michael tried to make out the expression on her face—anger or disappointment, relief or suffering—but then the head lifted and was Banes once again.

Michael looked down at his sleeping son. "Taking Sean was not part of the deal," he said. "He belongs with us."

"So you'll let one son go, but not the other."

"That's right. That was what we discussed."

"You wanted me to give him to another family, and let him do the things he's doing to you and your wife to someone else for a while."

Michael sat, silent, listening to the wind outside the cabin, the sound of Sean's breathing, the whistle of air as it slipped in and out of his small chest.

"That makes you a murderer, and a coward," Banes said. "You want to save your wife? What about the people who get him next?"

The lantern glowed on the floor between them. Banes rose from his chair, and fished in his pocket with his uninjured hand, removing a small slip of paper.

"This is where I was going to take him," he said. "I can't do it." He tore the paper in half, then brought the pieces together and tore them again, repeating the motion until they were useless bits of confetti in his hands, and let them fall to the floor. "Better to leave him in the ground where he belongs," he said. "That's your solution. It's what you should've done in the first place."

Banes bent at the waist and lifted the lantern. "Keep working at those handcuffs," he said. "Got to save yourself if you can." He went to the door, opened it, then paused at the threshold as if he were about to say something further. Then he stepped onto the porch, swung the door closed, and left them alone in the darkness.

33

A CERTAIN TYPE OF FEAR—SLICK AND NASTY—TAKES HOLD when you're lost in the woods, and it is far more frantic at night.

Jim reminded himself that there was a good chance Pierce and DeLuca were on their way. There was also a chance—and he did not like to acknowledge this—that he had wandered too far off course for them to find him. And since he was calculating the odds of things, it was also possible—maybe even likely—that they would all be too late to rescue Michael and the boys.

I should've waited in the clearing, Jim told himself. It hadn't seemed like the best option at the time, and it didn't seem like one now. He knew he would make the same decision again, if given the same choices. So instead of kicking himself, he should focus on solving the problem at hand.

"You're closer to the clearing than you think," he said. "You've just got to look for it."

Jim scanned the forest with his flashlight. He'd already established that nothing looked familiar. Now he was looking for something more nebulous. "You will know it when you see it," he said to himself. "Look at everything—up, down, and in between."

Moss grew on many of the trees. Didn't he learn as a kid that moss tends to grow on the northern side? If he could figure out which way was north, then . . . what? He'd approached from the south, but the trail twisted and turned its way through the forest. He'd circled the clearing, but didn't know exactly where he had gone off course. His intended destination could lie in any direction.

Jim turned off his flashlight to conserve the battery. Through the canopy of foliage, he saw the half-moon was high enough to shed some meager light on the forest floor. The clearing, he reasoned, should be a slightly brighter patch in the woods. He swiveled around slowly, and strained his eyes, searching for a lighter shade of black.

And there it was: an area of charcoal gray to his left. *Am I imagining it?* Most likely, yes. But it wasn't too far, and if it turned out to be nothing, he would turn around and come back.

He walked, holding one arm in front to fend off the branches, while the other carried his shotgun. It was hard to estimate the distance, but he was descending a gradual hill. He walked for another three minutes—timing it on his watch—before stopping to scan the tree line again. Were things lighter here? He couldn't tell. He looked back in the direction from which he had come. That section of forest looked lighter now. He thought of the way a mirage of water might appear on a desert highway, how it always seemed to lie slightly farther down the road—and how the things we seek are always in retreat, close enough to solicit us, yet seldom within our reach.

Like everything else I have tried today, this is not working. He sighed, started to turn back, and then stopped midstride. In his peripheral vision, he had caught a glimpse of light: not a vaguely brighter shade of darkness like before, this was focused and definitive. *How far off?* Again, it was hard to judge. *What does it mean?* He didn't know for sure. But it was something man-made—a porch light, perhaps—and that meant people, maybe even the ones he was searching for.

"Go careful, now," Jim told himself, and was reminded of his wife's words, how she—and many others—thought it might be better if the McCrays never returned at all.

"Margery, they were taken . . . If I can find them and bring them home, then that's what I should do."

She'd nodded, and Jim tried not to think of that patient, broadening smile. *"But how long will you look?"*

"As long as it takes," Jim whispered as he descended the hill. Then he cleared his mind and tried to focus on what lay ahead.

34

T WAS ONLY EIGHT THIRTY—TOO EARLY FOR BED—BUT KATE LAY on the double mattress anyway, with her eyes closed, and focused on falling asleep. She did her best not to listen to the silence.

Eight thirty was the most difficult time.

Right now, the boys would be brushing their teeth, changing into their pajamas, selecting a book to read before bed. Michael, sitting beside her in the living room, would yell for them to stop horsing around. A glass of milk for her—scotch on the rocks for him—would sit on the table within reach. The newspaper would be open, rustling, its pages like a curtain separating Kate from her husband. "Did you hear about Betty Savage?" she would ask. "Broke her ankle while gardening the other day. Took a step backward on uneven ground and down she went. Ellen Cassidy is helping her out for a while with groceries and the housecleaning."

"Maybe she'll learn some humility. The woman has something unkind to say about everyone."

No, Kate corrected him in her mind. *Only about us.*

"How would you feel about a trip to the ocean in mid-

September?" he'd say from behind the paper. "Once the weather cools a bit."

"You'd have to take time off work," she would point out. "And the boys would miss class. Is that a good idea so early in the school year?"

"Maybe not," Michael would say, turning the page. He would not mention it again.

"We should've gone over the summer," she'd say, and from behind the paper he would make a small noise and continue reading. She knew he didn't like the crowds, and preferred to go when the season had ended. "September would be nice, though," she'd say. "I'll bet the kids would jump at a chance to swim in the ocean."

"This is the one we want, Daddy," Sean would say, entering the room with his brother in tow.

Michael would lower the paper, fold it in his lap. With his left hand, he'd reach out and take the book from his son.

"*The Secret Garden* by Frances Hodgson Burnett. We finished reading this last night."

"We want it again."

Her husband would study the boys. "You don't want something new?"

"No, this one," Sean would say, and Danny would look at his brother and nod.

"The same story from the beginning," Michael would say, opening the book. "'Chapter One—There Is No One Left.'" After a short pause, he'd look over at her, his right eyebrow slightly raised. "They want the same one. What can I do?"

Kate would play along, trying not to smile. "I'm sure they don't mean the *exact* same story. Perhaps a similar one?"

Michael would turn to the boys. "You want a *similar* story, is that it? One with a beginning, middle, and end?"

"No, the *same* one. *This* story."

"Maybe they forgot what happened," Kate would say.

"Did you both forget?" he would ask. "You both have amnesia. Is that right?"

They would shake their heads.

"Oh," she'd respond. "Well, I guess you'd better read it to them."

"Give your mother a hug and a kiss good night," he would say. "And, if you can remember how to find your bedroom, meet me there when you're done."

They'd come to her then, climb onto her lap, and wrap their arms around her.

"Good night, Mommy," Sean would say, and Danny would squeeze her, planting a warm kiss on her cheek.

"Good night. I love you," she'd say as they scampered down the hall to join their father.

As she waited, she would sit, sipping her milk, and think of the ocean in September, the way the waves lifted her feet from the bottom, and settled her down again with each pass.

"How was the story?" she'd ask when Michael returned.

"Same as before," he'd say, reaching for his scotch and lifting the glass to his lips.

They would sit in silence for a while, comfortable in each other's presence. Eventually, she would rise, collect their glasses, and carry them to the sink. In this version of the memory, she is healthy, vibrant and full of energy, the idea of using a walker still a few years off.

She would return and stand behind him, trace her index finger along the back of his neck.

"If you can remember where it is," she would say, "meet me in the bedroom when you're done."

Then she would walk to their room, sit on the edge of their bed, and wait for him in the dark.

35

RICHARD BANES SAT ON THE PORCH STEP AND STARED OUT at the night. The field in front of him was cloaked in shadow. The half-moon above provided only enough light to spark the imagination, making the trees look like ghastly creatures observing him from the woods. Twice he saw something scamper across the open field, or at least thought he did—a quick blur of paws, an arched and bristled back. Raccoons were common in this region, and spent their nights scavenging for food. The light from the lantern might attract them, though there was nothing for them to eat. Banes had anticipated a short stay here—a day or two, at most—and only two mouths to feed instead of three. But things had not gone according to plan. A bad situation had deteriorated into something far worse. He could feel the infection that coursed through him now, clouding his judgment. He was missing two fingers. Their food was gone. He had no plan. And if the older child was right, he'd be dead by morning.

"But if you hurt him—if you hurt either of us . . . ."

Banes caught a spot of movement in his peripheral vision—something low and quick, coming for him across the grass. His eyes scanned the field, the woods to either side.

"Don't get all paranoid," he told himself. "Things are bad enough."

But were they? Couldn't they get worse?

"I don't want to be dead by morning," he said, but there was no one there to listen, only a scared and lonely man, flinching at shadows.

"*Sooner or later, he's going to kill you. He doesn't want to do it, but he can't help it.*"

Banes sat listening to the incessant chirp of the crickets, the low hoot of an owl from the forest. He felt his chest loosen and coughed once, twice, into his clenched fist. If there was blood, he didn't notice it—as he didn't notice the advancing infection along his left hand and forearm. In the context of night, the images before him were differentiated only by subtle shades of gray: massive tree trunks merged together and then upward; blades of grass, bristling in the wind, became a wolfish pelt protruding from the earth.

The pressure was mounting in his lower abdomen. He tried to ignore it, but its urgency compelled him. He tried to recall the last time he'd urinated, and found he could not. Except for the faucet and small sink, there was no indoor plumbing in the cabin. A hundred yards to the left was an outhouse, but it seemed like an unnecessary journey. Instead, he rose and stepped off the porch into the grass, turned right, and moved along the cabin's exterior until he stood in the six-foot space between its rear and the rocky cliff behind it. There he un-zipped his fly and emptied his bladder.

The night sounds had stilled around him, and he did his best not to disturb the quiet, directing his stream into the dirt instead of the rock face in front of him. When he finished, he rezipped his fly, straightened his belt, and made his way back across the grass.

"*You should get your gun while you're out there,*" the boy had said. "*You forgot to bring it in after you shot yourself in the fingers.*"

Banes pictured the kid's face in his mind, the eyes that studied and mocked him.

"*I didn't forget, okay? I decided to leave it out there for a while, that's all.*"

"*Why?*"

"*Why do* you *care? Mind your own business.*"

He was glad he'd left it in the grass. When he saw Michael enter the cabin, he'd been able to retrieve it. He wrapped his fingers around the wooden grip, removed it from beneath his waistband.

"*Are you afraid you'll shoot yourself again? This time in the head?*"

"I'm not going to shoot myself in the head," he whispered, but his words were hesitant, as if he was making a promise he wasn't sure he could keep.

He had always liked the weight of the .38-caliber revolver, but it did little to comfort him now. He remembered how easily the gun had fired when he fell. The two missing fingers on his left hand throbbed as if they were still there, beckoning to him from where they must still be lying in the grass.

For the last few days, Banes had harbored the suspicion that he might be going insane. True, it was not a condition that had plagued him in the past. But the recent events had been wild and unpredictable—and beyond his ability to control. If he had heard the story from someone else and not experienced it for himself, he would have scoffed at it and questioned their mental stability. But here he was: incapacitated by a small child; picturing fearful things coming from the woods; afraid his own weapon might do him harm when his attention was elsewhere.

So when he rounded the corner and encountered a man approaching the cabin from the woods, Banes recognized it for what it was, a hallucination. Whether it was brought on by the infection, or his dwindling sanity, or his own frenzied imagination was of little importance. *Remember*, he told himself, *the man is not there. Go easy now*, and he took a step backward, fading deeper into the shadows.

The figure was tall and slightly pudgy. It appeared to be an older man, the movement of his body stiff and awkward, the feet hesitant on the uneven terrain. When he reached the front steps, he paused, swiveled his head around as he took in the small porch, the cabin's huddled exterior. Now that the man had stepped into the circle of light from the lantern, Banes could make out the dirt and grime that had worked its way into the folds of the man's face, deepening the lines around his mouth and forehead. His eyes were pinched and wary, his shoulders hunched over a shotgun held at the ready, a silent, lethal thing.

He's here to kill me, Banes thought, and felt no terror at the realization, only recognition that this was a situation— hallucination or not—that he knew how to control.

His hand tightened around the grip of his revolver. *Careful now*, he thought, *you don't even know if he's real*. Either way, Banes decided to take a shot at the thing. If the bullet passed through, if the image vanished as quickly as it had appeared, at least then he would know that his eyes—and his mind—could no longer be trusted. He would walk away, enter the woods, and never come back. He would be done with it, all of it. More than anything right now, that's what he wanted.

The revolver went off in his hand, the report deafening and unexpected. He felt a *whomp* beside his right foot as the slug buried itself in the ground. *Finger must've been on the trigger*, he thought, right before the man's shotgun roared and the corner of the cabin exploded less than a foot from his face. A cloud of pulverized wood hovered in the air, obscuring his view, and something wet ran down the side of his neck. Banes stumbled backward, tangling his feet underneath him, and went down hard in the grass.

For a frantic moment he crawled around searching for the gun before realizing that he still held it in his right hand.

The man was coming around the corner of the porch now, the shotgun ready, finger tight on the trigger. Banes rolled onto his back, brought his gun up, and fired. His shot was well placed but a moment too soon—and the bullet zipped past his attacker a half second before he stepped into its path. Then the muzzle of the shotgun thundered as the man fired again, an uncompromising flame of death and obliteration.

No way he misses, Banes thought in the moment before the blast, and he found there was some relief in this. If he had to die, he wanted it to be at the hands of something he understood. He took a half breath and braced for the impact.

It will hit me in the chest like the hand of God himself. I will be flung through the air—dead before I land. If I am lucky, my last breath is already behind me.

He felt nothing, and saw nothing but the vast emptiness of the sky above.

This is how it is then, he thought. But then he expelled the snatch of air inside him, and found that his lungs still worked, and his torso was more or less intact.

Later, when he had time to reflect on it, Banes would realize that the shot had passed over him. The man had fired blindly, expecting him to be standing instead of lying on the ground. Even now, the man did not see Banes waiting in the grass. He was looking over and past him into the shadows. None of this registered for Banes in the moment, though, only the fact that he was still alive. He raised the revolver and fired.

The man took the round in the chest, the impact spinning him in a half circle before he fell to his knees and crumpled to the ground.

Banes was on his feet then, walking forward, gun raised. The man lay on his stomach, the shotgun underneath him. He was badly wounded—maybe fatally so—but still moving, his feet scissoring in the grass.

"Don't move," Banes said, but the man rolled over onto his back and brought the muzzle up. Banes pulled the trigger again.

The man's head rocked backward—a vigorous half nod—before going completely still. In the glow of the lantern, there was no mistaking the rift in his scalp, the spray of blood on the grass around him.

"Aww, hell," Banes said. "Why'd you have to go and do that?"

He closed his eyes, and tried to shield himself from the replay in his mind: the quick nod; the flesh tearing; the final spatter of crimson.

He walked over to the body. The man's finger remained curled around the trigger. Banes kneeled and pulled the shotgun free, then stood and tossed the gun away from him.

"Whatcha *doin'* out here, old man?" he asked the motionless figure. "You come for me?"

The man didn't respond, the blood on his scalp already starting to congeal in the thin patch of hair along the top of his head. A five-pointed star was clipped to his belt. SHERIFF, the badge read, and below that COTTONWOOD, CALIFORNIA.

"You've come a long way to get shot," Banes said. "I wish to hell you hadn't. I didn't set out to shoot anyone. I'm no killer."

He turned and paced the yard.

"A man comes after me with a shotgun. I didn't know he was a sheriff. I've got a right to protect myself."

Back and forth he went in front of the cabin.

"It's not murder. It's self-defense."

The crickets were back at it again. He heard something screech in the distance, an animal standing its ground.

"*Sooner or later, he's going to kill you. He doesn't want to do it, but he can't help it.*"

"How'd I get mixed up in this?" he asked, not wanting to face the answer. A string of bad choices that started long ago had landed him here. He wanted to go back and do things differently from the beginning. It wouldn't be all that hard, opening one door instead of the other. He wasn't a bad guy, and didn't deserve to be standing over a corpse in the dead of night.

"I'm sorry," he said. "I'm sorry and I want to take it back."

"*. . . you'll be dead by morning.*"

He lifted the gun to his temple, and willed himself to pull the trigger. Twice now it had gone off of its own volition. Was it too much to ask for one more time?

"*Are you afraid you'll shoot yourself again? This time in the head?*"

Banes lowered the weapon. *What am I doing? This is not what I want. The kid is pushing me, even now from below the ground.* Was that possible? How much power could one child have?

He looked up at the moon, a revolving sphere of radiance and darkness.

"What's done is done," he said at last, and went to the lantern, lifted it by the handle. Chances were, more men were coming, if not tonight then tomorrow for sure. He couldn't wait around any longer. He had to get out of here. But first, he had to finish what he started. The world would be better for it.

36

NEITHER MAN SPOKE, ONLY HURTLED UP THE INCLINE, LEGS pumping, air slicing swift and sharp in the hollowed cavity of their chests. The soles of their shoes dug into the soft earth. Pebbles skittered down the hill behind them. They did their best to train their beams of light in front of them, but their flashlights dipped and weaved as they ran, rendering each forward stride a gamble. Several times they stumbled, went to one knee or put out a hand to break their fall. Then they were up and running once again, the sound of the gunshots spurring them on like reins cracking over the frantic drum of their hearts.

They arrived at the open field five minutes after the final report. It took them another thirty seconds to circle the clearing, to confirm the trail ended here and it did not pick up again on the other side.

"The shots came from that direction," Pierce said, his voice sounding more certain than he actually felt. He stepped into the woods, and began to push through the brush.

"Are you sure?" DeLuca asked. In his mind, he had placed the shots about thirty degrees to the right of where Pierce was heading.

"As sure as I *can* be," Pierce said. "It's a best guess. There's not much time to—"

"Go then," DeLuca said, urging his partner forward. He reached up and placed his flashlight in the crook of a tree, the beam shining in the direction they were heading. If Pierce was wrong, the light could act as a beacon and guide them back to the clearing.

They moved as fast as they could over fallen tree trunks and through large patches of bramble. DeLuca followed a short distance behind his partner, avoiding the small branches that were pushed aside and then whipped back in the wake of his passage. On several occasions, DeLuca stopped to search for the small circle of light from his flashlight. It was faint now, a weak and distant star in the vastness of space.

They descended a hill, the ground beneath them falling away. The next time DeLuca looked back he could no longer see the beacon meant to illuminate their return. From here on out, there was no safety line.

"There," Pierce finally said. He switched off his flashlight, lifted his hand, and pointed off into the distance on their left. The source of the light was hidden from view, but the area around it was clear. They walked toward it, mindful now of the noise they made as they pushed through the forest.

"It's a cabin," Pierce whispered as they drew near. "The light is coming from a window on the side of the structure."

"The gunshots," DeLuca whispered back. "So many for such a small place."

Pierce nodded in the darkness, focused on the cabin. De-Luca was right. A firefight in a place that small would be over with a few shots in a matter of seconds. The fight they heard had lasted longer, and the shots were spaced apart.

"It happened outside, then," Pierce whispered, and they

continued forward—quiet as they could—until they stood at the edge of the field, some two hundred yards away from the cabin.

"Look," DeLuca said, and pointed over Pierce's shoulder to a motionless shape in the grass.

"Shit, I hope that's not Jim," Pierce said, but DeLuca was already heading across the field in the man's direction. "Be careful," Pierce whispered, and stepped out onto the grass himself, moving toward the cabin's front door, the stock of his shotgun pressed against his shoulder, the muzzle up and ready. If someone emerged—anyone but the kids—they would do exactly as Pierce ordered or feel the impact of a twelve-gauge round in their chest.

The night had gone quiet, and Pierce stood close to the porch, staring at the door and the light spilling through the side window.

"Coming toward you now," DeLuca whispered. He didn't want to startle his partner and get shot himself.

"It's Jim," DeLuca said when he reached him, and Pierce felt his stomach tilt, his mouth fill with saliva. The night had grown chilly, but beads of sweat stood out on his forehead and the back of his neck. Under different circumstances, he would have leaned against the wall or taken a knee as his strength left and his body grappled with the news. But he did neither of these, only nodded slightly, kept his gun raised, his finger on the trigger, and considered what to do from here.

If Jim was dead, where were the others? In all likelihood, the kidnapper was still in the cabin. Then the boys were probably in there too—and maybe Michael. If so, storming the place would put too many lives at risk. Instead, they could wait and hope to ambush the kidnapper when he emerged. But there was always the possibility he would kill the boys while they waited outside. Was it likely? *No,* Pierce decided. *If he was going to kill them, he would've done it by now.* But then again, maybe he already had. They must get a look inside. They couldn't assess their next move without knowing the situation in there. And right now, they needed any advantage they could get.

"Think you can make your way around to the window?" Pierce asked, holding his voice to a whisper. "Get a look at what's going on in there?"

"Sure," DeLuca said, then hesitated for a moment.

Pierce turned his head to look at his partner. "What is it?"

DeLuca placed a hand on Pierce's shoulder, and glanced back at the body before answering. "It's Jim," he said, sounding both scared and relieved. "He's still alive."

37

"WHAT THE HELL HAPPENED OUT THERE?" MICHAEL asked as Banes opened the door and entered the cabin. The left side of the man's neck was covered in blood.

"You brought company is what happened," Banes said, his voice thunderous. He placed the lantern on the lip of the sink, and peered into the mirror. "Look at that," he said to himself, and Michael saw it too. The lower half of his left ear was missing.

Michael looked down at his son. Miraculously, Sean slept on, the whistling of his breathing like the flow of air through a thin reed in the high wind.

"*Aww, hell.* Ain't I a piece of work." Banes turned, looked at Michael and smiled, causing the gash in his forehead to widen like the mouth of a fish. "I'm not as pretty as I used to be," he said. "You'll be joinin' me in that department real soon."

"I don't understand," Michael said. "Who—"

"The fat old lawman," Banes said. "And who knows how many others you brought."

"I brought no one."

Banes grimaced, and scrunched up his face. "Oh," he said.

"My apologies. I guess that was all in my imagination. Still," he continued, "doesn't explain the missing ear." With his injured hand he pointed at the macerated flesh hanging from the side of his head. "Or am I the only one seeing it?" he asked. "Tell me: does this look normal to you?"

"I didn't bring anyone," Michael repeated. He knew things would get much worse if he couldn't convince this man that he was speaking the truth.

"Do you know *why* I told you not to bring the cops?" Banes asked. "I mean, besides the fact that I didn't think it was good for either of us." He paced the room now, head down. The blood on his neck glistened in the light. "I said to myself, 'If he brings the cops, there's a good chance someone's gonna get shot.'" He stopped, looked at Michael. "In case you don't know, the legal system frowns on cop killing more than it does kidnapping and grand theft auto. For cop killing, they go for the electric chair. They want to see you fry. I think we can safely assume that's in play now."

"I'm telling you," Michael said, "I *did not* involve the police. What sense would it make for me to bring them? I'm as guilty as you are here."

"You'd be quick to deny that, I'm sure. From their end, it looks like I acted on my own." He was back to pacing now. "Maybe you knew they'd try to kill me. That would be a good way to keep me quiet. Dead men tell no tales."

"They followed me here. I don't know how, but they did," Michael told him. "It's the only way."

Banes walked over to the mattress, knelt down on one knee, and dug underneath for a moment, pulling out a box of ammunition that fit easily into the palm of one hand. He stood, went to the chair, and slowly lowered himself into it. "Doesn't matter," he said, opening the box and reloading the gun. "They're here now. One of them's lying dead in the grass and the others are coming. That man out there"—he gestured toward the door—"the blame for that rests on *your* shoulders, not mine." He lifted his right hand, scratched at the stubble on the side of his face. "But here's the flip side to cop killing," he said. "Once you cross that line, it doesn't matter what you do afterward. They can't electrocute you twice, can't make the punishment any worse. In that sense, I can act with impunity—go on a killing rampage if I want. The punishment's the same in the end."

I can act with impunity—go on a killing rampage if I want. Michael felt himself go cold with the statement. He tried to reason with him. "What happened out there was self-defense. You didn't know it was a cop. He just started firing. You were trying to protect yourself."

"They won't see it like that."

"You should surrender, let us go. I'll take responsibility, and tell them what happened. I won't let you take the fall for this."

Banes lifted his head and stared at him. The left side of his face was lost in the shadows. "How stupid do you think I am?"

"I don't think you're stupid at all. If anyone's acted stupidly here, it's me. I can explain that to them. That man out there was a friend of mine. He's dead because of me."

Banes said nothing for a while, merely sat with his head lowered, as if he'd drifted off to sleep. Michael wondered if he might have lapsed into unconsciousness. Part of him hoped he was dead.

"Even if I believed you," Banes said, his eyes closed, chin still resting on his chest, "it won't make a difference what you tell them. They'll fry me just the same. Can you imagine what that's like, all that electricity passing through your body? They make you wear a diaper. Grown men piss themselves. That's what's

waiting for me now." He took a few deep breaths, tilted backward in his chair, and propped himself against the wall. "Your
kid said I'd be dead by morning. A few hours ago, I didn't believe him. But now"—he leaned forward, settling the chair back
on all four legs—"I think that's about right." In the dim light of
the lantern, he appeared decades older than the man Michael
had met in the bar a month before. "I'm okay with that," Banes
said, "being dead by morning. Our days are numbered, yours
and mine—even his," he said, nodding toward the sleeping boy
on the floor. "There comes a time when the price of living is
more than we can pay."

"You should let us go," Michael repeated, "give yourself
over to the authorities. It's the best way forward from here."

"I don't think so," Banes said. "I'm a man with no future.
I'd rather die tonight than spend the next few years in prison
waiting for the juice." He dug his right hand into his pocket,
brought out a small key, and slid it across the floor to Michael.
"Take the cuff off his wrist," he said, "then fasten it around the
post and slide the key back to me."

"No," Michael said, his heart walloping in his chest. "I'm
not going to let you—"

Banes was on his feet in a flash with the gun raised. It was
scary how much fury he still had left inside him. "You're not
letting me do shit!" he thundered. "You do as I say or I will kill
you both right now. It doesn't make much difference to me
either way."

"Where are you taking him?"

"*Do it!*"

Michael scooped up the key and removed the cuff from his
son's wrist.

"Now lock the cuff around the post and slide the key back
to me," he said, and Michael did as he was told.

The key made it halfway across the floor. Banes went to it and instead of bending over to retrieve it, kicked it toward the corner of the room farthest from Michael. Then he crossed the remaining distance between them, and lightly kicked the boy in the back of the leg. "Wake up," he said, "time to get a move on. You and I got places to go."

He kicked him again. Sean opened his eyes and stood, his breathing now worse than ever. Banes tucked the revolver into his belt. With his good hand, he clutched the back of Sean's shirt, and nudged the boy toward the door.

"You should get him to a doctor," Michael said, "soon as you get out of here. Drop him off at a hospital. They can take it from there."

Banes turned and studied him. "Where do you think we're going?"

"He's your ticket out of here," Michael answered. "They won't touch you as long as you've got a hostage."

"You don't get it, do you? It's over. What kind of an ending do you think this is going to be?"

"Where are you taking him? Where's Danny?"

"What do *you* care? You wanted him gone. He's gone," Banes said. "Pretty soon, you won't have to worry about either one of them. Sean here is going to join his brother." He grabbed the lantern, opened the door and pushed the kid through it, and didn't bother to close it behind them.

"Wait!" Michael called. "You don't need to do this!" But all he could see was an empty porch and a small circle of grass in the retreating light. They lingered off to the right a moment, then crossed his line of sight before heading in the opposite direction. Then the cabin went dark, along with everything beyond it. "He won't hurt them," Michael whispered. "He's not a monster." But Banes, like everyone else, believed Danny was a different kind of monster—and so maybe, by association, his brother was as well.

"*Better to leave him in the ground where he belongs,*" he'd said. But what did that mean? Had he already killed Michael's younger son and disposed of the body? *Had he buried him alive?* Was that where he was taking Sean now?

Michael strained to make out any shapes through the open doorway. It was no use—only shadows and wild imaginings. He listened for the sound of voices or footsteps, the commotion of a physical struggle. In his mind, he saw Sean break away and run for the trees. But where would that get him? How far could he go?

"*I need you to do whatever it takes to get Sean and Danny back,*" Kate had said, and he had promised, knowing—*even then*—that he could not keep his word.

He pulled on the cuff, tried to slide it over his wrist, and felt the metal bite into his flesh. "I'm sorry," he whispered, and then he looked up. The light was returning. Banes was coming back—*too soon*, he thought. Did he change his mind? Did something go wrong? Had he decided to let Sean go?

Through the open door, Michael saw, or thought he saw, a man at the edge of the woods holding a shotgun. He was down on one knee, hunkered low, visible for only a fraction of a second as the circle of light passed over him. If Banes saw him, he didn't pause, the light from the lantern growing steadily as he made his way back to the cabin. *He missed it*, Michael thought, and then wondered if that was true. If he *had* seen it, he would do exactly what he was doing now, head for the cabin and hole up inside. From there on, it would be a standoff.

Should I warn them, Michael thought, *tell whoever is out there that they've been spotted?* But then Michael might be giving them away. Still, if Banes made it back to the cabin . . .

He had to make a decision. In a few seconds, Banes would be at the door and it would be too late, a missed opportunity.

Michael drew in a breath, and readied himself.

"*HE SEES YOOUUU!*" he yelled. It was followed by a brief snatch of silence, enough for him to feel his heart thump three times in his chest.

After that, everything went to hell.

38

HE WAS THIRSTY AND HUNGRY. SOMETIMES HE FORGOT. HIS hunger was like a mouse, moving around in his stomach on a wheel. He could hear it turning inside him. *Screech, screech, screech* went the wheel as the little mouse feet ran quick, then stopped, ran quick, and then stopped.

It was hard to be hungry when your brother was in trouble, chained to a stove and his breathing going *squeak, squeak, squeak* like the mouse. Danny wanted to help, to do something to make it better, but he didn't know how. He only knew that hunger goes away when you're scared but it doesn't go away forever. It comes back to bother you, and makes its noises in your stomach even though your brother is in trouble.

Being thirsty was worse. It was a fly that buzzed around in his head and wouldn't let him think. It marched along his tongue: back and forth, back and forth. The fly feet felt different from the mouse feet—prickly and sticky. They walked and walked and never went away.

It was dark here and there was almost nothing to see. The floor was cold and hard and wouldn't let him sleep. He had tried anyway, hoping this place would go away for a while. He missed his bed, missed his family. It had been a long time since he had seen his mother. He tried to picture her face in his head, and it was hard. He was forgetting what she looked like.

"*Good night,*" she would say, sitting on the side of the bed, tucking his green blanket around him, then pulling it up over his shoulders. "*It's time for sleep. Close your eyes and think happy thoughts. Tomorrow will be another wonderful day.*"

It was not easy. Happy thoughts were hard to find in the middle of the night.

Something crawled across his arm. He sat up and tried to brush it away, but it was already gone. Danny got to his feet, and went *stomp, stomp, stomp* in the dark. His body gave a little shiver. He wrapped his arms around himself, and shivered again.

He knew what it was like to wake from a nightmare, to open his eyes in the dark and be afraid. On nights like those, he would go to his brother, and shake him until he woke up and took him to their parents' room, where Danny would sleep between his mom and dad until morning.

He could not go to their room now. Sean was not in the other bed. There was nothing here but the mouse and the fly inside him.

Danny closed his eyes and tried to think of something good. If he had any friends, he would've thought of them. But kids don't want to be your friend when you can't talk. When you knock on their door, their mothers tell you they can't come out and play. Kids who are different should learn to play by themselves.

"You're a poisonous child," Kenny Travis told him one day. Kenny lived two houses away. At twelve, he was too grown-up to play with Danny, and had never spoken to him before. Danny was kneeling in the grass, playing with his trucks, and didn't know Kenny was there until he stood over him, looking down.

"Your mother is sick because of you—that's what my parents say. Lots of people are sick because of you. No one wants you here. You should go away."

Danny had thought Kenny was going to hit him. Instead, he kicked one of his trucks and sent it tumbling across the yard. Then he turned and walked away.

That was the first time anyone had told Danny he had poison inside. It scared him. If he'd been able to talk, he would've asked his mother about it. Maybe there was a way to get rid of it. Maybe they should take him to the doctor. Crying silently, he went to find Sean, and led him to where Kenny's bike lay in the grass. His brother would understand. He wanted Sean to tell him it wasn't true, that of course there was no poison inside him. Instead, his brother walked right over to Kenny, who was kicking a ball against the side of his house, and punched him in the nose, even though Sean was smaller and two years younger. Kenny ran into his house crying, his face bloodied. After that Kenny wasn't allowed to play with either of them because one was poisonous and the other was a fighter.

Danny shook his head. These were not happy thoughts.

He wondered what his brother would do if he was here. Sean always made a game out of things that were boring or scary. In the dark, Danny pretended he could see him, standing beside him and scratching his head, thinking up a new game for them to play.

"We need to find something to drink," Sean told him. His voice and his breathing were strong now. "I'm thirsty as hell."

Danny nodded. He liked it when Sean cursed. It made him feel tough and powerful. *The two of them were thirsty as hell.*

"Come here," Sean said. He took Danny by the shoulders and moved him toward the wall until he stood alongside it. "Put your hand out, like this," he said, placing Danny's right palm against the cold, moist concrete. "Now put your other hand out in front so you don't run into anything."

Danny did as he was told.

"Now walk forward, real slow. If you come to something, feel it with your hands to find out what it is. Maybe you'll find a flashlight, or something to eat or drink. The important part is to keep searching. Don't give up until you're sure there's nothing else in here. You'll be like a pirate, hunting for hidden treasure."

Where are you? Danny thought, but couldn't say it. And even if he could, his brother wouldn't hear him. His brother was somewhere else.

"Never mind that," Sean told him. "Pirates are tough. They do what they want. I'm here if you want me to be. But it's up to you to find the treasure. I'm counting on you. Don't let me down."

I won't, Danny thought. He moved forward, one hand against the wall, the other out in front of him.

"*Arrrrrrrr,*" said Sean. "*Thar be buried treasure in here somewheres, matey. I kin smell it.*"

Arrrrrrrr, thought Danny. He could hear music, men laughing around a fire, the slap of waves against the shore. He paused long enough to adjust his sword and pull the leather patch over his right eye. Then he continued his search.

39

FOR BANES, STEPPING ONTO THE FRONT PORCH WAS LIKE returning to the scene of the battle. It was funny how quickly he'd forgotten that the dead man would be there, sprawled on the grass with the shotgun beside him. *It could've been me*, Banes thought to himself, and in many ways it was hard to believe that it wasn't. When he'd tripped over his own feet and fallen backward onto the grass—when the man stepped around the corner and fired at close range—Banes had already come to the realization that he was about to die.

No way he misses, he'd thought. *It will hit me in the chest like the hand of God himself.* But it hadn't come, none of it.

And yet, in the space of those few seconds, the idea had taken hold. He'd felt the slight give of the earth beneath his feet, his heart churning within his chest, the night breeze on his skin. *I'm alive*, he'd told himself, but it was like clinging to the shattered remnants of a dream in the hour after waking.

He continued down the steps, holding on to the back of the boy's shirt and nudging him along. On the grass, they turned right and walked to the corner of the building. Banes wanted to get a good look at the spot where he had fallen. Nothing would be there now but a matted patch of grass. But he wanted to be sure, needed to prove to himself that he wasn't still lying there, a massive crater in his chest, his eyes staring blankly at the sky. "I am not dead," he whispered. The boy in front of him made a small noise, as if this remained a point of some contention.

"This way," Banes said, and jerked the boy around, heading for the opposite side of the cabin.

A hundred yards ahead stood the outhouse, a solitary structure against the backdrop of the woods. They passed it, and entered the loose gathering of trees that bordered the field. The stone cliff face to their left rose high into the night sky, but he didn't look at it. He kept his eyes trained on the space in front of them.

The old man honored his end of the bargain, Banes thought. If there was such a thing as a soul, his body had surrendered his, leaving behind a mass of useless flesh, and a shotgun whose barrel still cooled in the chill of the grass. He could see him roll onto his back and raise the muzzle as he prepared to fire. Banes hadn't hesitated. He had pulled the trigger and watched as the man's head snapped backward from the impact the bullet made with his skull. Standing over him, Banes had felt neither relieved nor victorious—only hopeless and empty. The fact that it was this man and not him lying there was a mere technicality that could soon be corrected. *Dead by morning*, he thought. And what did it matt—

He stopped, and brought the kid to a halt with a hard tug on his shirt.

Is that how it happened? Am I remembering it correctly?

He closed his eyes, and tried to picture it again.

I stood over him, then reached down and pulled the shotgun from his grasp. I remember tossing it aside.

He could see it now, lying a short distance away, perpendicular to the body. The more he thought about it, the more certain he felt. Only . . .

A few minutes ago, that's not how it was. The gun was closer, lying next to the body. Within easy reach.

What did it mean?

You're crazy; I saw him die, he reassured himself. But he hadn't seen that exactly. He had only witnessed the head shot and assumed it was true.

He took a bullet in the chest, as well. Let's not forget that.

Right, he thought. *Only that hadn't stopped him either.* Chest wound or not, he had turned onto his back and tried to fire.

"I've got to be sure," he whispered, and again the kid made a sound, as if the whole thing played into his predictions. "Shut up," Banes said, and the kid didn't reply, only continued his wheezing.

They headed back to the clearing, the prisoner in front of him, the lantern raised to the level of his head.

If we return to the spot and he's not there . . . , Banes thought. But he didn't know how to finish, and didn't know what he would do afterward.

I've still got the boy, he reasoned. *He won't fire while I'm holding him in front of me.* But was that true? After taking a shot to the head, could a man be trusted to act rationally?

Where's your gun? You left it in the cabin.

A moment of panic passed over him until he remembered: it was here, tucked in his belt.

You have no free hand to hold it. With the boy in one hand and the lantern in the other . . .

"Here," he said, and held the lantern in front of him until the kid took the handle. "Raise it up. Keep it high."

He switched his grasp on the kid's shirt to his left hand. It was painful and his grip was more tenuous with the tips of his index and middle finger missing. But he could do it—*had* to do it. He needed his right hand for the gun.

The cabin was dark, just as he'd left it.

He could be in there now. It's the first place I should check.

No, no. Check the grass. If he's there, you should shoot him again to be sure.

"Move it," he told the boy, whose progress had slowed. He gave him a small shove, and in that moment noticed a figure off to his left. The man stood inside the cluster of trees where the woods merged with the open field. Banes kept his eyes straight ahead.

The others. They've arrived. No telling how many of them are out here.

Standing here in the open, it became apparent how vulnerable he really was. If they could get off a clean shot . . .

Get back inside the cabin. Right now. It's your only chance.

He tried to maintain the same pace forward, to give nothing away. Up ahead, on the far side of the porch, he saw the man lying in the grass where he'd left him. Banes strained his eyes to pick out the shape of the shotgun in the shadows. Had it moved closer? Was it in the man's hands now? It was hard to know for sure.

They were almost at the front porch now. When they reached the steps, he would turn, ascend them backward, and hold the boy between himself and the man he'd seen lurking in the woods.

What if there's another cop waiting for you inside the cabin? You'll have your back to him. It'll be an easy shot.

He paused, thinking.

Go sideways up the steps, so you can keep an eye in both directions.

Yes, this was a good strategy, and his best chance of making it back inside. He would keep the boy close to his body. They wouldn't fire if there was a chance of hitting—

"*HE SEES YOOUUU!*"

Banes froze. It was the father, calling out to the man. He'd seen him too. If they were going to take a shot at him, now would be the time.

He pivoted to face the man in the woods, holding the kid in front of him. There he was, standing in the grass, handgun raised and pointed in their direction.

Banes extended his own weapon over the boy's shoulder and fired. The man dove to his right, and rolled over once in the grass.

"Is this what you came for?" Banes yelled and fired again. Once. Twice. It was hard to tell whether he'd—

His head exploded, a blinding spray of heat and pain. The left side of his face was on fire, daggers of glass digging into his skin.

He shot me, he thought. *Took a chance and fired right past the kid, hit me in the head.*

The light rolled away from him, and left him lying on the steps in the darkness.

You aren't shot. If you'd been shot in the head, you'd be dead by now.

In his mind, he saw it again: the man's head snapping backward, the body going still.

Banes touched his face, brushing it with the tips of his fingers—the ones that weren't already amputated. It was more pain than he could bear. The skin was blistered and hot to the touch.

Why is your hand not holding the kid?

He looked down at his open palm, as if the child might still be there.

He's gone. He hit you with the lantern.

"Son of a bit—" Banes started, then heard the crack of a

handgun, and felt a bullet zip by his head and bury itself in the wood behind him.

Crack. Crack.

Two more shots, and he was on his knees, hunkered behind the rail.

Get inside, get inside, his mind pleaded, but he wanted to find him, the one who'd caused him nothing but trouble from the beginning.

He could no longer see out of his left eye, and scanned the field with his right, the images blurring and jumping in front of him. If the man was still lying on his stomach in the grass, Banes couldn't make him out, only the figure of the kid sprinting toward the woods. He steadied his hand against the rail, took aim. Fired.

He missed, the bullet either too high or too low, off to one side or the other—it was impossible to tell from here. Another gunshot followed and a section of rail detonated two inches to his left. He ignored it, and aimed again, lining up his sights as best he could.

Now or never, he thought, squeezing the trigger twice in rapid succession.

He never saw whether he hit his target, for his second shot was accompanied by another one, louder and off to his right. He took the brunt of the impact in his right flank, the force of it shoving him sideways.

The dead man. The one I left lying in the grass. Somehow he's up on his feet and coming after me.

He raised his gun and fired in the man's direction, but the hammer snapped down with a click and nothing else. He was out of bullets, and completely exposed on the porch.

Get inside, his mind screamed, and this time he did as he

was told, squirming through the open doorway on his stomach. The shotgun went off a second time, but he was already most of the way inside. He felt his left foot jerk, as if he'd been kicked hard in the side of his boot. He didn't bother to look, only pulled himself the rest of the way across the threshold, grabbed the lower edge of the door and slammed it shut behind him. Even then, he didn't stop. He army-crawled across the floor to the mattress, pulled the shotgun out from where it lay against the wall, racked it once, and waited.

He was breathing hard, couldn't seem to catch his breath.

In the corner, his body pressed tightly against the stove, sat the man who'd sparked all of this trouble in the first place.

Time to finish this off, Banes thought, and trained his weapon on the door. *Did they hear me rack it? Do they think I still have the other kid inside?*

He didn't know how long he lay there waiting, but eventually it became clear they weren't coming. They must have decided the best course of action was to wait him out.

I'm not hurt too bad, Banes told himself, even though he could barely breathe and felt his belly turning rigid, his intestines twisting inside him. He was cold, and vaguely aware that he was sweating. Before long, he would pass out—either from the pain or the blood loss, it didn't matter. When that happened, Michael would call to the men outside and tell them it was safe to enter.

"Just a few more things," Banes whispered, and forced himself to move. He grabbed some books from the shelf and stacked them in the windowsill, obscuring the view. Then he slid the chair to the door, and wedged it under the knob. In a remote place like this, locks were of little use, and his uncle—even as paranoid as he was—hadn't bothered to install one.

"You should give yourself up," Michael said.

Banes crawled toward him with the shotgun. "Your boys are dead because of you," he croaked. He leaned forward and vomited on the floor, the pungent odor filling the room.

"There's no way out of this."

"Not for any of us," Banes agreed. A wave of dizziness passed over him. He lifted the gun, steadied it.

"Shoot me and they'll hear. They'll bust through that door and take you, one way or the other."

"I know," Banes said. He brought the gun back, and swung it with everything he had left. The stock of the shotgun connected with the man's head, the jolt of the impact traveling up the barrel. Michael's body went slack, slumped to the left, and Banes collapsed as well.

For a long time, he lay there, unable to do anything except focus on his breathing. He was wading through a marsh, could taste the brackish water on his tongue, the reeds wrapping themselves around him, gripping his legs, attempting to pull him below the surface. In the distance was a light: the glow of the Coleman lantern, perhaps. The kid would be there, or maybe someone else. He tried to focus on it, refused to look away. "Not much farther now," Banes whispered. He managed to get his elbows out in front of him, and dragged himself across the room. The water deepened, rose to the level of his chin. The floor was spongy now, and he sank into it, felt the mud sucking at his body. *One last breath*, he thought, but there was nothing there—only silt and sludge that cascaded into his mouth when he opened it, filling his lungs, enveloping him in silence. Banes gagged, tried to cough, but even that was too much effort.

His right leg kicked out at nothing. His body shuddered. Then he went still.

40

"HOLD PRESSURE ON IT," PIERCE SAID, SLAPPING A HAND over DeLuca's and pushing down on the wound.

They were fifty yards into the woods now. The older boy was lying on his left side so they could tend to the gunshot wound to his right flank. His breathing was long and labored, the air moving in and out of him in tight screeches. His body seemed to cling to it, not wanting to let it go.

The boy had gone down on the last shot the man had fired. Pierce—already running toward him—was there in a second, scooped him up, and sprinted for the cover of the woods. He'd heard DeLuca fire the shotgun—twice—but didn't stop to look back. Instead, he laid the boy on the ground, dropped to his knees, and risked using the flashlight to see where he'd been hit.

There were two wounds—one entrance and one exit— through the right side of his body just above the bony crest of his pelvis. The thin chest moved in and out, his eyes glazed over with shock and pain.

"Bleeding's not too bad," DeLuca said, and continued to apply pressure.

"What d'you think it hit?" Pierce asked him. "Kidney sits somewhere in there, doesn't it?"

"Somewhere," DeLuca said, shaking his head. "I don't know exactly."

"Well, it had to hit something, right?"

"Maybe," DeLuca said. "Maybe it just"—he looked at his partner—"passed through."

Pierce looked down at the boy, placed the palm of his hand on the kid's forehead. "You willing to risk his life on that?"

"No," DeLuca said, "I'm not."

A short distance away, Jim moaned, and tried to roll over. DeLuca had dragged him into the woods earlier, and taken his position in the grass near the cabin. They had hoped to catch the kidnapper off guard. It almost worked, but the man had held the boy too close to risk taking the shot, and then there was the lantern swaying back and forth, the bodies of man and boy merging in the shifting light.

"I'd better take a look at Jim too," DeLuca said. He left the boy in the care of his partner, crawled over to where the sheriff lay.

The most obvious injury was the shot to the head. A bloody ridge extended from the top of his forehead and followed an arcing path around the dome of his scalp. DeLuca placed a hand behind Jim's head, and felt a raised cylindrical bump that moved beneath his fingers. *Skull fracture*, he thought, *a piece of bone perhaps*, but a moment later the thing slipped through the gash and fell into the palm of his hand.

DeLuca slipped the small object into his pocket, unbuttoned the man's shirt, and searched for a second injury. There was a large bruise on the left side of his chest—Jim winced when he touched it—but no entrance wound that he could find. He rolled Jim onto his right side to look at his back, and still nothing—only dirt and flecks of grass, a few superficial scratches.

He returned the sheriff to his back, and buttoned his shirt. There was a hole in the left breast pocket. He stuck his index finger through, and felt the crunch of metal underneath. De-Luca reached in, retrieved the object, and held it between his thumb and index finger. The cigarette lighter was shattered, its thin steel casing split in half, one side still in Jim's pocket, the other hanging by a corner. Its size and shape corresponded to the bruise he'd just discovered, although he found it hard to believe the lighter was strong enough to withstand the force of a bullet. He studied it incredulously, then switched it to his other hand, reached into his pocket, and dug out the object he'd retrieved from Jim's head wound.

It was a bullet, slick and bloodstained—dented at the front— but otherwise intact.

"Never pierced the skull," DeLuca whispered. *And the other one?* He looked from the bullet to the lighter, back to the bullet again. The other shot must've struck him at an angle, hit the lighter and glanced away.

He shook his head, contemplating it. What were the chances of either one of these trajectories? A thousand to one? *Ten thousand?* And for both to happen like that, back-to-back, with the same man? The odds must be a million to one. *Or maybe*, he thought, *maybe none of this was chance at all.*

He remembered what the sheriff had told them in his office that first morning after the boys went missing, how people in the town of Cottonwood had gotten it into their heads that Danny McCray was no ordinary child.

You've been good to those boys, DeLuca thought, eyeing the man who had escaped death twice in the space of a few seconds. Was it luck or protection, or maybe something else entirely? Chances were, he would never know.

"What do we do from here?" Pierce asked when DeLuca returned to his side.

DeLuca gave it some thought, ran through the short list of options in his mind.

"I hit him with a shotgun round. I know I did."

"Did you kill him?" Pierce asked. "If you did, or at least *think* you did, then that changes everything."

DeLuca thought about it, played the scene over in his mind. "I don't think so," he said. "He may die from his injury, but . . . not right away."

"So he's still alive in there. The father too. As for the other boy . . ."

"I didn't see him earlier when I looked through the window," DeLuca said, but he couldn't be sure. For something like this, they had to be positive.

Pierce leaned over the child. "Where's your brother?" he asked. "Was he in there with you?"

Sean McCray worked on his breathing. His eyes were distant, focused on a place far away from here.

"We've got to get him out of here," DeLuca said. He caught his partner's attention, dropped his voice to a whisper. "If he dies . . ."

"We both go. We both stay. Or one of us goes and one of us stays," Pierce said. "Those are the options."

"One of us has to go," DeLuca replied. He looked down at the kid. "He needs to get to a hospital. Jim too, if we can."

"Can't leave the father and the other kid here," Pierce said.

"Unless we storm the place. Take the son of a bitch right now."

"It's a big risk with two hostages still inside. Of course, it's a risk to do nothing. He could decide to kill them at any time."

"If he was going to, he would have done it already," DeLuca said. "I put one round in him. He might not live more than a few hours. I think we should wait him out." He looked back at the cabin, turned to his partner. "One of us goes and one of us stays."

Pierce sat back on his heels. "Shit," he said. "I don't like it, splitting up like this."

"Another plan then. Do you have one?"

The senior detective shook his head.

"Let's stop wasting time," DeLuca said. He crawled over to the sheriff, and shook him gently. "Jim. You with us?"

The man grunted, his response muffled and incoherent.

"Get up, Jim. On your feet."

Jim rolled to his side, tried to push himself to his knees, and then slumped back down again.

Pierce shook his head. "Let him be. The man's been shot in the head, for God's sake. Even if we can get him up, he'll never make it all the way back to the car on his own two feet. And I can't carry them both."

"No, but you're strong enough to make it with the kid. Jim will be okay to stay here with me for a while. We'll wait this guy out."

"Okay." Pierce checked on the kid's bleeding. It was slowing, but hadn't stopped. He stood with the boy in his arms. "Be careful," he said. "Unless something happens to force your hand, don't go in after him by yourself. I'll bring an army of backup as soon as I can."

"You know the way to the clearing?"

"Yeah," he said, turning and surveying the woods. He started up the hill, the body of the boy already heavy in his arms.

"Partner," DeLuca called.

Pierce stopped, swiveled around. "What?"

"The clearing's that way," he said, and pointed.

"You sure?"

"Yeah. Up and over the hill. Once you clear that rise, you should see the flashlight I lodged in the tree. Head straight for it."

"Thanks," Pierce said. "And be careful. Don't underestimate this guy. And don't go getting yourself killed."

"I'll do my best," DeLuca said. Then he turned and settled himself on the forest floor, eyes on the cabin. He looked down at his watch. It was still a long time until morning.

41

KATE SNAPPED AWAKE.

Something was wrong. She could feel it.

As bad as the situation already was, she knew this was worse. Much worse. It had fetched her from a fitful sleep, the sheets soaked with sweat, her hands opening and closing in the wake of a dream she couldn't quite remember.

He's falling. You reach out to catch him, but he's already gone.

The world seemed to slip sideways, and opened up beneath her, endless miles of empty space.

Kate kicked off the sheet, got out of bed, and paced the room.

Look how strong you are. You're so much better than you've been in a long, long time.

It was true. There was no denying it. The walker stood abandoned in the kitchen. When she'd gone to bed, she hadn't even bothered to take it with her to the bedroom.

It's the new medication, she told herself. The trip to Sacramento to see Dr. Eichner the month before had been worth the time and expense. She had Michael to thank for that, the way he'd taken charge, and insisted that she take the medication despite her own reservations.

"This is the one that's going to work," he'd said. "Dr. Eichner was very optimistic."

She'd balked at that. "Nothing else has made a difference. Insurance doesn't pay for everything. The cost of this is—"

"It's going to turn things around for you," he'd assured her. "You'll see." And on that point her husband had been right. Things were different now. Her strength was on the rebound.

For the past week and a half, though, a voice countered. *It's only been on the rebound since Danny was taken.*

No. That wasn't true. She'd started feeling better almost right away, long before Danny was taken. It had been several weeks now.

A week and a half is all it's been, maybe less. It's right there in front of you. Why do you refuse to look at it?

"I refuse to look at it because it isn't true," she said, her voice loud and defiant in the still of the house. She left her slippers by the bedside, walked to the kitchen in her nightgown.

"*I need you to do whatever it takes to get Sean and Danny back. Promise me: whatever it takes.*"

She could see her husband watching her, hear him promise. But his face had been difficult to read, his eyes like two dark stones protruding from the water.

Where are you? she thought. *What are you doing with my sons?*

She stopped, and listened to the soft mutterings of the house.

What are you doing with my sons? Why had she framed it like that?

You know what's going on here. You've known it from the beginning.

I don't, she told herself. Nothing was rational. What kind of person would take two small boys? None of it made any sense.

The refrigerator's motor hummed, whispering things she could not understand.

"*This is about two sweet children . . . You will find them, Detectives, and you will bring them home to me, safe and unharmed. Is that understood?*"

"Yes, ma'am."

Safe and *unharmed*, useless words written on cardboard placards. They tumbled and scattered in the wind.

One of them has been hurt. One of them has been killed.

"You don't know that," she said, but the words were uncertain. Lately, she told herself quite a lot about what she did and didn't know.

Kate went to the sink, filled the kettle with water. She would make herself a cup of tea, placed the kettle on the range to boil.

You don't have to know that they've been hurt. You can feel it.

"No," she said, taking a seat at the table. "I don't feel anything."

Then what are you doing out here at one o'clock in the morning?

Couldn't sleep, was all. It was as simple as that.

Footsteps behind her, a voice in the hallway: "You okay, honey?"

She turned in her chair and saw him standing in the shadows with his hand against the wall, his head bent, returning to the kitchen from their children's bedroom.

"Michael?"

The figure moved, stepped into the light.

"It's me," her sister said, walking forward. Lauren paused, cocked her head to one side, as if she were listening to the sound of distant music, a song she recognized but could not quite place. "Michael is gone, remember?"

"Of course." Kate swiveled back around, faced the front door and whatever lay beyond. "I was just thinking about him, is all."

"Trouble sleeping?"

"There's no such thing as a good night's sleep when your children are missing."

"Right. I'm sorry." She stepped to the counter, straightened a few things that did not need straightening.

"I'm making some tea," Kate told her. "You're welcome to have some if you want."

Lauren went to the range. "You want me to light this?"

Kate turned to look. She had forgotten to light the burner. She nodded, looked back at the door.

For a few minutes, they were quiet, sitting across from each other with their fingers laced in front of them, waiting for the water to boil. The clock on the wall went *tick, tick, tick* and said nothing else.

"I can't stand it," Kate said at last. "Not knowing what's going on out there."

"If anyone can find them, Michael can."

"You've said that before. Tell me, why is it that he can find them when no one else can? How does he know where to look?"

"I don't know," her sister admitted. "But I believe in him. Don't you?"

Kate was silent. Her eyes returned to the door, waiting for it to open. Eventually, the kettle whistled and Lauren stood to turn off the burner, then retrieved the tea bags from the cabinet above.

"I had a dream tonight that I can't remember," Kate said at last. "It woke me, and wouldn't let me fall back to sleep."

Lauren placed a cup before her, and returned to her seat on the other side of the table.

"Sometimes it seems that my whole life is like that," Kate continued, "a dream I can't quite remember. At night I think about it: how much is real, how much forgotten." She took the string between her thumb and forefinger, bobbing it up and down. The tea bag broke the surface, then sank below again. "I've been sick for a long time," she continued. "Recently, I've been feeling better. Stronger. And do you know what? I've already started to forget what it was like to be ill." She smiled incredulously, shook her head. "How is that even possible?"

Lauren lifted the cup to her lips, took a tentative sip. "We have the ability to remember," she said. "But mostly, when it comes to agony, we live in the present." She placed the cup back on the table, looked down at her fingers. "It's like a train, you know? Massive when it reaches you. Inconsequential when it's gone. It loses its power if it isn't happening right now."

Kate thought about this, wrapped her hands around the warm ceramic. "What will I do if they don't come back?"

"They'll be back."

"When I woke up tonight, I had this strong feeling that one of them was already dead."

"That's your fear talking," Lauren said. "It can't be trusted. It'll latch on to anything."

"It's so strong."

"You can be stronger."

Kate pushed her cup aside, crossed her arms in front of her. "Promise me I'll get my family back. Tell me it'll be okay."

"It will be. You'll see."

Kate nodded, and dropped her eyes to the table. The clock on the wall went *tick, tick, tick* and said nothing else.

"You never talk about Gary—what it was like to lose him, how difficult it is to continue on in his absence."

"He was my husband," Lauren said. "It's the hardest thing I've ever had to face."

"I'm sorry."

"Me too. It's like part of me has been carved away."

Kate swallowed, the saliva thick and viscous in her mouth. "Do you blame him? Do you blame us?"

"I blame no one. My life is too short and too precious for that kind of poison."

Kate brought her hand to the side of her face, and wiped away the tears. "There are people who say this family is pois—"

"It doesn't matter. None of that matters now. There's a time for letting go."

They stared across the table at each other, saying nothing.

"He can't help it," Kate finally whispered. It had been in her thoughts for a while now. This was the first time she'd said it out loud. "What happened to Gary, what happened to you . . ."

"Stop."

"He didn't mean to do it," she said. "He doesn't mean to do any of it."

Lauren stood, the legs of her chair scraping against the floor. "Good night," she said, and a moment later she disappeared down the hallway.

He doesn't mean it, Kate called after her, but the words were only in her head now, a senseless chant playing over and over. It meant nothing in the end.

Something is wrong—even worse than before.

She stood, collected the cups, and took them to the sink. Lauren was right. She had to stay positive.

He's falling. You reach out to catch him, but he's already gone.

"That's your fear talking . . . You can be stronger."

She tried to quiet her mind. Whatever was happening out there, it was nothing she could control.

"He was my husband. It's the hardest thing I've ever had to face."

"I'm sorry."

"Me too. It's like part of me has been carved away."

Kate turned out the light, and returned to the bedroom. The walker stood abandoned in the kitchen. She was stronger and didn't need it.

"I had a dream tonight that I can't remember . . . I've been sick for a very long time."

"Do you blame us?"

"I blame no one."

She lay down in bed, closed her eyes. There would be no more sleep, the conversations spinning around inside her head, spilling together and falling apart.

"I believe in him. Don't you?"

How long had it been since they'd sat together on the couch, the promise passing between them?

"Whatever it takes," Michael had said. But his face had been difficult to read, his eyes like two dark stones protruding from the water.

42

RICHARD BANES WAS DEAD BY THE TIME MICHAEL BROKE through the surface of consciousness and opened his eyes. Morning was still a long way off, the room nebulous and unstructured, a cast of vague shapes hunkered in the corners. Michael could hear his own breathing, and when he focused on the rhythm of it, could tell that he was the only one.

"Banes," he called. "Where are you?"

No response—not even a moan, or the shifting of a body on the mattress.

"Banes. Wake up. It's later than you think. I can hear someone coming."

Nothing. Only the unmoving hulk on the mattress.

For the next few minutes, there was little Michael could do except stare at the form, allowing his eyes time to adjust to the darkness. Gradually, the details became clear. He could see the torso was not moving. The outline of the man's teeth was visible, his mouth partially open. A moment later, the whites of his eyes also surfaced in the dark, wide and staring.

Dead, Michael thought, and his body shuddered. The man was gone. Still, there were questions that he needed answered.

"Where did you take him?" Michael said. "What did you do with my son?"

Banes stared back, and said nothing. He'd put Danny in the ground. Isn't that what he'd said?

"He's dead, isn't he," Michael said. The possibility was unthinkable, a cold hand gripping him from below. He was talking to himself now. There was no one left to listen.

He glanced toward the chair Banes had wedged between the doorknob and the floor, imagined it pushed back against the wall, the man sitting in front of him. *"Your kid said I'd be dead by morning. Our days are numbered, yours and mine—even his. There comes a time when the price of living is more than we can pay."*

This brought him around to Kate. She was dying too—faster than she deserved. What price had he been willing to pay to try to save her?

"The folks I was going to take him to—I can't do it." Banes had torn the paper again and again until the scraps fell from his hands. *"Better to leave him in the ground where he belongs."*

Michael stared at the wasted body on the mattress. "He's dead," Michael said out loud, testing the idea. He wasn't certain if he was referring to Banes or his own son. Maybe there was still time to save Danny. Maybe there was still time to set this right.

The detectives were out there somewhere. They were watching the cabin, waiting. They would come if he called out to them.

"He's dead," Michael said again, his voice stronger now, more insistent. He said it again. And again. It wasn't long before he was yelling.

"He's dead! Do you hear me? Get in here and help me find my children!"

He rattled the handcuff, pounded his other hand on the floor. "Get in here! What are you waiting for?!"

Eventually, the knob turned. When the door met with resistance, the man on the other side gave it a hard kick. The back of the chair cracked, and the wood buckled. Two kicks later and the backrest snapped in half, and the rest was sent skittering across the floor.

"Jim," Michael said, but it wasn't the sheriff—only the younger detective, standing alone in the doorway, his body silhouetted in the moonlight.

He came alone, Michael thought, but it rang false even as the assertion passed through his mind. *No, that's not it. They've been weeded out. First there were three and now only one.* There was a strange symmetry to it. Wasn't it the same for him and the boys?

The detective's gun was drawn, trained on the crumpled body on the mattress.

"He's gone," Michael told the detective, meaning his son, not Banes.

Tony DeLuca crossed the room, and knelt down to assess the corpse. The muzzle of his gun never wavered from the dead man's head. "What happened here?" he asked, and he wasn't merely asking about Banes.

"Right now, it doesn't matter," Michael answered. "We need to find my son."

The keys to the handcuffs were on the floor by the door. DeLuca removed the cuffs, and helped Michael to his feet.

"Your older boy has been shot. I don't think it's serious, but we didn't want to take any chances. Detective Pierce is taking him to the hospital."

"Shot? The son of a bitch shot my son?" Michael's hands balled into fists. He wanted to pummel the dead man, to slam his knuckles into Banes's face over and over until there was nothing left.

"Yes," DeLuca said, "but he's in good hands now. I think he's going to be okay."

Michael paced the floor, seething. *What have I done?* he asked himself. *What have I gotten them into?*

"Right now," DeLuca was saying, "I need you to focus. Your other boy, Danny, is still missing. He wasn't with Sean, and he's obviously not here in the cabin. I'm assuming this man"—he looked down at Banes—"took him somewhere. Somewhere close. Do you have any idea—"

"I don't know," Michael said. He walked to the sink, and gripped the counter in both hands, working to pull himself together. "He kept saying he put him in the ground." Michael shook his head. "I hope that doesn't mean what I think it means."

"It means we'll find him," DeLuca said, and Michael felt certain this was true. They would find his son. There was even a chance Danny might still be alive. As for the other possibility, Michael had prepared a small room in his heart for that as well. He had started building it a long time ago—a place he kept locked and vacant.

"Let's go," he told the detective, and they left the cabin, leaving Banes as he lay.

Beneath the open sky, they went in search of a boy who had never spoken a word or called out for help—not once in his short and jumbled life. *He is not dead*, Michael reassured himself. *My son is not dead.* But his skin was slick with sweat, the fear rising inside him. *We're coming, Danny*, he thought. *Daddy's coming.*

IV

PROTECTING THE INNOCENT

43

B
Y THE TIME THEY REACHED COTTONWOOD IT WAS LATE IN
the day, the shadows already sprouting like vines across
the yards and sidewalks. They took a short detour and
drove by Century Grocery on their way home. Stan Eddleworth's yellow 1952 Chevy Bel Air was there, nosed into its
usual spot. For Michael, seeing it brought on a sense of déjà
vu—the feeling of coming home to find nothing had changed,
the path of their lives simply waiting for them to pick up where
they'd left off.

Sean had spent ten days at Sacred Heart Hospital in Medford, Oregon, recovering from the gunshot wound that had
pierced his right flank. It missed his colon by the smallest of
margins, and exited just as cleanly. The doctors had worried
about blood loss and infection, and kept him in the hospital for
observation and antibiotics. Kate had arrived late in the afternoon that first day, and hadn't left his bedside since.

"He's going to be okay," Michael said, standing behind his
wife, the two of them staring down at their sleeping son.

"What happened out there?" she asked. It was the final day
of Sean's hospitalization. Michael had spent the last week and
a half searching the woods with a team of volunteers and local

law enforcement officers. The men had found Jim Kent lying in the woods near the cabin, shot twice, confused, dehydrated, but still very much alive. Banes was inside, his body rigid on the mattress. It was the shotgun blast to the torso that killed him, and a portion of his left foot was obliterated.

Danny was never found. If Banes had put him in the ground as he said, nine days of searching had yet to uncover the location. They didn't know whether he was alive or dead when Banes first hid him there—and even the most optimistic volunteers had to admit the obvious: after nine days, they were now searching for a body. Two of them actually. The woods had a way of gobbling people up, and their search for Detective Tony DeLuca had taken precedence.

"Don't tell me you couldn't find him!" Kate had shrieked at her husband following that first futile day of searching. Her face was a mask of horror: sunken cheeks falling in on themselves; lips parted as if she might suddenly vomit; dark eyes wide and wild. "Danny is *out there*—lost somewhere in the woods. You can find him. You *will* find him. All you have to do is gather enough people to go looking."

"We had at least fifty people out there tod—"

"Well, get fifty more—a hundred, I don't care." She walked to the other side of the room, a caged animal desperate for a way out. "Just find him, Michael. Promise me you'll find him."

Michael nodded as the grief and responsibility ripped through him. He tried to talk and felt the clench of his throat, the words he wanted to say that refused to come. He swallowed, closed his eyes against it. "Whatever it takes," he managed, realizing—a moment too late—that he'd made her this same promise in their living room the day after their boys first went missing. He'd looked at his wife and vowed to find them. And he had. But now Sean was here and Danny was not. What kind of father lets his boy go? *What kind of father goes into the woods and only brings home one?*

Now, ten days later, their liberty blue Mercury rolled slowly through their neighborhood on its way to the small house on Willow Street. The evening was warm and pleasant this early in September, yet still they saw no one—only cars parked in driveways, front doors and windows closed against the coming night. The Cottonwood Cemetery on First Street stood across from the elementary school, as if patiently waiting for the years to pass and the young bodies to grow old and weaken, destined for their own plot in the acrid soil. In the short time he was away, Michael had almost forgotten about the air of sickness that permeated this place, the contraction of each family inward.

His own house—headstone white and sitting in silence— was no different from the others. With its interior lights extinguished, it was enveloped in darkness, waiting for its family to return.

Michael parked the car in his driveway, stood at the front door staring down at the keys in his hand. He inserted one into the lock, turned, and pushed the door open. He reached inside to flip the switch for the kitchen light, then stepped aside and allowed Sean and Kate to enter. Standing in the doorway, Michael was overcome by the sense that he did not belong here and was not worthy to come inside. He tried to shake it and told himself he had done all he could. There was no point to second-guessing, replaying it in his mind, hoping for a different outcome. He had failed them. Even if he had salvaged a few good things—the remains of his family, a chance at survival, a place for them to begin again.

Kate was standing by the kitchen table when he entered, her hands clasped in front of her. Sean had already retreated to his room—something he would often do in the days to come.

Michael set the keys on the countertop. His wife jumped at the small sound, her shoulders hunching upward, arms drawing closer to the sides of her chest.

"Sorry," Michael said, uttering the apology that seemed to always hover on his lips.

She turned to him, large tears already streaming down her face, her fingers cupped against one another. Even now, in mourning, Michael could see that much of her strength had returned over the past several weeks. He watched it slowly dissipate now, could almost see it cascade down the angles of her body like rainwater. *She will rebound. She will survive this injury*, he reassured himself, not knowing if his words were true or not.

"I . . . I don't know what to do," she said, and that one sentence conveyed all the despair she had held inside until returning home.

Michael stepped forward and caught her before she fell. He took her in his arms and whispered weightless, vacant words that scattered into nothing at their feet.

Kate didn't reply, merely held on to him as if she were standing in a swiftly moving river and would be swept away in an instant if she let go.

"We will get through this," he promised. "There is another side." And on that assertion he was right.

44

T HANKS FOR COMING," JIM SAID, GREETING MICHAEL AT THE door and offering him a seat. A standing fan in the corner of his office whirred dutifully as the sheriff circled his desk and plopped down in his chair. "Thought it would be cooler by now," he said, lowering the window shade against the afternoon sun.

Michael nodded. He could hear the faint sound of passing vehicles from the street below.

"How are Kate and Sean holding up?" Jim asked.

"As best they can."

"Right." He looked down at his desk, then back at Michael. "That's all you can hope for, I guess. Horrible experience, the whole thing."

"I appreciate your concern. What you did for my family . . . the risks you took . . ."

"I wish I could've done more."

"We all do." Michael drew a hand across his face, and realized he'd forgotten to shave for the second day in a row.

Danny liked to watch me shave, he thought. *Used to sit on the counter by the bathroom sink and help me apply the Barbasol.*

The two men sat in silence for a while. A fly landed on the corner of Jim's desk. He leaned forward, and shooed it away.

"It's kind of you to accommodate me like this," Jim said at last, glancing around the room. "I've slowed down a bit lately, tend to stay put more than I used to. I'm getting older, I guess—hell, we all are—but lately I've been getting pain in my chest if I overdo it. Doctor says I should take it easy for a while, that it could take longer than expected to regain my strength."

"Your heart took quite a thump."

"It did. Although the lighter took most of it." Jim reached up and touched that area of his chest. It was still tender from the impact, even three weeks later. His fingers fumbled around inside his left breast pocket, and fished something out.

For a moment, Michael expected to see the old lighter, split down the middle but still riding around in Jim's pocket as a reminder of how close he had come. Instead it was something much smaller, a cylindrical hunk of dented metal.

"They found this during the search," Jim said, "inside the woods, some three hundred feet from where I was hit. They think it's the bullet that struck me—the first one, anyway." He turned it over several times between his thumb and index finger. There was a practiced look to the movement, something he'd done many times before. "Maybe it is," he said. "Or maybe it's just one of many that were fired that day." He shrugged. "There are some things we'll never know for sure."

From the other side of the desk, Michael looked at him. "What can I help you with, Jim? Why am I here?"

The sheriff shook his head. "The truth is, I don't know exactly. You've spoken with the investigating detectives on several occasions. They have your statement. I keep asking myself: Why bother a man who is struggling with the loss of his child? What more can another conversation bring to light?"

"But here I am."

"Yes, here you are, humoring an old man who is probably going soft in the head. I feel I owe you an apology. It keeps me awake at night—that and the questions that remain unanswered, the people who are still out there, waiting to be found."

"It's been three weeks. I don't think they're waiting for anything. I think they're dead."

"I don't like to think of it like th—"

"What is it you want to ask me?"

Jim pressed the back of his right hand against his mouth. The bullet—a forgotten thing—still rested between his thumb and index finger. "I want to hear it from you," he said. "You've told them, now tell it to me. What happened out there? Tell me everything you remember."

Michael laced his fingers, considered his response. *What happened out there?* Kate had asked him the same question. How many times would he have to tell it? How much longer could he bear her incredulous gaze?

"I remember thinking the police weren't doing enough." Michael focused on the stifled glow of the shaded window just beyond Jim's head. "When the kidnapper contacted me, he demanded a ransom, and I told him I would bring it." He swallowed. "It was all the savings we had, but it didn't matter. He threatened to kill the boys. The money was my only chance to get them back."

"What happened to the money? It wasn't found on the premises."

"He took it with him while Sean and I were chained to the stove. When he returned, he was no longer carrying the satchel. I figure he must've hidden it, maybe in the same place he hid my son."

"Why didn't you let us know? We could've helped y—"

"He said to come alone. No cops. I wasn't going to risk the lives of my children."

Jim looked down at the bullet, and waited for him to continue.

"It took a while to find them. Even with directions, it was confusing in the woods. When I reached the cabin only Sean was there, chained to the stove. The man arrived a short time later. I handed over the money, and asked him to let us go as he'd promised." Michael's eyes were on the desk now as he recalled the conversation. "The kidnapper—Banes—was in bad shape when I got there. He'd fallen and struck his head during their initial trek to the cabin. The wound was large and infected. He'd also had a mishap with his gun, and shot off part of two fingers. Bad luck, I guess. Or something else. Either way, he was rattled, confused and irrational. He chained me to the stove, and said he'd already gotten rid of Danny."

"What do you mean, 'gotten rid of'?"

"I don't know. He wouldn't say. Only that he blamed Danny for what happened."

"Blamed him how?" Jim asked, but Michael didn't answer. The sheriff had known his family long enough to understand his meaning.

"You arrived after the sun went down," Michael said, "the detectives a short time later. I think the details of those encounters are pretty clear."

Jim frowned. "I remember him shooting at me, returning fire. After that, it's all a blur." He reached up with his left hand and touched the scar that stretched across the top of his head. He lowered his hand, and looked at his fingertips as if there might still be blood. "They say they found me the next morning, lying in the woods. I don't remember that." He looked at

Michael. "Yesterday I got turned around in my neighborhood and had trouble finding my own house. The doctor says it's probably temporary, but it feels like it's getting worse."

Careful, Michael thought. *Maybe that's true and maybe it isn't. Jim Kent is sharper than he seems.*

Jim leaned forward in his chair. "According to his partner's statement, Detective DeLuca shot the kidnapper at least once at close range with his shotgun. An injury like that is apt to be fatal."

"It probably was. Eventually."

"But you didn't witness the state he was in when he crawled back inside the cabin."

Careful now.

"I don't know if he was crawling at all," Michael answered. "I wasn't there."

"Where were you?"

"I was inside the cabin when the shooting began. By the time it stopped, I had made it through the side window, the one above the sink."

"But you were handcuffed to the stove."

"I was able to pull my hand free—tore up my wrist pretty good doing it. But I'd been working on it for a while. When he left the cabin with Sean, I gave it everything I had. I shaped my hand like this"—he held his right hand up to demonstrate, formed a sort of cone with his palm and fingers—"and the skin around my wrist was bleeding pretty good by then. The lubrication helped. More than anything, though, I think it was the sheer panic of knowing my boy was out there amid all the shooting. I pulled as hard as I could, and my hand came free."

"So you went out through the side window?"

"That's right."

"It was a single pane of glass, not the type that slides open."

"I broke it."

"With what?"

"My foot," Michael told him. "I kicked it out and squirmed through. That part was easy."

"What did you do next?"

"I put some distance between myself and the cabin."

"But Sean had been shot."

"I didn't know that. I didn't know where Banes had taken him."

"Why not go to the detectives, once you'd escaped?"

"By that time, they were shooting at anything that moved. Approaching them in the dark would've been a good way to get myself shot."

Jim sat back, stared at Michael. His body language was familiar. This was the fifth time Michael had told his story. In each of the previous interviews, there had been a moment like this, when the man on the other side of the table decided whether or not he believed any of this. It didn't matter. With each telling, Michael found that he cared less about whether they believed him or not. He'd thought his story through. It provided the explanations they needed.

"And then?" Jim asked.

"I kept looking, moving deeper into the woods, hoping to find some sign of my boys."

"But you never did."

"No," Michael said. "Instead, I got turned around—lost—like we all did out there." His eyes flitted to the window and back, as if he'd seen movement there. "At some point I realized I couldn't find my way back. Then I came to a dirt road cutting through the woods."

"A fire road," Jim said. There were dozens in the area. In retrospect, it was obvious. How else could the cabin have been constructed? The supplies had been driven most of the way, then carried for the last quarter mile or so. The hidden cabin deep in the woods hadn't been that far removed from the currents of civilization after all.

"I tried following it out, but the roads crisscross all over the place. You really have to know where you're going."

"So it took a full day for you to make it back to the high-way?"

Michael shook his head. "Part of one. A handful of hours, really."

"And then you returned to the house, to the beginning of the trail. The officers at the scene say you arrived around four P.M."

"I'm pretty sure it was earlier than that."

"When you were told that Sean had been shot, you didn't want to go to the hospital?"

"They said that he was stable. Danny, on the other hand, was still missing. I wanted to join the search."

"There was a pickup truck stolen that morning from a drive-way less than three miles from the cabin. It was discovered two days later at the Grants Pass fairground. You know anything about that?"

Michael scowled. "A stolen truck? No. This is the first time I'm hearing about it."

"What happened to Detective DeLuca?"

"I don't know. Got lost, I suppose. Like the rest of us."

"He had a gun. Why didn't he fire off a few shots to help the search party find his location?"

"Maybe he fell, hit his head. Or maybe he was simply out of bullets." Michael glanced at the bullet still nestled between the thumb and forefinger of Jim's right hand. "I didn't know Detective DeLuca very well," he said. "Met him only that one time at the house the morning after the kidnapping. Still, he seemed like a nice enough guy. He was trying to help us find my son. If he did get lost in the woods—if he died out there because of us—I'm sorry as hell that it happened."

"Is that what you think really happened? You think he got lost in the woods?"

"I don't know, Jim. What do *you* think?"

The sheriff sighed. "I don't have any answers either," he said. "Only wild, unjustified speculation."

"And what does it tell you?"

"Nothing," he said, returning the bullet to his pocket. "I was slow and careless and got myself shot. If I'd been quick enough to kill Banes myself, things might've gone a lot differently. As it was, I was too dazed to offer DeLuca any assistance. I lie awake at night struggling with these things. That and the loss of your boy."

Michael placed the palm of his hand on Jim's desk. "I should be getting home, check on Kate. Was there anything else you wanted to ask me?"

"How is she doing?" Jim asked. "Really."

Michael shrugged. "Some days are better than others."

"She seems stronger."

Michael considered this. "Losing Danny has taken a lot out of her. Emotionally, she's a wreck."

"And physically?"

"It's hard to tell," he said. "She sits in the dark for hours, lies in bed for much of the day."

"She's grieving," Jim said. "It will pass."

On Jim's desk, Michael's hand began to tremble. They both looked down at it. Michael slapped his other one on top to get it under control. The shaking marched up his arm, and became progressively worse for about twenty seconds before leaving as quickly as it came.

Michael sat back in his chair, closed his eyes, and rested.

"You okay?" Jim asked. It was not the first time he had seen this happen. In Cottonwood, it seemed everyone had something.

"Yeah," Michael said. "I'm okay. I should get going."

Jim set his hands on the armrests and rose from his chair. "I'll walk you out," he said, opening the door. "Tell Kate that Margery and I send our love. We've been praying for you and your family."

"Thank you, I will," Michael said. He turned at the bottom of the stairs, and shook the sheriff's hand. "When I went off to find them," he said, "you didn't have to come looking for us, you know. You could've left it for the others."

"I couldn't have done that."

"I know," Michael said. "It's not in your nature." He stepped back, and reached into his pocket for the keys to the Mercury. "I'm glad you did. I'm glad it was you who was out there."

"I did the best I could. It wasn't enough."

"That's not your fault. It's not something you need to carry around with you like that bullet of yours."

Jim nodded. "I'm glad you think so. Now, go take care of your family."

"I will," Michael said. He walked to his car parked against the curb, opened the door, and climbed inside. The engine started on the first try. Michael turned the wheel to the left, and pulled into the street. At the corner stop sign, he braked, made a right, and disappeared into the afternoon haze.

45

FOR A SHORT TIME, KATE HAD GOTTEN BETTER. When she arrived at the hospital in Medford to visit Sean, the difference in her health had been obvious. Her body was still thin, the face hollowed out beneath the ridge of her cheekbones, but she appeared taller, her spine less bent by the weight of her illness. There was a fluid quality to her movements as she walked down the hospital corridor, a palpable vigor Michael hadn't seen in years. It was strange, he thought, how memory deceived you, how it became increasingly difficult to conjure up a person as they once were when the reality of their decline was ever present. He'd forgotten, for example, how beautiful she was, how his body used to respond when she touched him. For a few fleeting seconds, she was the woman he'd fallen in love with more than a decade before. To his surprise, he could still feel the soft brush of wind against his face as the Ferris wheel lifted them into the night, as he leaned forward and fell into that first kiss, the one by which all others would be measured. *"You found them! Somehow you found them!"* she'd exclaimed in the prim, unadorned hallway of the hospital, hugging him tight. But her next question was "Where's Danny?" And it all fell apart after that.

A sick heart will weaken the rest of the body, and this is what happened to Michael's family in the weeks and months that followed. Whether she was physically improved or not, Kate lost her will to live. She spent most of her time in bed, or sitting in the living room under the pale light of a single bulb, the rest of the room in shadows. Michael could understand the depth of her grief—felt it himself—but he still couldn't reach her. He couldn't even discuss it with her. To mention it made the sorrow unbearable. And so the house remained silent, a shrine from which they could never escape.

In his brother's absence, Sean became doleful and subdued. "Where did the man take him?" he wanted to know. "Why can't we get him back?" Nightmares visited him often, not centered on his own experience, but on the loss of his brother. When he cried out in the middle of the night, it was Danny's name he said over and over again until Michael turned on the light, took him by the shoulders, and shook him awake.

Michael assumed both Sean and Kate blamed him for what had happened. *How could they not?* he asked himself, and this was another type of sickness that grew and soured between them.

The residents of Cottonwood had a similar reaction. As much as they had feared and silently condemned his young son, they did not appear relieved by Danny's absence. Nothing was ever said to him directly, but Michael saw how people looked at him—the way conversations faltered when he entered a room. The entire town seemed to hold him responsible. *If he hadn't left the keys in the car. If he'd told the police about the ransom demand, and hadn't gone off on his own to try to rescue them.* It was a cowardly way to condemn a man. But such is the blind, mindless trudge of public opinion, and fighting it, Michael knew, would only make it worse.

In his classroom at Anderson Union High, Michael's effectiveness as a teacher had become undermined by his notoriety. The science classes he taught were well-attended, the lectures followed with rapt attention. But early on, Michael was aware that the eyes of the students were on *him* and not the chalkboard, their fascination having more to do with his own tragedy than the subject at hand. *It will pass*, he told himself those first few weeks, then it became his mantra for everything that season, from his incapacitating guilt to the pervasive silence that dominated their home. "It will all pass," he repeated in the shower, during his short drive to work, as he sat alone at the kitchen table at night. But as the months went on, Michael came to realize that it would not pass, at least not anytime soon, and he wrestled with the mounting conviction that he had made a serious mistake.

"You're a good teacher," Dennis Volkmann, the school's principal, said during his semiannual review in early December. "But the standardized test scores in science for the students in your classes have taken a downturn."

"If the students don't study, don't apply themselves—"

"It's never been a problem before," Volkmann interrupted him. "This is something different. Quite frankly, I think they're distracted."

"By what?" he asked, knowing the answer but needing to hear the man say it.

"By you," the principal responded. "It sounds callous, I realize. But you've been through a lot, Michael. It's hard to watch you try to function in the classroom and not be distracted by it."

Michael looked across the desk at the portly administrator. There was a small coffee stain near the top of his tie, a few inches below the knot.

"I think I'm doing a good job here," he replied. "The work helps me, provides a . . ." He stopped there. He was about to say distraction.

Volkmann nodded. "You're a fine teacher. Everyone knows that. It's just that . . . well, this is hard to bring up, but . . ."

"What?"

The man shifted in his seat, resting a chubby hand on the surface of his desk. "There have been a few complaints. From some of the families."

"Complaints? About me?"

Volkmann shrugged. "It's political. Makes me angry, the way people speculate about things they don't understand." He shook his head. "There are some folks, misguided as they are, who feel you didn't fully cooperate with the investigation." He smoothed his tie, laced his fingers across his considerable belly. "Now, you know I don't pay attention to gossip. But the school board does and, quite frankly, I'm a little under the gun here. My options are"—he offered an apologetic smile—"limited."

"You called me in here to fire me."

"Fire you? No, no. Of course not." The man held up his hand, vanquishing the idea. "It's just that . . . well, if I'm to be completely honest . . ." He hesitated, appeared to mull it over, as if the recommendation wasn't already front and center on his agenda. "Maybe you should think about taking a leave of absence, some time for you and your family to recover. Your salary for the rest of the school year would be covered."

Michael took a moment to respond. "A bribe. You're offering me a bribe to step down without a fuss."

"Heavens no," the man said, and to his credit actually seemed shocked by the accusation. "This would simply be something akin to a medical leave of absence."

"Medical."

"Well," he said. "Stress and grief can play havoc with the body. You know that."

Michael shook his head, considering it. "I don't think a leave of absence will help. I'm not convinced that's what's best for me and my family."

"I understand," Volkmann replied. He stood and offered Michael a limp handshake. "Just give it some thought, will you? We should also keep in mind what's best for the students. Shouldn't we?"

And just like that, he was out of a job. *It's not so bad*, Michael thought on the ride home. *We'll figure something out.* They had always gotten by in the past. But the truth was, he wasn't worried about the money—at least not yet, anyway. What worried him most was that there was nowhere for him to go—to escape the oppression of the place he still called home. He couldn't face them, couldn't exist in that space for long periods of time. The hallway to the boys' bedroom was too silent, the guilt from their suffering too crippling.

There were countless moments when he wanted to take it back, all of it. When he replayed that day in his mind, he imagined bringing Danny *into* the store instead of leaving him in the car. He went to the police with the whereabouts of the kidnapper instead of trying to go it alone. In the cabin that night, he tried harder to convince Banes that he should turn himself in. He left the shredded scraps of paper on the cabin floor instead of piecing them back together so he could read the address written there. He left the covering of the shelter open instead of sliding it closed.

I could go back. I could return for him and bring him home.

It wasn't impossible. He'd gotten rid of the address, but still remembered the way.

There was a time, not long ago, when Michael had allowed

himself to believe in a different kind of ending, one in which his wife recovered, rediscovered her health, and reclaimed her place among the living. In this reality, the town of Cottonwood emerged from its cracked and trampled shell, Sean flourished, and a new life unfolded before them. It would be their second chance. But all second chances are tethered to the first. And things that are left in the dust have a tendency to track you down, and clutch at your heels with their scratched and dirt-caked fingers.

Michael pulled into his driveway, and turned off the engine.

When he closed his eyes and thought back, he could still see the single-story ranch house, set off from the road and tucked among the pines in a small town west of Eugene. The well-tended garden out front had teemed with orange poppies and sunflowers, tall and proud in the early morning light. A green Oldsmobile 88 coupe sat quietly in the driveway; a snatch of sunlight shone off the polished chrome of its bumper.

It was 7:32 in the morning. Most of the streets he'd taken were still empty.

Michael brought the pale green Chevy pickup to a halt in front of the house. The place was quiet, its occupants likely still sleeping. He heard the braying howl of a hound dog from within as he slid from the truck, approached the front door, and knocked. It took a moment for the door to open, and then for the man to settle the dog and acknowledge him from the other side of the threshold.

"Help you?" he asked, his voice calm but expectant. In a glance, he took in Michael's tattered appearance, the grime from the past twenty-four hours that was still layered on his face.

"I'm Michael McCray." He offered his hand. The man shook it, and his skin was soft like leather, the flesh warm and yielding. "I'm here with the"—he paused, thinking—"with my son. I believe Richard Banes has been in contact with you."

"Oh." The man smiled, his face crinkling, subtle lines appearing at the corners of his mouth and eyes. "I was expecting *him*, not you." He looked past Michael toward the truck. "Where's Richard?"

"Couldn't make it," Michael said, keeping his voice as neutral as possible. "Things . . . didn't work out the way we'd hoped. We ran into a bit of—"

"We'd prefer not to know—my wife and I," the man said, cutting him off. "It's better this way. Cleaner. Don't you think?"

Michael stared down at his own mud-spattered shoes, then back up at the man, whose hair was thinning and speckled with gray. Still, he seemed able-bodied, lean and well-muscled, the remnants of youth faded but not entirely gone from his complexion. If Michael had to guess, he'd place his age around fifty.

"We're a bit of a mess."

The man frowned. "Been a long night?"

"It has."

He glanced over Michael's shoulder again. "Is that truck yours?"

"Not exactly."

The man nodded as if this was the answer he'd expected. He brought a hand to his chin, cupped the stubble that had sprouted there overnight.

"You might want to get it out of sight then. We don't have many visitors here, but there's no sense tempting fate. Move the truck around back. That should be fine for now."

"Thank you," Michael said, exhaling softly. He hadn't realized he'd been holding his breath. He turned, and started toward the vehicle.

"I'm Henry. My wife's Ruth. I'll tell her to set some extra places for breakfast."

Michael stopped, and turned to face him. "We appreciate that, Henry." He gestured toward the truck. "That's Danny. He doesn't talk much."

"Well, that's just fine with me, Michael. People talk too much as it is. The world needs some good listeners. Do you need help carrying anything inside?"

Michael shook his head. "Just my boy," he said, glancing back at the cab of the Chevy where Danny slept. "I can manage him."

46

RUTH STOOD AT THE RANGE IN THEIR SMALL KITCHEN COOK-
ing breakfast. Michael and Henry said very little, merely
sat at the table sipping their coffee. The bloodhound's
name was Maggie Mae. A three-year-old purebred, she had a
sensitive nose that twitched at the smell of eggs and bacon.

Exhausted from his ordeal, Danny slept in the adjacent
room. Michael's search for him had been a frenzied, nightmarish process, the beam of Jim's borrowed flashlight swinging
back and forth as he stumbled through the woods, calling out
to his son over and over until the sound of his voice became
part of the forest itself. *"Danny! Danny, where are you?"* he'd
yelled, praying for an answer, while telling himself it wasn't
too late. If he'd been thinking clearly, he would've realized:
Danny doesn't speak. He can't answer. Instead, he told himself lies
to stave off the panic. *Pockets of air can become trapped in the soil.
Under the right conditions, a boy who is buried alive could survive for
several hours. There was still time to save him. There was still time to
make this right.*

He and the detective had split up, DeLuca heading west
along the cliff face and Michael heading east. Eventually, he'd
come across a fire road about a half mile from the cabin, twist-

ing its way through the woods. *Would Banes have taken him this far?* Michael wondered. He didn't think so. Still, it was impossible to know for sure. He hadn't seen any sign of his son—and the cliff was behind him now, lost in the trees. If he continued, he wouldn't be able to find his way back. So he returned to the cabin, hoping there was some clue he had missed before.

The chair was in pieces, the playing cards scattered across the floor. The books that Banes had used to block the detectives' view inside were still stacked along the windowsill. The flashlight beam illuminated their spines. The titles—*Is Communism Un-American, The Red Menace, Surviving a Nuclear Invasion*— were focused on a different kind of nightmare.

Michael got down on his knees, and gathered the shreds of paper Banes had torn the day before. The man's body still lay on the mattress. Michael did his best to ignore it, to avoid looking into those wide, staring eyes.

"Where did you put him?" Michael asked, and his voice was strained and desperate in the small confines of the room.

"*Better to leave him in the ground where he belongs,*" the dead man whispered. "*That's your solution. It's what you should've done in the first place.*"

"Shut up," Michael said. "Where did you take my son?" He was suddenly furious—at himself as much as Banes—and snatched up one of the chair's broken legs, hurled it across the room. It glanced off the wall, struck the windowsill, and a few of the books toppled to the floor.

Michael paced the room, tried to think rationally.

When he left with Sean, Banes said he was taking him to join his brother. What did that mean? That the hole hadn't been filled in yet?

"*They used to drown the witches. The guilty ones rose to the surface.*"

"*And the innocent?*" Michael had asked.

"*Sometimes they drowned, as well. We'll have to see if he rises to the surface. See if I drown. Be getting dark soon. This one thinks I'll be dead by morning."*

Michael stepped on an object lying on the floor—one of the books, its pages splayed, words staring up at him like the eyes of the dead man on the mattress. He picked it up, glanced at what was written there.

> Where politicians fail, it is the duty of every American to take what precautions are necessary to protect them-selves and their families from a military incursion at home. Preparation is the key to survival. It is the goal of this book to serve as a roadmap to the steps you can take today to keep your family as safe as possible in the event of a foreign invasion.

"Jesus," Michael muttered, turning the pages. There were diagrams of bomb shelters, photos of duck-and-cover drills with schoolchildren in fetal positions under their desks, maps of projected radiation fallout exposure across the country in the event of a nuclear strike. He returned it to the windowsill.

Where politicians fail, it is the duty of every American . . .

He circled the room, but found nothing else.

Banes had stood here and torn up the address: *"Better to leave him in the ground where he belongs. That's your solution."*

. . . to take what precautions are necessary . . .

Michael leaned against the counter, eyes on the wall.

Preparation is the key to survival . . .

If there was something to find, it would've been built near the roadway. That kind of digging required heavy equipment. To do it by hand would've been impossible.

Michael left the cabin at a run, then stopped about fifty yards away.

What will you do about Detective DeLuca? What will you tell the others?

He thought about how things might play out from here. He needed a story to fall back on, no matter what—a story for *just in case.*

The window. The open handcuffs. The cabin has to match the story.

He turned around, and went back to the structure.

Take the books with you. Put them in the satchel with the money. If you could figure it out, then so will they.

"Here you go," Ruth said, sliding a plate in front of him.

"Thank you, ma'am."

"You want me to wake him for breakfast?"

"No," Michael said. "Let him sleep."

They ate in silence, their metal utensils clicking against the plates. Michael hadn't eaten in nearly two days; still, he managed only a few bites—and each one sat like a moss-covered stone in his stomach.

When they were done, Ruth stood and cleared the dishes, pretending not to notice the food left on Michael's plate.

"Tell me," Michael said. "How did you come to know Richard Banes?"

"He contacted us," Henry said. He reached over and poured himself another cup of coffee. "Said he got our name from the adoption agency out of Portland."

"You've adopted before?"

"No. We looked into it. About seven years ago."

"If you don't mind me asking . . ."

"I don't know how much you've heard about these agencies." Henry lifted the mug to his lips, and took a sip. His eyes went to Ruth. She stood at the kitchen counter, watching him.

"Not much," Michael admitted.

The man was quiet for a moment, considering. "I've heard

politicians describe it as an epidemic in this country, a drastic rise in the number of unwanted pregnancies in young, unwed women. Sex outside marriage, it's more acceptable now, I guess. A girl gets herself in trouble, has no legal option but to have the baby." He glanced at his wife again, then down at the table. "We were never able to have a child of our own. Yet here are all these young women, giving birth to babies they don't even want."

"If that's the case, then why not adopt?" Michael asked. "Through the usual channels, I mean."

"Something about it bothered me—bothered both of us," Henry said. "There isn't much sympathy for an unmarried woman with a child, or much of a chance for her to find a respectable husband after that. It's not a choice really, giving up the baby. They leave town, have the kid, and it's immediately given up for adoption." He sighed, crossed his arms in front of him. "The agency discourages contact with the mother. I didn't know that when we applied. Adopting couples are expected to take the child and go."

"I insisted," Ruth said. She had a red-and-white-checkered dish towel in her hands, the same pattern as the tablecloth. "I wanted to meet the mother."

Michael looked back and forth between the two, waited for them to continue.

Ruth placed the towel on the counter. She came to the table, and sat down in front of them. "She didn't know," she said. "When I talked to the mother, and asked her if this was really what she wanted to do, that's what she said. That she didn't know and didn't have a choice." Ruth smoothed the fabric of the tablecloth with the palm of her hand. "She was nineteen years old. Her father had arranged things with the agency. No one had told her she had a choice."

"It was the same with most of the others," Henry said. "A whole generation of women giving up their babies, other people making the decision for them."

"We couldn't do it," Ruth said. "Not that way. Not if they didn't know."

Michael nodded, and reassured himself that what he was doing was different. Dr. Eichman had sat behind his desk and told him Kate had four to six months to live. "*She will suffocate*," he'd said. "*Sooner rather than later.*"

The few bites of breakfast still sat undigested in Michael's stomach. *I'm going to vomit*, he thought. *Sooner rather than later.*

"So you walked away," he managed, "from the agency?"

Henry cleared his throat. "Yes."

"And they remembered you, seven years later? Still had your name on their books?"

"That's what he told us when he called," Henry said. "Banes said he was representing a couple through a private adoption. Said it involved a special child—one who couldn't speak— whose parents were sick and no longer able to take care of him."

Michael nodded. He didn't see the need to contradict this. Enough of it was true. Maybe Banes had known the young mother Ruth had met through the agency. Maybe he had paid someone off at the agency to go through their books. However he'd gotten their information, it didn't matter now. Henry and Ruth seemed like good people. They would take care of his son.

Ruth shifted in her seat. "I'll ask you the same question I asked that nineteen-year-old girl seven years ago. Are you sure about this, Michael? Are you sure this is what you want to do?"

No, Michael thought, *I'm not sure*. He could feel it now: the bile rising in his throat, the grief of this new reality washing over him. *I want to take it back, not just this moment, but all of it. If I could go back, start when he was younger . . . I could teach him— train him somehow—to redirect it, to lock it away where it couldn't hurt us, couldn't hurt anyone.* Or maybe, he reasoned, if we could go back . . . maybe this time Danny would be normal. If they rolled the dice again, would it always come up the same? What if it missed him, this thing his son carried inside? What if it passed right over him, landed on someone else? What if it didn't affect Henry and Ruth the same way?

It didn't land on someone else. It landed on him.

Yes, but what if it—

There's no use thinking about that now. The time for other choices is over. Do what you came here to do.

"My wife is sick. She may die. It's . . . no good for us all to be there."

Henry placed a hand on Michael's forearm. "In the end, if it comes to that, she'll *want* you all to be there."

"There's more to it than that," Michael said. "It's . . . complicated. A private matter. This is best for all of us."

Ruth leaned forward in her chair. "Stay with us awhile, a few days at least. You might change your mind."

"I can't stay," Michael said. "My wife. She needs me."

The woman looked at her husband, and Henry nodded, the decision passing between them.

"You'll want to spend some time with him before you go," she said, rising from the table. "I'll go check on him."

Ruth left the kitchen, heading for the guest room where Danny slept. Maggie Mae sat at the door, staring back at the two men. Henry stood, let her out the front door, and returned to his seat at the table.

"Can I ask you to promise me something, Henry?"

"If I can."

"Promise me you'll never bring him back."

The man shook his head. "That's a hell of a thing to say. A *hell* of a thing."

"*Promise me.*"

"No," he said. "Ruth is right. You might change your mind. You might decide to come back for him yourself."

"So don't be here if I come back. Be somewhere else." Michael ran a hand across the back of his neck. "I went through Banes for a reason. I wasn't supposed to know where you live."

"We make a modest income, Michael. We can't just pick up and—"

"There's a satchel on the table in the other room. There's money in it, enough for a new start. I want you and Ruth to have it."

"We can't take your money."

"It's payment for the job Banes was supposed to do. He didn't live up to his end of the bargain. I don't want it back. It's part of Danny's future now, wherever you decide to take him."

"What happened to Banes?"

"He couldn't make it. It didn't work out."

"What are we getting ourselves into?" Henry asked. "What exactly are you giving us?"

Michael turned to him, and answered as honestly as he could. "I'm giving you my son."

47

SOMETIMES MICHAEL WONDERED IF IT HAD HAPPENED AT all, since so much of their life was as it had been before. If Kate was any better, it no longer showed. She withdrew into her private bubble of mourning. Michael tried to reach her, would sit beside her in silence, engage her when he could. It was difficult—and seldom effective. Kate said little, and looked at him even less. He was afraid to touch her.

When she did speak, the things she said haunted him.

"Do you think he's warm enough? Is he finding enough to eat?"

"*Where do you think he is?*" Michael wanted to ask her, but didn't. "*Do you imagine he's still in the woods?*"

There was a disorienting quality to it all. He felt like he was standing on a high and narrow ledge, the weight of his body on his heels, with nothing but air and open space before him.

"You can use leaves to keep you warm," she said. "If you crawl under them, like a blanket."

Michael looked down at the cup of tea on the table. He'd set it there an hour ago, and had yet to see her bring it to her lips. It would be cold by now. Maybe he should make her another, a fresh cup.

"The weather's getting colder. He doesn't have a coat."

Say something, Michael told himself. *Tell her what you did. Tell her Danny is okay, that he's living with a new family who loves him.*

If you do, she will never stop searching. She will look until she finds him. Then she will bring him home. Everything will start again. And it will have been for nothing.

"It won't get really cold for another month." She stared across the room, her face devoid of expression. "When do you think the first snow will fall?"

You can't tell her. Not ever. That's what you decided.

Michael swallowed. At night he dreamed of Danny, sitting beside him on the porch before he left that late August morning, before he climbed into the truck and drove away from the single-story ranch house west of Eugene. When he closed his eyes, it was like he still sat beside him: the scent of his son's hair as Michael leaned over and kissed him on the head; his small hand resting like a bird in the palm of his own.

Bring him home and your wife will die. Sean will be next.

"I think he's in a safe place," he said, opening his eyes. "With people who love him."

"Why wouldn't they help him to find his family?"

"He can't talk. He's six years old. He doesn't remember where he used to live."

"But they would take him to the police, wouldn't they? The police would figure it out. People know about the kidnapping."

Michael wrapped his arm around her, felt his wife's body turn rigid at his touch. He withdrew, and placed his hands in his lap.

He was not working now, and spent his days doing pointless things. It was hard to focus his attention. Sometimes there was a flash of light in his right eye. And when he covered his left with the palm of his hand, his vision became blurred and fragmented.

You're lucky you found him, he thought, *on that morning near the cabin.*

He had almost missed it, even though he knew what to look for. The bomb shelter was close to the fire road on the other side. He descended a small hill, walked another few hundred yards until he found it. A medium-size boulder sat on the concrete slab that was flush with the ground, covering the opening. Michael rolled it aside. Then he got down on one knee, lifted and pulled, and felt as much as heard the slab slide along the concrete lip. It was heavy, and it required all of his strength to move it. When he was done, there was a dark circular hole in the ground, a few feet in diameter.

Nothing leaves, he thought. *Whatever goes down there stays there.*

"Danny," he called, peering into the dark. How far down did it go? Ten feet? Twenty?

Maybe it keeps going. Maybe it never ends.

"Danny," he called again. "Are you there? Answer me."

He can't answer you. He doesn't speak.

Of course. How could he have forgotten?

Michael placed a hand inside, and felt for a ladder. He missed it somehow during his first pass, and found nothing but damp, empty space, like the gullet of a creature that had risen to the surface. *Try again*, he told himself, and this time he was slower, more deliberate. Halfway around, his fingers touched metal: the rungs of a ladder that descended into the darkness.

"There are lots of things to eat in the woods," Kate said, and Michael jumped, the words startling him.

He looked down at his hands; they were still in his lap. "I made you tea," he said.

"Oh," she responded. She studied the cup as if it was a strange, foreign thing she had no idea how to use.

"It's probably cold by now. I can make you another."

"Mmm," she said, and nothing else.

"Have you seen Sean?" Michael asked. "Is he back in his room?"

"Their room. It belongs to them both."

"Right," he said. "That's what I meant."

"Did you?" she asked, her tone neutral, hard to interpret. She still stared at her cup, as if uninterested in his response.

"I should go check on him."

She sat there lost in her thoughts, perhaps unaware that he was still in the room.

Michael got up, went to the hallway, then looked back at her. "Maybe we should go outside today. Get some sun." He glanced at the clock in the kitchen. It was 3 P.M. How much time did they have? These days, it was dark early. "Kate," he said when she didn't respond. "*Kate*."

"Hmm?"

"Do you want to go outside today?"

"Oh," she replied. "It's getting cold."

"You can wear a jacket. We all can. It'll be—"

"I don't think he has one. Does he, Michael? I can't remember if he was wearing one when he left."

"No," he said. "It was summer."

"I hope he's not cold. I hope that at least."

Michael turned away from her, walked down the hallway, and stopped. The door to the boys' bedroom was closed.

What if he's in there? What if you walk in and Danny's sitting on the bed? Will you go crazy? Take him away again? Find someone else to do the job?

"Danny is gone," he whispered, but it wasn't true. His son was still here, everywhere he looked.

He imagined pushing open the door and finding the two boys lying in their beds.

"Read us a story," Sean would say, propped on one elbow.

"Which one?" Michael would ask, moving to their book-shelf and getting down on one knee.

"This one," Sean says, snatching up the book on his night-stand.

Michael glances at the title. "*The Secret Garden*. We finished reading this last night."

"We want it again."

"You don't want something new?"

"No, this one," Sean says, looking to his brother for confirmation. Danny smiles, giving them both an enthusiastic nod.

"The same story," Michael says, "always the same story."

"Yes," Sean replies. "The same one."

"Maybe you forgot what happened. You have amnesia. Is that it?"

"What's amnesia?"

"It's when you can't remember."

"We remember. We just like the way you tell it. And don't forget to do the voices."

Michael would cross the room then, and take the book from their small, trusting hands. He sits on the edge of one bed, flips to the opening page, and reads, "'Chapter One—There Is No One Left.'" He pauses, and looks up at them—their eyes upon him, waiting for him to continue. Then he lowers his head, and begins to read.

48

KATE MCCRAY DIED ON A COLD AND OVERCAST WEDNESDAY in mid-January. Her funeral was well-attended, though influenza and a host of other winter ailments had plagued the town over the past few weeks. Jim Kent was there, as was Detective John Pierce from the Shasta County Sheriff's Department. They were polite, empathetic. But they did not stand with him during the eulogy. No one did except his son, the one he'd managed to save, the one who'd returned to Cottonwood where he belonged.

A cold spell had hit Northern California, and the ground was hard, the early morning grass crusted with a thin film of ice from the night before. Michael stood at the graveside wearing his dark suit and overcoat, his hand resting on Sean's shoulder. He bent to his ear and told him it was time to place the flowers on his mother's casket. The child nodded and stepped forward, laying a clutch of purple orchids—Kate's favorite—on the dark mahogany. He stood there, head bowed as the wind sliced across the field and licked at his soft blond hair. It had gotten long, halfway to his shoulder. Like many other things these past few months, it had escaped Michael's attention.

"Winter is a season of rest," Pastor Reed began. His speech was slightly slurred, the result of a recent stroke, but he'd been adamant about conducting the ceremony. *Stroke or no stroke, it was his duty*, he'd said. *The McCrays had been members of his congregation since he'd married them twelve years before. He had baptized both of their children.*

"Kate McCray was born and raised right here in Cottonwood," the pastor continued. "She spoke her mind, laughed freely, and was loved by many. As most of you are aware, she endured a long and debilitating illness, but fought hard every step of the way. She was an inspiration for the many who knew her, an example of the enduring strength of the human spirit." He paused here, scanned the faces of those in attendance. They stared back, a collection of chess pieces waiting to be moved. "I've heard some suggest that God does not smile on the town of Cottonwood, that illness and tragedy have found a home within our midst."

Michael's eyes slid across the familiar faces in the audience, their expressions solemn, unreadable, eyes fixed on Pastor Reed, or on the flowers now splayed across the casket.

"But I say unto you: there is no place on earth devoid of suffering. The flesh of God's children is not impervious to disease or the ravages of time. Our bodies are only temporary vessels, designed to assist us in carrying out our service to the Lord and to each other." He stopped, and waited for the wind to die down before continuing. "Who among us will never fade or falter? The glory of God is not in the permanence of *this* life, but in the gift of life ever after. Kate McCray has earned her rest, and taken her place beside the Lord. And though she will be missed, she will also be remembered—and honored—by all who knew her. Let us pray."

A sea of heads bent in unison.

"Heavenly Father, thank you for the life that we have been granted, for the time you have given us to experience the miracle of your creation. Let us be thankful for *all* things, for you are with us during times of illness as well as in health, during sorrow as much as joy. You stand beside us during our darkest moments of grief, and you offer us hope for the days ahead. Help us come together as a community and a family, to support and shepherd one another through the valley of darkness. Please watch over Michael and Sean during this difficult time. May they draw strength from each other and find comfort within our fold. We surrender the life of Kate McCray to your hands as she ascends into heaven. For thine is the kingdom, the power, and the glory forever and ever. Amen."

49

MICHAEL ASCENDED THE SMALL HILL, HIS BODY MOVING slowly. In the depth of winter, it had been difficult to remember the warmth of spring, the longer days of sunshine that give birth to flowering things. Over the past four months, Michael found he could do little else except mourn the loss of his wife. The house that Kate had taken such pride in maintaining when she was well fell into disarray, each room a memorial to the person who had once lived there. With nothing to do with his time, Michael decided to teach Sean at home for the remainder of the academic year. There were lesson plans and texts to follow, but Michael's tremors had become worse, almost constant. He had lost the vision in his right eye. It was difficult to concentrate, to focus on the pages, and so he left it to Sean to negotiate the texts, to manage his own education. It hadn't gone well. The boy was falling behind. But what choice did he have? Michael understood his son's resistance. He didn't want to return to school, and Michael couldn't force him to go out and be among his friends. *Did he have friends?* Michael didn't know. He'd lost track of what his son did with his days.

He tripped, stumbled forward, went down on his knees in

the soft grass of the field. It was beautiful here. Serene. Even in his compromised state he could appreciate that. May was a good month for flowers. The soft breeze made them dance and sway in the morning light. Four years ago, he'd sat in the car with his family near this spot, and listened to the radio broadcast as the New York Giants won the National League pennant. The worst of Kate's illness hadn't yet taken hold. She and the children had played in the grass.

"Is the game over?" she'd called. "Turn off the radio and come join us."

Michael got out of the car, and walked over to where they were playing. "Bobby Thomson just won the playoffs with a three-run homer in the bottom of the ninth."

She laughed. "You listen to too much baseball. Nobody cares about Bobby Thomson."

"They will," he said, scooping up Danny. "After this, they'll care a lot." He planted his face in the boy's belly, went "Yum, yum, yum" until Danny smiled, squirmed in his arms, but didn't laugh. Why was his younger son so quiet? He would've liked to hear him laugh every once in a while.

There was a tug at the leg of Michael's pants. "I want to be a baseball player when I grow up," Sean said.

Michael got down on one knee to look him in the eye. In his left arm, Danny began reaching for his mother. Michael placed him on his feet, and watched as he toddled over to where Kate sat in the grass, coaxing him, her arms opened before her.

"Your brother's going to be the baseball player," Michael told his older son. "He's much faster than you."

"He's not faster," Sean said, scowling. "He can't even run."

"Look how fast he goes," Michael said, and pointed. As if on cue, Danny stopped and turned around to look at them. The sudden movement was more than his developing balance could handle and he fell down in the grass, rolling twice before coming to rest on the slanted terrain.

"Are you okay?" Kate asked him, giggling. She crawled over to where Danny lay, helped him to his feet, and plucked a few strands of grass from his hair.

"I'm a lot faster than that slowpoke," Sean said.

Michael raised an eyebrow. "Really? Let's see." He pointed to the far side of the meadow. "You think you can run all the way to that tree over there?"

Sean turned to look. "Yeah. That's easy."

"Okay. You run to that tree and back. I'll time you. We'll see if you're faster than your slowpoke brother." Michael reached out, and placed a hand on Sean's shoulder. "Hold on now, don't go yet," he said, looking at his watch. "Let's wait until the second hand gets around to the . . . okay, ready? Get set. *Go!*"

Sean sprinted across the field, his small hands clenched into fists, arms pumping.

Michael walked over to where Kate was sitting, and plopped down beside her.

"He *is* fast," she said. "Look at him go."

"And there goes the other one," Michael said. Danny had started after his older brother. He made it a few yards before tripping over his own feet and sprawling in the meadow.

Kate laughed, hand over her mouth. It emerged as a snort. "He's as clumsy as I am," she said, but Michael didn't find that funny. There was something wrong with Kate's coordination. The doctors had explained that one of her feet wasn't working as it should. They said there was a possibility it might grow worse over time.

He wrapped an arm around her waist, turned to kiss her on the cheek. But she was gone, lost in the sunlight.

"Do you remember how it used to be?" she asked him. *"Between the two of us? Do you remember how you used to love me?"*

Michael looked around and found he was alone in the field. The car, the family, even the ball game, all years ago.

"I never stopped loving you," he said.

"I know," his wife whispered. *"But now you love me in a different way. I'm okay with that. It happens to everyone."*

"Who among us will never fade or falter?" Pastor Reed had asked the gathering at Kate's funeral. *"Our bodies are only temporary vessels, designed to assist us in carrying out our service to the Lord and to each other."*

Michael got to his feet. The right one dragged a bit—*just like Kate's*, he thought—but he could still walk, and when he made it to the road he simply stood there, thumb out, until he caught a ride back into town.

"You okay, mister?" the young man asked as Michael climbed into his car. "You're limping. You hurt your leg or somethin'?"

"Nah. I'm all right," Michael replied, then turned and gave him a smile.

"Yeah, okay," the boy said. "None of my business." He flipped on the radio, and they listened for a while as the sun glinted off the yellow hood and the road unfolded before them.

"That was Bill Haley and His Comets with 'Shake, Rattle, and Roll,'" the deejay announced when the song was over. "And for those of you with a hankering for a little upbeat blues, this next song is a debut single from a young man out of Memphis. Originally written and performed by Arthur 'Big Boy' Crudup, here's Elvis Presley with 'That's All Right.'"

"You heard this one yet?" the kid asked, reaching forward and giving the volume knob a quarter turn.

"Nope," Michael answered.

"It's pretty good. Be interesting to see what else he comes up with." He glanced over at Michael. "Whatcha doin' out here anyway?"

"Just visiting. It's a place we used to come to."

"You and your family?"

"Yeah."

The boy nodded. "I'm thinkin' about gettin' married. My girl and me, we've been together for a while." He cracked a smile. "My old man says I'd better marry her before I get her pregnant. Kids . . . now *that* changes everything."

"Is that right?"

"Sure is. At least that's what people tell me. You have any kids, mister? I'll bet you have a couple."

"Two boys."

"Well, there you go. Two's a good number. And brothers, that's somethin'. I've got a brother myself. My mom says we were inseparable when we were younger. She says it was hard to know where one started and the other left off. But hey, that's the way it's gotta be, right? Brothers gotta stick together."

"Right," Michael agreed. "Brothers gotta stick together." He held his arm in his lap, and tried to keep it from shaking. Then he closed his eyes, rested—and listened to a man named Ray Charles singing "I've Got a Woman"—until they made it into town.

50

THEY HAD DINNER LATE THAT NIGHT. OVER THE PAST MONTH, it had taken Michael longer to prepare their meals. The vision in his right eye was nonexistent now, and the acuity in his left worsening at an alarming rate. *What's wrong with me?* he wondered. *Brain tumor, maybe. Or the same disease that took Kate.* In a way, it didn't matter. There was no fixing this. The time for fixing things was gone. Before long, he would be completely blind. The shadows would wrap around him until his sight sputtered once and winked out forever. It terrified him, knowing it was coming. Considering all he had lost, couldn't he have kept just this one thing? Was it too much to ask not to die in the dark?

"Dad, I'm hungry."

"I know," Michael said. "Soup will be ready soon."

On the range, the soup began to bubble. Michael stood to turn off the heat. There was a ladle in the drawer, bowls in one of the upper cabinets. He managed to set them on the counter. But his left hand wasn't working properly and his right arm shook with tremors, an almost constant part of him now. "Do you mind scooping this?" he asked, turning to his son.

Sean came to him, ladled the soup into their two bowls, and

took them to the table. "Spoons," Michael reminded him, and Sean grabbed those too.

They sat down and busied themselves with the meal. With his fingertips, Michael traced a path along the worn edges of an envelope that had arrived in their mailbox three weeks before. He'd handled it countless times since then, staring at the enclosed picture of Henry, Ruth, and Danny with a mixture of relief and bitter regret. How had it come to this? How much effort had they gone through to find him, to track down his address?

"Is there any bread?"

"I think so. It's in the refrigerator." He watched the boy rise and make his way across the kitchen.

When the letter first arrived, Michael read the single, hand-written page with difficulty. His vision had worsened since then. He could no longer make out the letters, only their vague shape, the way they lifted and fell on the page. It didn't matter. He'd memorized what was written there—locked it into his brain and couldn't get it out.

Dear Michael, it read.

He lifted a spoonful of soup to his lips, and blew on the steaming liquid before slipping it into his mouth, swallowing. Some of it spilled on the table.

We wanted to let you know that we're doing well, the letter said. *We've been in Flagstaff for the past few weeks, but will have moved on by the time you receive this. Danny's speaking now—only brief phrases, but enough to communicate. He asks about you sometimes, wants to know when you're coming back for him. It breaks our hearts. He's such a sweet boy. We're blessed to have him.*

We pray for the health of your family, knowing that all things are in God's hands. Wishing you the very best. Henry, Ruth, and Danny

Speaking now, Michael thought. *Danny was speaking.* He tried to imagine him here, sitting with the two of them as they ate. It was difficult. His mind kept returning to the forest.

The perfect circle of darkness. His hands and feet on the rungs of the thin metal ladder descending into the bomb shelter. Then a small hand touching the back of his calf at the bottom.

"Thank God. Thank God you're alive." Michael reached out, and hugged him in the dark.

The slight and trembling body. Silent tears. Danny clinging to him underground.

"I'm going to get you out of here. It's time to take you someplace safe." Even as Michael climbed, the child held on to him, arms and legs locked around his father.

At the surface, there was enough light to inspect his son, enough time for them to get—

"Michael. Oh my God, Michael, you found him." DeLuca's voice, approaching from behind him.

Michael lowered his head, closed his eyes. *No. Not now. Not when I was so close to ending this.*

Trot of footsteps across the forest floor. A few seconds later, the detective stood beside them.

"What in the hell *is* this?" the man asked, staring down at the opening.

"Bomb shelter," Michael said. He paused before saying the next six words that would start them down a different path, the six words he could never take back. "Children. It's where he puts them."

"Where he puts . . ." DeLuca's voice trailed off, the realization slowly sinking in.

Michael was still on his knees in front of Danny. He looked up, locked eyes with the detective. "There are more of them down there. I don't know how many."

DeLuca's mouth opened, and his face crumbled into something raw and horrible. "Are there any . . . are they all . . . ?"

Michael let his eyes fall to the lonesome void of the entrance. He glanced at his son, then back at the detective.

DeLuca sat on the ground near the lip of the opening, lowered his feet into the darkened space until they rested on the rungs of the ladder. "I've . . . I've got to take a look." He swallowed, gagged on his own saliva, then climbed down and disappeared.

"Dad?"

"Yeah." Michael looked up, and studied Sean from across the table.

"I miss Mom. Danny too." His spoon slipped from his hand and clattered inside his empty bowl.

"I know," Michael said. "I miss them too."

"Sometimes it hurts so bad, I feel like I'm breaking inside."

Michael nodded. "I feel it every day." He glanced at the door, and imagined them walking through it. Sometimes, if he listened, he could hear them in the house. "Do you know what I do to make it better?"

"What?"

"I invite them inside me. I talk to them. Hold them in my heart."

Sean gave it some thought. He shook his head. "I'm starting to forget what they looked like."

"We have pictures," Michael said. "I'll put more up around the house. We also have memories of the things we did together. You won't forget them. You don't have to worry about that."

They sat together in silence, the two of them recalling the good things they remembered, and struggling to come to terms with the rest.

"The kids used to say that Danny had a poison inside him," Sean said after a while.

"They don't know him like we do."

"Sometimes I wonder"—the boy looked up from his bowl then—"if Mom got sick because of it."

"What happened to your mom had nothing to do with your brother."

"She got worse and died anyway, even when he was no longer here."

"Yes," Michael agreed. "She did."

"And you're getting sicker," Sean said. It was not a question.

Michael didn't reply. He just looked across the table at his boy.

"So maybe it's me. Maybe I'm the one with the poison."

Michael ran his finger along the edge of the envelope.

Danny's speaking now—only brief phrases, but enough to communicate. He asks about you sometimes, wants to know when you're coming back for him.

"There was no poison," Michael said. "It wasn't in any of us."

You don't know that. If it was Sean . . . if you sent the wrong son away . . . you could've saved her . . .

"*She will suffocate.*" Dr. Eichner lifted the glass of whisky to his lips, and took a sip.

"*Could it be a person?*" Michael asked. "*One person infecting another?*"

The doctor frowned. "*How do you mean?*"

Michael shook his head, and tried to clear his mind of the conversation. "The only poison is what we allow ourselves to believe," he told his son. "If we don't believe in each other . . . we're already ruined."

They sat in a cone of light from the overhead lamp. There was a grating noise, a vibration in his hands as he slid the concrete slab back into place.

"There's no one else down here. Michael, what are you doing? What are you—"

The house was otherwise dark and quiet. Michael had rolled the boulder back in place, and covered the slab with dirt and leaves. Even standing here, directly above it, there was no noise, no indication there was a man trapped below.

"I'm sorry, Dad. If it's me, I can't control it."

"It's not you. You have nothing to apologize for."

You thought it was Danny. You thought it was Danny and you sent him away. You gave away your boy, killed a man to cover it up. In her final time on this earth, you robbed your wife of her son.

Sean was out of his chair, standing beside him now. "I never meant to hurt anyone," he said. "I'm doing everything I can to hold it back. With the bad man, it was different. I wanted him to die."

"No, you didn't."

"Yes," he said, "I did."

He's such a sweet boy. We're blessed to have him.

"Your kid said I'd be dead by morning." Michael looked up, and it was Banes at the table now. The dead man rocked back in his chair, and studied them both. *"I'm okay with that, being dead by morning. Our days are numbered, yours and mine—even his."* Banes reached out, placed a hand on Sean's shoulder. It was missing two of its fingers. *"There comes a time when the price of living is more than we can pay."*

Sean touched his father's arm. "You're getting sicker. I'm afraid you'll die soon. Just like Mom."

"If that happens, Aunt Lauren will take care of you. She loves you. So do I."

Michael had already spoken to Lauren about it, a difficult but necessary conversation. Sean hadn't stayed with her in a long time, since before her husband, Gary, passed, when Danny was still a newborn. Nine months ago, Lauren had helped Michael again when he stood on her front porch and told her he was going after his children. Lauren was the one he turned to when his family needed tending.

"*I don't . . . I don't like that house, Michael.*"

No. She didn't like it here. After her struggle with breast cancer and Gary's passing, Lauren preferred to stay away.

There was a tug on the leg of his pants. "*I want to be a baseball player when I grow up.*"

"*You think you can run all the way to that tree over there?*"

Sean began to cry, his body shaking. His son's grief carved a hole in his chest, and made Michael ache for everything that had led to those tears. Still, it was good to get this out in the open.

It's him. Sean's the one who brings the sickness. It was never Danny.

"*This is about two sweet children named Danny and Sean Mc-Cray,*" his wife said, leaning across the table. "*They are six and ten years old. Danny doesn't talk much, but his brother watches out for him. You will find them, Detectives, and you will bring them home to me, safe and unharmed. Is that understood?*"

"Hey, buddy," Michael said, "how about we promise each other something."

"What." Sean wiped his nose with the back of his hand.

"How about we promise that we won't give up on each other, that we'll stick together until the very end. No matter what happens. Because we're family."

It's a little late for that.

Yes, Michael told himself. *It was a little late for that.* But here they were, only the two of them now. In the time they had left, it was better to face this together.

"I'm scared," Sean said.

"Me too."

"I don't know what's going to happen next."

"I don't know either," Michael said. He placed a hand on his son's shoulder. "I love you," he said. And it wasn't only Sean he was talking to, but Kate and Danny as well. He could feel their presence around him, the simple reassurance of family.

Sean leaned into him, wrapped his arms around his father's neck, the way he did when he was younger. "Don't let go," he whispered.

"Never again," Michael told him.

And in the time he had left, Michael kept his promise.

Acknowledgments

In September 2015, I took a road trip to the small town of Cottonwood, California. I'd started writing this novel before then—had chosen the setting—but I needed to get a sense of the place. It took a good part of the day to drive there, and my first stop was at Travelers Motel.

Residents of a small town can easily spot an outsider and the trouble they've brought with them. Standing in the parking lot and surveying the premises, I soon attracted the attention of the proprietor.

"Can I help you?" she asked.

I turned, half-expecting to see a shotgun in her hands. (I don't know why I expect such things, but my imagination leans toward the dark side. If there's a way of shutting it off when I'm not writing, I haven't discovered it.) Instead, her hands were empty. She smiled.

"This may sound strange," I said, "but I'm a writer planning on setting my next novel in Cottonwood. I've come to learn about your town."

When you tell people you're a writer, there are generally three types of responses: suspicion, pity, or genuine interest. Her response coincided with the third.

"I'm an avid reader," she said. "And you should talk to my

husband. He's lived in this town a long time. He could tell you a thing or two about Cottonwood."

And so I followed her inside and got the scoop on the town from two of its locals. Some of what they told me made it into this book, and some of it didn't. But all of their stories were fascinating, and their enthusiasm made me glad I'd stopped at Travelers Motel first. So, thanks to M. Alicia Wilson and her husband, Robin Lee Wilson, for their gracious hospitality. And thanks for not greeting me with a shotgun, although that would've been memorable as well.

Thanks also to Bill Caughlin, who directs the AT&T Archives and History Center. He answered my questions and explained the process of long-distance telephone service in the 1950s. Back then, tracing a phone call wasn't as easy as it is in the twenty-first century. But it could be done, with a little ingenuity.

Shelley Daniels from the Shasta Historical Society provided me with details of what did and did not exist in Cottonwood in 1954. I've taken some creative liberties in the depiction of the town for the purpose of this novel. I also accept sole responsibility for any historical errors you might encounter along the way.

Thanks to my agent, Paul Lucas, for his continued guidance and wisdom. He is my advocate and the caretaker of my stories. I would not feel right about trusting them to anyone else.

My phenomenal editor is Jessica Williams. It is my tremendous good fortune to work with her. She brings out the very best version of each novel. Thank you, Jessica—once again—for your patience, insight, and creative vision. This story is so much stronger because of you.

Thanks to the many great people at William Morrow for everything from production, to marketing, to publicity, to cover design. This is our third book together, and I look forward to many more in the years to come.

The Quiet Child is a story about the complexities of family, and I am grateful for my own family as it continues to evolve. The relationship between Sean and Danny captures, I hope, the deep connection and loyalty of brothers. As such, I dedicate this novel to my brother, Mark, whose humor sustains me, whose thirst for adventure inspires me, and whose spirit remains untamed in a civilized world. He has found a way to live boldly—at least in my eyes—and although I am the older brother (and a little taller), I still look up to him as an example of how life ought to be lived.

And finally, thanks to you, reader, for lending me your imagination. It's a good thing we have going here, and I'd like it to continue. I look forward to the next time we come together. Until then, be good to each other, and to yourselves.

John Burley
December 1, 2016

About the Author

JOHN BURLEY is the award-winning author of *The Absence of Mercy*, honored with the National Black Ribbon Award, and *The Forgetting Place*. He attended medical school in Chicago and completed his emergency medicine residency at the University of Maryland Medical Center and the R. Adams Cowley Shock Trauma Center in Baltimore. He continues to serve as an emergency medicine physician in Northern California.

ALSO BY JOHN BURLEY

THE QUIET CHILD
A Novel

Available in Ebook and Digital Audio

It's the summer of 1954 and the residents of Cottonwood, California are dying. At the center of it all is six-year-old Danny McCray, a strange and silent child the townspeople regard with fear and superstition, and who appears to bring ruin to those around him. When a stranger arrives, Danny and his ten-year-old brother Sean go missing. In the search that follows, everyone is a suspect—even their own parents—and the consequences of finding the two brothers may be worse than not finding them at all.

THE FORGETTING PLACE
A Novel

Available in Ebook and Digital Audio

"*The Forgetting Place* is a deep dive into the darkest recesses of the human psyche. Surprises wait at every turn."
— Lisa Unger, *New York Times* bestselling author of *Crazy Love You*

A female psychiatrist at a state mental hospital finds herself at the center of a shadowy conspiracy in this dark and twisting tale of psychological suspense from the author of *The Absence of Mercy*. In this chilling follow-up, author John Burley—a master at medical and psychological detail—showcases the many ways in which the dangers of the outside world pale in comparison to the horrors of the human mind.

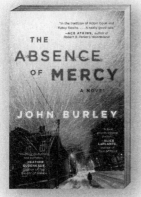

THE ABSENCE OF MERCY
A Novel

Available in Ebook and Digital Audio

"A true psychological thriller down to its very core . . . will both thrill you and cause you to turn away at the same time, this is one debut novel that will definitely make you lock your windows and doors in suburbia before heading off to bed."
— *Suspense Magazine*

John Burley's *The Absence of Mercy* is a harrowing tale of suspense involving a brutal murder and dark secrets that lie beneath the surface of a placid, tight-knit Midwestern town. With its eerie portrait of suburban life and nerve-fraying plot twists, *The Absence of Mercy* is domestic drama at its best for fans of Harlan Coben, Laura Lippman, Jennifer McMahon, and Lisa Gardner.

Available wherever books are sold.

THE
QUIET
CHILD